T0243486

MORTAL RADIANCE

MORTAL RADIANCE

Kathryn Lasky

**SEVERN
HOUSE**

First world edition published in Great Britain and the USA in 2024
by Severn House, an imprint of Canongate Books Ltd,
14 High Street, Edinburgh EH1 1TE.

severnhouse.com

British Library Cataloguing-in-Publication Data
A CIP catalogue record for this title is available from the British Library.

ISBN-13: 978-1-4483-1384-6 (cased)
ISBN-13: 978-1-4483-1385-3 (e-book)

All Severn House titles are printed on acid-free paper.

Typeset by Palimpsest Book Production Ltd.,
Falkirk, Stirlingshire, Scotland.
Printed and bound in Great Britain by
TJ Books, Padstow, Cornwall.

Praise for the Georgia O'Keeffe series

"The intricately plotted mystery puts a new spin on several historical figures"
Library Journal Starred Review of *Light on Bone*

"Lasky provides vivid descriptions through O'Keeffe's eyes that bring the setting and timeframe to life"
Library Journal Starred Review of *Light on Bone*

"Step aside Miss Marple, Eugenia Potter, and Kinsey Millhone – Georgia O'Keeffe is the new sleuth in town! . . . Vivid prose brushstrokes bring the legendary artist, the Southwest landscape she loved, and a complicated plot with historical and imagined characters to life"
Katherine Hall Page, author of the award-winning Faith Fairchild series, on *Light on Bone*

"Georgia O'Keeffe as an amateur sleuth? A daring idea that works like a charm for the highly talented Kathryn Lasky . . . And the portrait of the artist is superb"
Peter Abrahams, author of *The Tutor*, on *Light on Bone*

"Kathryn Lasky draws Georgia O'Keeffe's New Mexico with her own skillful hand . . . I couldn't put it down"
Gregory Maguire, author of *Wicked*, on *Light on Bone*

"O'Keeffe's righteous vision does not flinch from the truth, and we follow her gaze in fascination through this masterfully woven story"
Joseph Finder, *New York Times* bestselling author of *Judgment* and *House on Fire*, on *Light on Bone*

"The characters are rich, the setting is sublime . . . a
memorable and beautiful book"
Brenda Buchanan, author of the Joe Gale mysteries,
on *Light on Bone*

About the author

Kathryn Lasky is the author of over one hundred books for children and young adults, including the Guardians of Ga'Hoole series, which has more than eight million copies in print, and was turned into a major motion picture, *Legend of the Guardians: The Owls of Ga'Hoole*. Her books have received numerous awards including a Newbery Honor, a Boston Globe-Horn Book Award, and a Washington Post-Children's Book Guild Nonfiction Award. She has twice won the National Jewish Book award. Her work has been translated into nineteen languages worldwide. She lives with her husband in Cambridge, MA.

www.kathrynlasky.com

I feel there is something unexplored about women that only a woman can explore.

Georgia O'Keeffe

PROLOGUE

She was uncertain how long she had slept, but there was such peace and quiet in the chapel. She could hear the cottonwoods stirring softly outside. From the floor where, two hours ago, she and Mateo had made love before he left, she looked out the narrow arched window of the chapel. Three stars were suspended in the night. Just like the First People legends her mother had told her. The stars, her mother would whisper, were born not in heaven but on earth. The tiny star seeds were drawn to the sighs of the cottonwood trees that stirred in the wind, and burrowed themselves in their roots, spreading out in all directions. Those sighs were like music to the star seeds, and they began to climb up the roots and settle in the twigs and branches of the tree.

Soon, all the stars in the earth began to come and hide out in the cottonwood twigs. But the Spirit of the Night and the Spirit of the Wind knew somehow where the star seeds were hiding. They felt the stars needed to be seen by all and not hidden away. So together they created a storm, and that snapped the branches of the cottonwood. As the branches broke, the stars shot from them into the sky. 'And, Flora,' her mother always said as she tucked her into bed, 'if you break a twig in just the right place, you will find the shadow where a star once hid.'

But now another shadow slid across the moonlit, earthen floor of the chapel. A strange paralysis, a numbness, crept over her body. She tried to fight, but suddenly she could not move; she could not even scream as the rock came down and smashed her face, and then again and again. But she did not feel the subsequent ones. She was gone before the first of the stars began to melt into the dawn.

Please join in celebrating the life of English writer
D.H. Lawrence
September 11th, 1885 – March 2nd, 1930
Eleven a.m. at the Lawrence Chapel
April 5th, 1935
San Cristobal, New Mexico – just off the Old Kiowa
Road

ONE

'Yoo-hoo!' A voice trilled from outside the small chapel.
'Oh dear.' Georgia O'Keeffe sighed while on her knees
and crouched over a stained-glass window on the floor.
'Here comes trouble,' she murmured as the voices drifting down
the forest path became louder.

'*No molesta*, Signora Georgia,' said the young woman on her
hands and knees on the other side of the stained-glass window.

'I've almost finished the caulking.' A voice came from outside,
where the window would be installed in the eastern wall. 'It should
be dry by the time of the memorial service – just a couple of days
from now, right?'

'Yes!'

'And Georgia and I have almost all the tacks in. Two women,
we work fast!' Flora Namingha's eyes sparkled as she winked at
Georgia.

Such a beautiful girl, Georgia thought. She and Mateo were
indeed a striking couple. Both Navajo and both artists, together they
seemed to embody the grace and sheer elegant beauty of the land
– their land. That earthy, ruddy blush of the very soil and rock.

'Here we come!' trilled the voice.

'NO!' Georgia bellowed.

'Hold on, ladies,' Mateo called out. 'We are about to mount the
stained glass into the window frame.'

'Georgia, you in there?' Frieda Lawrence, the widow of D.H.
Lawrence, called out. The light suddenly diminished as a large
shadow blocked the light coming through the door. A thick German
accent drilled the air.

'Yes, I'm in here, but stay away! We're at a delicate point in
the operation here.' Georgia sighed. It had been more than three
years since she'd last seen Frieda. A dose of Frieda went a long
way. Lawrence was still alive then but had died shortly after he
and Frieda returned to their villa in France.

'You're the boss, darling,' a cultivated voice replied.

'She is not,' Frieda growled.

Georgia rolled her eyes at Flora, who giggled softly. A strand of her jet-black hair came loose from her bun and brushed her cheek.

'They never cease,' Georgia whispered.

'Hold on, ladies,' Mateo called out. 'We need to concentrate while we move it.'

Georgia had been asked to design the two stained-glass windows, one in the east and the other in the west wall of the chapel. The glass had been made by Mateo Chee, the extraordinary Navajo glassmaker she had met at the Native American Crafts Exhibit in New York five years earlier. She was thrilled with the commission and did it at no cost.

She was now eager to observe how the sun came through the windows that depicted some of her favorite flowers, flowers that she had so often painted but were now given another life in glass. And they were beautiful. She imagined a bouquet of light – jimson weed, iris, calla lilies and poppies. The colors of the flowers would spill across the floor like a liquid palette of rose and orange and pale crimsons.

'All right, ladies,' Mateo said, entering the chapel, 'I'm ready for you. Flora, over here. Georgia, over there.' He nodded, indicating the other side of the stained glass. 'And I'll take the top.' He took a deep breath.

'OK, on the count of three. One, two, three – here we go.' It seemed like a miraculous moment: suddenly, the earthen floor was sliding with color.

'Take the paper off the one on the opposite wall now. So we can see the setting sun and, with the eastern light, the promise of tomorrow.'

The promise of tomorrow. Georgia liked that phrase. She lived with the promise of tomorrow. It was her favorite time to paint out in this country. It was why she got up well before dawn to go out into the desert and paint. 'Live in the moment,' people say, but in Georgia's mind it was live in anticipation of the moment. *Be prepared*, she thought. *By gosh, I am a real Boy Scout.* She nearly giggled out loud. Her husband, Alfred Stieglitz, always said that he regretted that he was born too early to be a Boy Scout. Alfred – a Boy Scout? The whole idea was ridiculous. And she told him so.

'Low blow, Georgia!' he had muttered.

She had apologized.

The paper was now off the other window, and the western light, so much more intense on this late afternoon, slid into the room. She was nervous. This was an entirely new art form for Georgia. She had never designed a stained-glass window before. And to have designed it in New York and then Lake George, where there was no light like the light in New Mexico – well, she felt as if she had been groping in the dark the entire time. It was like painting a portrait without a face. She had to recall the light that so entranced her, but it seemed to have worked. She had a sudden feeling of being unbound, unbound from the canvas and floating in this new medium of ethereal light. It was as if she were fusing with a gossamer world sliding with color.

'Look at this!' Flora exclaimed jubilantly as she bent down to help Georgia get up. 'Look at what you two have done.' She seized Georgia around the waist as Mateo encircled them both with his arms. The three of them began to slowly move through the shifting dapples of tinted light. Georgia felt as if she were suspended in some Elysian region, neither heaven nor earth. She was in this instant fused with a new palette – a palette of air and light and color.

Frieda and her good friend Sybil – Lady Sybil Hatch – entered the chapel. Frieda was in her German Hausfrau dress that was stained and the hem half out, while Sybil looked as if she were riding to the hounds in a fitted tweed hunting jacket and gleaming knee-high riding boots. She was in a sense a British hybrid, an aspiring member of the Bloomsbury set, but also landed gentry teetering on the brink of bankruptcy, trying to maintain her late husband's estate, Stonebridge.

'Lovely! Lovely,' Frieda said, looking around as the colorful shadows poured through the window. 'I so like the notion of my dear Lorenzo here with the sliding colors. Yes, yes, his spirit is here. I feel it. His . . . his spirit, his Geist. The very color of his soul.'

'You know, that was my point exactly,' Sybil said. She squeezed her eyes shut for a moment, imagining that long, handsome face, the black hair flopped over his forehead, the penetrating dark gaze of his eyes.

'What was your point, Sybil?'

'Frieda, tell me why one would contain a spirit like Lorenzo's in an urn?'

'Maybe not an urn. Something else?' She turned and looked at the rectangular formwork of the concrete altar that was soon to be installed. On top was an urn destined to contain Lorenzo's ashes.

'Not an urn!' Mateo said. He was clearly aghast. 'But Flora designed this urn especially for ashes that will be set on top of the altar.'

Flora reached out and touched him. '*Calma! Cara, calma.*'

'No, Flora, you are the artist,' Mateo said firmly.

'You say this so cavalierly, Frieda,' Georgia muttered. 'It can be something else? An urn for ashes is what you commissioned. Flora here is the maker of this lovely urn. Would you ask Lorenzo after finishing a book to change what that book is about?'

'Oh, don't worry!' Flora said quickly, but Mateo's face had darkened. 'It can be used just as easily for flowers.'

'His ashes should not be *contained*,' Sybil persisted. 'It's against his nature, against all that he sought to find here in the desert – and did find.'

'What do you know about what he sought? His nature? I am his wife,' Frieda growled. '*Fick dich!*'

'What?'

Fuck you!

Georgia blinked. Sybil most likely was ignorant of the meaning. Georgia knew the two words because, on occasion, when Stieglitz was extremely upset with a landlord, he would mutter this imprecation during a heated conversation.

Georgia decided right then that she wasn't going to get involved in this argument with Frieda or Sybil, even though she had accepted Frieda's commission to design the windows with Mateo. She'd said enough already. She hadn't come out here to argue.

She had to live in the moment of being back on this land she loved – not Santa Fe right now, but Taos until the memorial service was over, then back to the Ghost Ranch. Finally, she was away, away from New York, a good two thousand miles away from Stieglitz. Not to mention the rowdy, boisterous life of the family at their summer encampment on Lake George. She had agreed to come to the dedication of the chapel almost three years before – before the breakdown that had put her in Doctors Hospital in New York for three months, before the Ghost Ranch and before she had met Ryan McCaffrey, the sheriff of Santa Fe County. Unexpectedly, she and Ryan had fallen in love. She felt no guilt whatsoever – not since Dorothy Norman had turned up in New York and become part of the cause of her initial breakdown.

She still loved Alfred, but she had told him nothing about Ryan. Why should she? He was so far away, and she was here. Alfred was indiscreet, and she was terminally discreet. Of course, it was easier for her to be discreet at this distance than for Alfred with Dorothy. Separate coasts accommodated her perfectly, whereas Dorothy was constantly in Alfred's studio and made occasional visits to Lake George. She sighed.

The subject of the urn had thankfully changed to Sybil's favorite topic, her daughter Bunny.

'You know, Frieda,' Sybil was saying, 'I think my little Bunny has snagged Eldon.'

'Eldon who?' Frieda asked.

'Eldon Burke, the son of the Chicago millionaire.'

The name rang a slight bell in Georgia's head.

'Well, that will be nice for you,' Frieda commented tersely.

'Yes, you know it's hard to keep up Stonebridge. I would hate to have to do what so many do and open it up for tourists – serving tea, gift shop. All that rot!' She made a phlegmy noise in the back of her throat.

For Georgia, this was a new rendering of the old story of the Gilded Age, when rich American young ladies crossed the Atlantic to find poverty-stricken titled aristocracy, but in reverse. This was a British girl coming to seek her fortune in America.

'I think I'll excuse myself now,' she said abruptly. Why hang around while these two silly ladies argued? She'd come back in a couple of hours when the sun was truly westing, yet the light would not have completely faded in the east, a cusp of light. And she would balance on that cusp, like a dancer on pointe between earth and air.

TWO

The sun was sinking as Georgia returned to the chapel two hours later. She couldn't believe it – the two women were standing in the drive as she arrived. They appeared still to be arguing about something. These two needed each other in some peculiar way. It reminded her of Stieglitz's sister Selma and his mother, Hedwig – jousting, he called it. It was a kind of sport, each one trying to shove the other off balance.

The light was not quite right yet, so she went just halfway down the path to the chapel. There was a magnificent Ponderosa pine with a bench beneath its branches. The first time Georgia painted this tree had been six years earlier, in 1929, a year before the death of Frieda's husband, D.H. Lawrence, from tuberculosis. She had been a guest at the nearby ranch of Mabel Dodge Luhan in Taos. The idea of painting the tree had in some unfathomable way rooted it in her brain, and now that she was back, she wanted to paint it again.

She loved it. There was a distinct fragrance of vanilla drifting in the air, so common to these trees. She sat down on the bench and looked up through the filigree of branches. The bickering voices faded. She kept her focus on the sky. Georgia wasn't going to get involved with Frieda or Sybil about this argument. No, not at all. She was escaping the chatter, the skin of the earth, and felt herself melding with the soul of the coming twilight.

Tomorrow she would return before dawn, but she wanted to take one last look before darkness obliterated everything. The angle of the sun would be perfect now in the west window.

Getting up from the bench, she began walking down the trail to the chapel. It would take a mere two minutes at the most. However, as she approached, she heard noises, gasps and groans of pleasure, coming from the chapel. She stopped to listen more closely. She bit her lip slightly and looked down at the ground, grinning. Someone was making love in that chapel – vigorously! In her mind, it was not a desecration but a consecration possibly, a blessing of sorts, letting the radiance of the setting sun through the stained glass spill over their bodies. It was lovely to imagine those two bodies entangling – the curves, the ellipses of light and flesh, a geometry of ardor and fading light. And all of it transpiring in a chapel!

She turned and walked back up the short incline and on to where her Ford Model A was parked.

In the driveway, Sybil and Frieda were now standing next to a barrel mounted on wheels. Frieda clutched an empty cloth bag in her hand.

'You what?' Sybil was screeching.

'I put them here! I knew you'd be upset. I just didn't want to tell you – not yet. But I did it.' She pointed to the barrel. 'A Sears, Roebuck special – a one-point-three-horsepower concrete mixer. Swivel action for easy dumping, and it rolls. How about that?' She appeared to swell up triumphantly, her thick yellow hair blowing out in a frothy cumulus around her head. She could have been a Valkyrie.

'The ashes there!' Sybil stomped her elegantly booted foot, gasping. 'In with the cement for the altar!' She pointed with an accusatory finger as if it were a creation of Satan.

'Yes, it's done, and now let's see them steal this!' Frieda fumed. 'Tony came by very early this morning to pour it for the altar. It should be dry by tomorrow, and there my dear Lorenzo will rest in peace, I hope.'

Georgia was stunned, and her only thoughts were to get away. Get back to Los Gallos, Mabel Dodge Luhan's rambling house, where she was staying for a few days before going back to the Ghost Ranch. She closed her ears to the relentless squabbling and tried to recover the thought of the images of those two bodies entangled in love and lust and light.

THREE

By the time Georgia drove through the carved wooden gates into the flagstone courtyard of Los Gallos, the rain was bucketing down. Colorful painted ceramic roosters perched on the high adobe walls. She stopped the car and was halfway out when a slender man with an umbrella strode up to the door of the Model A. He had prominent cheekbones and a sharp nose that conferred on his face an undeniable elegance.

Leaning in through the car window, he announced, 'Well, she has arrived.' Spud Johnson, Mabel's secretary, gave a bit of a pause after 'arrived' and rolled his eyes.

There was a beat or two before Georgia responded. 'Oh, her!'

'Yes, we don't yet have to address her as "Your Grace" – not until the deal is sealed, as they say. She's not a Your Grace or a Majesty. She is simply Mrs Simpson. For now, I'm the only queen around here!' Spud giggled softly.

'Where is Our Grace?'

'Our Grace as in Mabel?' he asked.

'Yes.'

'Inside. Looking quite grumpy. You know the battle over where the ashes will go. But maybe Mrs Simpson will distract her.'

'Not from the ashes.' Georgia sighed. 'Spud, I think you might say there has been closure on that issue.'

'What?' Spud opened wide his dark eyes. 'How did that come about?'

'Easy. Frieda dumped Lorenzo's ashes into a cement mixer.'

Spud gasped. 'Darling, you have to be kidding me!'

'Nope, not at all.' Georgia wished Spud would not call her 'darling', but he called everyone that. There was nothing 'darling' about her. But dear Spud was such a nice fellow that she couldn't bear to criticize him. Not only was he a nice fellow but he was a good poet. However, there was not much time for poetry, since he was in fact an extremely efficient manager of Los Gallos and tended to Mabel's correspondence and finances, and oversaw all the activities both social and otherwise for the guests.

Have a bad back? Spud knew the best healer in the pueblo for a smudging ceremony. Need a gentle horse for an elderly guest? He knew where to find one. He was especially deft at getting rid of boring guests. He was also discreet. When someone was having a roll in the hay with someone they shouldn't, he kept it to himself. He was, in a sense, the all-seeing, all-knowing personage of the ranch. Mabel's husband, Tony Luhan, had built the ranch, but Spud made it run like a well-oiled social machine.

'Any chance I can move out of the Big House and into my old digs – the Pink House – away from all this? Have they finished the plumbing repairs?'

'Almost.'

'I'll use a bucket. I so miss my old studio up there.' She sighed. And she so missed the solitude of it. The gossip had already begun to swirl among the guests as to why Wallis Simpson, the lover of the Prince of Wales, would be here in New Mexico at Mabel Dodge Luhan's Bohemian retreat. Who could be less Bohemian than the mistress of the Prince of Wales? Wallis Simpson, married and divorced twice, a dubious few years spent in Shanghai – an 'athlete of the bedchamber', one scurrilous journalist had dubbed her. *I don't even want to think about this stuff.* Georgia just wanted to focus on the commission. Create stained glass to honor the memory of a great writer.

'Come along, dear.' Spud took her arm. They went up the steps to the main house. 'Brace yourself,' he whispered as they walked into the foyer and then the sala grande.

The living room had been enlarged and was divided by twisting columns into two areas, each with its own fireplace. With the thick adobe walls and New Mexico fireplaces, it was as if the Alhambra had met the Alamo. Apparently, many more guest rooms and casitas had been added to accommodate the crowds that now flocked to Los Gallos.

In the seventeen years since Mabel had bought the property, it had become a lodestone of sorts in the Southwest for artists and a host of luminaries who would make their way there. Georgia thought of them as 'domestic' expatriates – the artists, writers and visionaries who had begun to come to this desert Utopia as they rejected the urban landscapes in the east. Mabel's salons in New York and else- where had all moved west to Taos, which was now the beating heart of the universe artistically, spiritually and psychically, a sort of

heady cocktail of tequila, mesquite and peyote – a desert martini,
as it were. And the latest ingredient was something called chakras
– the seven vital points in one's body that need to stay open and
receptive for the flow of energy.

These chakras must not be blocked, for if they are, one can
become vulnerable to myriad physical and psychic disorders, from
heart conditions and constipation to delusions and schizophrenia.
One heard random references to such symptoms – the depletion of
sexual desire or reverse of the lack thereof. Or, God forbid, the
fourth chakra is blocked, which can result in bitter anger or jealousy.
A healer from the pueblo came once a week to provide 'unblocking'
sessions – all, of course, on Mabel's dime. Mabel had encountered
an Indian from Bombay in New York – Swami Shankara – who
attended her salons in New York and Georgia. Stieglitz had met him
once and persisted in calling him 'Rabbi' – not to his face – because
he reminded him of the rabbi back in his hometown of Hoboken,
Rabbi Abramowitz.

Georgia immediately caught sight of her hostess standing in front
of the gigantic fireplace in the living room with another woman.
The two made an odd couple. One was knife-slender, dressed in
a suit with sinuous curves, a long cigarette holder in her hand, a
contrast to the squat Mabel in one of her shapeless dresses with
a colorful Navajo blanket, a serape, worn at a slant across her front.
Her dark hair was cut in a neat little Buster Brown style, complete
with bangs across her forehead, giving her head a decidedly boxy
appearance. She looked the same as she had almost six years earlier.
But the house had changed – sprawled really, in a pleasing way –
from when Tony started building it in 1918. Heavy wood furniture
mixed with more delicate English antiques, obviously imported from
her New York apartment. Oriental rugs were side by side with the
bold designs of the Navajo woven ones. The art on the walls was
also what one wit called '*igenous*', a blend of indigenous and religious – inlaid turquoise crucifixes with southwestern madonnas that
bore distinctly Mexican or Indian faces. And there were, of course,
several Marrano crosses, a cross inside a Star of David. These were
relics from the Jews who had escaped the Spanish Inquisition and
come to the New World to secretly practice their Judaism. Georgia
was especially fond of these Marrano crosses. To her, it was a kind
of coded art: disguising something you were, a Jew, with something
you would never be, a Christian.

Mabel gave a tiny shriek as she spied Georgia.

'Georgia, dear! Come here!'

Georgia made her way across the room.

'Wallis, meet Georgia.'

Wallis, who was already deathly pale, somehow turned paler. There was a complete blankness.

'What an . . . an interesting gown,' she offered.

Georgia looked down at her cream-colored dress with pintuck pleats. 'I, uh, made it myself.'

'Really! All those tiny pleats. You must be very nimble with your hands.'

Mabel flushed red. 'Wallis, Georgia is a painter. Georgia O'Keeffe.' She raised one eyebrow that seemed at this moment to function as a large question mark with a caption: 'You have heard of her, haven't you?'

This could be a New Yorker *cartoon*, Georgia thought.

'Really, now.' But it was clear that Wallis had no idea to whom she was speaking. 'And . . . and what do you paint?'

Mabel's eyes opened wider, as if she too were waiting for an answer. Mabel was obviously not in the mood to help Georgia out here. Indeed, she almost – in her implacable way – appeared amused.

Georgia tipped her head slightly. She was unsure how to reply. She waved her left hand vaguely as Spud had just put a glass of champagne in her right hand. 'Uh, you know . . . here.'

'Here?' Wallis repeated. She waved her right hand, and one could not miss the sparkling diamond bracelet on her wrist. It seemed to announce: 'I'm here. You can continue with your turquoise and silver, but have a little taste of what's to come – the crown jewels.'

'You mean right here in this building? That is what you paint?'

Jesus Christ, thought Georgia. *She thinks I'm a house painter!*

'No! I mean the here-ness of this country. The light, the desert, every place you look, stand, walk, the very air you breathe. The scents you smell. The scent of sage, the adobe of these walls. I am bombarded with images constantly. How can I not paint?'

'So you paint fragrances?'

Georgia gave a slight chuckle, then replied, 'In a scent,' with a quick smile. Wallis did not get the pun.

'Georgia designed the two windows for the chapel in memory of Lorenzo,' Mabel finally chimed in.

'Lorenzo?' Wallis's face had the ability of appearing blanker than blank.

'Lorenzo!' Mabel replied with force. 'D.H. Lawrence.'

'Oh, the author. But didn't he die years ago?'

'Yes, five years ago to be precise. But his ashes have been brought here, as it was his favorite place. There's been a bit of – how shall I put it? – *controversy* over where they should actually . . .' Mabel was straining for the proper word. 'Where they should reside – in an urn made by a wonderful potter or simply scattered across the hills he loved so much.'

'Not anymore,' Georgia said.

'What do you mean?' Mabel asked with alarm.

'No controversy. Apparently, Frieda threw them in a cement mixer.'

'What?' Mabel screeched. 'She didn't.'

'She did.'

'What can I do about it?' Mabel now gasped.

'Nothing, Mabel. What's done is done.'

Mabel furrowed her brow. If anything, she was the essence of stubbornness. Being stubborn was an art form for Mabel.

'Indeed, they are to be part of the altar in the chapel.'

Wallis flinched, and if it was possible for her face to turn paler, it did.

At this moment, a gentleman came up. Georgia had met him here years before.

'Mrs Simpson!' he exclaimed. 'I presume but have not yet had the pleasure.'

Wallis's color was restored.

Off to the side, Georgia noticed that Spud was winking at her. Dear Spud, he had sent Dr Bernard Ellington in obviously to rescue Georgia from this tiresome woman. In Georgia's mind, the doctor was equally tiresome. But Wallis seemed immediately charmed. Wearing an impeccably tailored suit, he stood out among the more casually dressed men. He had a pencil-thin mustache with a little gap in the center. A sharply pressed silk handkerchief saluted from his pocket. This fellow spends a lot of time on his appearance, Georgia thought, yet he affected a casual air. Maybe it was a studied casualness. She thought how uncomfortable it would make her if either Stieglitz or Ryan dressed this way.

As Georgia walked away, Wallis was explaining to the doctor

how the cairn terrier of the Prince of Wales had been bitten by a
viper while chasing a rabbit.

'I'm so sorry,' the doctor moaned and touched her shoulder.
She did not flinch, but tears sprang to her eyes. There was, in fact,
something just a tad viperish about her. Georgia could imagine a
forked tongue slithering out. Pathetic fallacy? Perhaps in reverse?
Instead of attributing human qualities to aspects of nature, perhaps
it was borrowing animal qualities to apply to those of humans. This
same doctor had once explained to Georgia the primitive nervous
system of a rattlesnake, which allowed the creature's jaws to continue
snapping for hours after its head had been severed. This Georgia
knew for a fact, as she had executed many a snake with her own
snake stick, which she always carried when she walked into the
desert. She imagined Wallis Simpson's jaws snapping away even
though her head was still attached.

'Tony, you aided and abetted this disaster. A cement mixer!'
Mabel was trying to keep her voice low.

Tony Luhan possessed at all times an impenetrable tranquility.
Georgia often thought of it as his invisible yet radiant armor. Standing
well over six feet tall, with his two long braids twined with silver
threads, nothing disturbed him. Unfaltering, never wavering, Tony
was the calm of any storm at Los Gallos. That was the essence of
his appeal for Mabel. As she once said to Georgia, 'He was Indian,
whole, uninjured and unsplit.'

'Angelo needed help with the cement mixer, that's all,' Tony
replied softly. 'I didn't know Lorenzo was in it.' He paused. 'His
ashes, I mean.'

Mabel wheeled about and glared at Georgia. 'When did you find
out, Georgia?'

'I found out when I was there to look at the chapel and the
windows. I heard Frieda and Sybil arguing.'

'Mabel,' Tony said, 'it's done now. Angelo and I set up the form
work and poured it. It will be dry by tomorrow – unless Lady Sybil
wrecks it. She's plenty mad.'

'So am I! The soul of Lorenzo trapped in concrete!' Mabel
said. 'Lorenzo needs to be on those beautiful Kiowa hills out by
the old trail. For once, I agree with Sybil. Generally, she's such
a nitwit.'

Tony murmured something in Tewa, the language of the Taos
Pueblo. Mabel shot him a fierce glance. Georgia knew only a few

words in Tewa, but one was *fuck*. The word was sprinkled liberally through many Taos conversations. Georgia decided to move on. She'd had a long day already, driving here from Santa Fe, where she'd spent the night with Ryan McCaffrey before he left for a conference in San Francisco. It had been so lovely to sit in his garden and sip a glass of wine. It was the first time seeing him after the months she had been back in New York. But then he had to take off for the conference, and she had to come to Taos. There was a rightness to their relationship that had nothing to do with morality or fidelity. It was more to do with balance. She felt completely balanced when she was with him, a state of mind that she now realized she had never really felt with Alfred. And it wasn't simply that Alfred had cheated on her most outrageously with Dorothy Norman.

She had only ever felt this with one other person in her life – Ansel Adams. But there had been no affair with Ansel. It was their vision that drew them together. There was a scintillating overlap in how she and Ansel viewed a landscape. They were each like one lens of a pair of binoculars that finally converged and made two distinct yet related images – never identical but alike in some mysterious way. She had hoped to go on a pack trip with him this summer, but Ansel was reluctant to leave his wife at home with the two children, one an infant, the other just two years old. She had wondered if she could convince Ryan to go with her. Maybe. He needed to take some time off. Perhaps after this memorial service for Lorenzo, they could do a pack trip together.

On the opposite wall from where she was standing, a new piece of art caught her eye. It appeared to be a Marrano cross inside a Star of David. Usually, the crucifixes were made of turquoise, but this one gleamed as bright as a sun from small, strategically placed overhead lights. She walked over to it.

'Lovely, isn't it?' Spud came up beside her.

'Yes, and very unusual. Most often the crucifixes are inlaid turquoise. What kind of stone is this?'

'Topaz – a very rare kind. Some call it Golden Sun topaz. Usually, they are brownish or orange. But Mabel heard about it through a gem dealer. Cost a pretty penny, let me tell you.'

At that moment, Wallis approached them.

'Ah, I see you are looking at something that caught my eye as well.

There are several of these crosses of six-pointed stars that Mabel seems to collect. What is their significance?'

Georgia slid her eyes toward Spud. He cleared his throat.

'Well, have you ever heard the term "Marrano", Mrs Simpson?'

'Uh, I don't believe so.'

'Well, a Marrano is a Christianized Jew.'

'Christianized Jew? I've never heard of such a thing.'

'It comes from the word "Moor" or "Moorish". The North African Muslims were known as Moors. When the Jews of Spain were expelled during the Inquisition, many came to the New World and settled first in Mexico and then throughout the Southwest. They would, for example, never eat pork and continued to worship their own God, but secretly. This is not just any star that the crucifix is set in. It's a Jewish star, the Star of David. It's quite valuable.'

A narrow smile crawled across Wallis's face. 'Well, leave it to the Jews to figure out a new way to make money. How sneaky of them. Trying to have their cake and eat it, too.' She laughed.

Georgia gasped. 'Mrs Simpson, I'm going to try to forget what you just said. I am married to a Jew. And let me tell you, there are several Jews in Mabel Dodge Luhan's circle of friends and many here at Los Gallos. So get used to it.'

'Well, I didn't mean to be offensive.'

'You are.' Georgia turned on her heel and left.

She breathed a sigh of relief once she got outside. A soft rain continued, and she tipped her face up toward the sky. She knew she couldn't stand out here all night, but it felt cleansing. However, right now she needed to get out of that room. It was filled with a tribe of Mabel's hangers-on, and yes, of course, some real friends of Lorenzo and Frieda's for the memorial and the dedication of the chapel in two days – if the cement had dried. She chuckled to herself. She had to go back in to get to her room, and the only way was to go through the living room. She sighed and entered the house.

'Well, that was something, wasn't it?' Spud nodded toward Wallis Simpson, who was now talking with Dr Ellington.

'Good God, Spud, is she not awful?'

'Don't worry. Mabel's on to her. She'll find a way to get rid of her quickly.'

'What, host a bar mitzvah here? Or maybe on Friday we could

light Shabbos candles at dinner.' She sighed and glanced around
the room. The heavy furniture, the giant candles flickering in the
twilight, the colorful weavings on the walls. Beyond the lively
chatter, the space – this room – seemed to possess something
hallowed, or rather a sense of the hallowed.

A woman was standing near the bar in a vaporous dress that one
could almost see through. She looked quite lovely, and she knew
it. She seemed to be striking poses. Her thin, beautiful arms gesticu-
lated softly as she animated some story she was telling another
person, whom Georgia believed to be a poet.

'Hey, Spud, who is that woman at the bar?'

'Oh God, Dorcas Moore – the next Isadora Duncan,' he replied.

'According to whom?'

'Herself. With a bit of a boost from Mabel.'

'By boost, you mean money?'

'Yes, and back when Mabel was trying to escape her gilded cage,
before she ever married Tony, they apparently had a roll in the hay.'

'Really? She doesn't look that old.'

'She is, believe me,' Spud said. 'She calls herself a pioneer dancer,
breaking new paths of form and movement, but she's also a pioneer
in plastic surgery. Facelifts.'

'Good Lord. I've just started to hear about that. I think Wallis
has had one,' Georgia offered.

'Oh, definitely. Not just the face but the neck, too. So tight I
wonder how she can swallow anything.'

'I guess that's why she's so thin.' Georgia looked back toward
Wallis as she took a bite of an hors d'oeuvre she had just picked
up. It did look rather painful as she swallowed. But what was this
woman doing here in Taos with Mabel? Shouldn't she be in Biarritz?
Or at the gambling tables of Monte Carlo?

'Well, Spud, you know me. I'm not cocktail material,' she said,
stifling a yawn. 'I think I'll go to bed.' She paused. 'And do let me
know when the work is done on the Pink House. I would love to
move back to my old digs.'

'Will do, my dear.'

She headed up to her room, wishing she could be in the Pink
House, plumbing or not, just to gain a little distance on the scene
in the Big House. But that wouldn't do. Mabel needed her court of
artists and painters close by for the celebration of Lawrence. How
Wallis Simpson got into the mix was mystifying, to say the least.

She stuck out like a sore thumb in Georgia's mind. Dr Ellington himself was a questionable guest. She supposed that Mabel liked him because he was the only doctor she knew who did not dismiss the pueblo form of medical treatment that depended largely on peyote. He was writing a book, *Sacred Medicine: Peyote and Spinal Stenosis, A Non-Surgical Treatment.* Catchy title.

Once back in her room, Georgia got undressed in front of the long mirror. The reflection she saw was that of a skinny body with jutting pelvic bones. *Oh dear*, she thought. *Going bald down there.* Her pubic hair loss was noticeable. She recalled decades earlier, when she was in art school at Teachers College in New York, her teacher Alon Bement would try to get models of all ages. There was one seventy-five-year-old, perhaps, who was completely bare – or would one say bald? – in the pubic area. And then there was a rather luscious redhead with an almost smoldering nest of hair down there. The class called her CF – short for campfire. CF slept with several of the students, both genders.

Well, let's see, Georgia thought. *I am almost fifty, just halfway between CF and Isabel, the seventy-five-year-old.* Thankfully, neither Stieglitz nor Ryan had commented on the hair loss. Stieglitz refused to use the Latin name, *mon verneris*, in reference to this part of her anatomy, as he thought it made it sound like a celebrated tourist attraction – 'Like Mount Fuji,' he had muttered. Instead, he called it Fluffy. 'Cozier, you know.'

Georgia liked the nude photos that Stieglitz had made of her over the years. He somehow got her into poses that were very classical. She was certainly never going to buy one of those little wigs for down there. What did they call them? A merkin! Sounded like a character out of Dickens. She slipped into her nightgown and set her alarm clock for four forty-five. Sunrise would be at five twenty. She was excited to see that first light streaming through the eastern stained-glass window that featured two pink calla lilies and a red canna unfurling. She needed to get there in the darkness and watch the light as it rose and brought life and color into the world. Life to her and Mateo's work. A birth of sorts.

FOUR

The chill of the night cast a somnolence over the desert that seemed almost tangible. The heartbeat of the snakes slowed. Their breathing was at a barely discernible level. Now, just before dawn, the moon was a haunting earthy red color and teetered in the west on the edge of the fading night. Georgia turned as she stopped the car and climbed out. To the east, the first vibrant orange of a new dawn stained the sky. She was excited to see how that light would appear through the east-facing window.

She made her way down from the top of the path where she had parked her car. The cement mixer was gone. Presumably, the cement altar with Lorenzo's ashes had dried.

She entered the chapel just as those first streaks of dawn were peeling away the shadows. The scent of newly poured cement was strong, but it didn't distract her from a rosy spill of light flowing across the earthen floor. Then the pink of the calla lilies grew more intense. She was mesmerized as light and stained glass combined in what appeared like a pellucid liquid splashed on a canvas. This transient bouquet was being gathered and crept down the sides of the new concrete altar. The concrete still had forms around it to maintain its shape while drying.

She was uncertain how long she had been watching this ineffable dance of light and color when she noticed a fragment of what appeared to be pottery, a shard from the vase that had originally been designed for Lorenzo's ashes. Black pottery from the pueblo of Sacred Water made by Flora Namingha, the granddaughter of the famous potter Rosita. And then she emitted a small shriek as she spied in the dark shadows on the floor, at the far side of the altar, a body. The left side of the face was smashed in. The black hair was drenched in blood. Like the fractured faces of a Picasso painting, the pieces began to assemble themselves into a human being. She gasped as she realized that she knew this person, this young woman. It was Flora Namingha! The potter and the pot, both broken and irreparable. Her eyes fixed on this macabre design of death.

A large, flat, bloodstained rock just inches from the victim's left ear declared itself the murder weapon. Flora's one eye was swollen shut. Georgia looked up. *Why?* she thought. Was she looking for an accident? A rock dropping from a chapel beam? Unlikely. She knew that she must not touch the rock. Fingerprints, after all. But could rock provide a surface for fingerprints? Was there any chance that Flora was still alive? Georgia bent over the body and lightly pressed her hand on Flora's shirt. There was stillness – absolute stillness. She shrieked as she saw the wrecked, once-beautiful face. She then held a trembling palm over the young woman's mouth and smashed nose to try to detect a breath. Nothing. The face was hardly a face. She might as well be looking at an earthquake. Where the nose would be was a gouged cavity. One eye was a swollen lump. The other eye was gone entirely, leaving just a bloody crater. It was a landscape of the most devastating violence imaginable. As she peered down at Flora's ruined face, she knew that the girl had made that dreadful passage from *being* to *body*.

She rocked back on her heels. Soundless tears welled up in her throat as if to resist this transit from existence to non-existence, from living to dead. She began to mutter the girl's name: 'Flora, Flora, Flora.' *Was it you I heard making love last evening? Was it you, guttural and gleeful in your pleasure?*

Georgia rushed up to Frieda's house and burst in.

Frieda stumbled out of the bedroom.

'Flora's dead. Murdered.'

'What?' gasped Frieda.

A second later, Sybil came out from another bedroom.

'Where is your telephone?'

Frieda pointed. 'But it doesn't work.'

'OK, I'll drive to Taos.'

'What's going on, what's going on?' Sybil called out.

'Flora's been murdered.'

The two women collapsed into each other's arms on the floor as Georgia rushed out the door.

Twenty minutes later, Georgia screeched to a halt in front of the Taos police station. She had left Frieda and Sybil in hysterics and driven straight back to Taos. The door to the police department was locked. *How can they lock such a door?* she thought. She began pounding on it. It was at least five minutes before anyone answered, but finally she heard the lock turn and a young boy opened the door.

'Yeah?' He wore a New Mexico State Police officer's badge.

'Where's the chief?' Georgia asked.

'Uh,' the boy stammered, 'in the can?'

'You mean the bathroom?'

'Not exactly?'

'Well, where exactly is he?'

The boy took a big breath. He had reddish hair, but he also had the high, aquiline nose bridge of Navajo people and the slight slope of their eyes. A mixed blood.

'Uh, ma'am, he's not taking a piss. He's in a jail cell. And we've only got one, so I hope we don't get any more drunks.'

'You're telling me the chief of the station is drunk? So you're now the chief?' She looked pointedly at his badge.

'Yes, ma'am. He says I should wear it when he's *aadalini*.'

'Drunk?'

The boy nodded.

'And you're now the chief police officer?'

'Uh, not exactly the chief. But the only cop. The only sober one.'

'There's more than one in there?'

'The chief's cousin Homer. He's a deputy.' The boy pressed his lips together and rolled his eyes toward the sky as if to say, *What can you do?*

'There are only forty-four cops in this whole state and two of them are drunk?' Georgia asked.

'There are only forty-four?' the boy asked, clearly in wonder. 'How did you know that, miss?'

'I have a friend in the police force.'

'Jeez,' said the boy. 'That's four-point-five percent of the whole police force here.' He paused for a second.

'Yes, four-point-five percent, I guess. They're here and they're drunk. You did that in your head down to the decimal point?'

'Yeah, I'm good at math.'

'Well, how are you on murder?'

FIVE

'Uh, my name is Jesus Yazzie, but you can call me Jessie,' the boy said, leading Georgia to the telephone on the chief's desk.

'Does the chief have a telephone directory here or, more specifically, a number for the coroner's office in Santa Fe?'

'Yes, ma'am. I organized that the other day. Chief's not the best at organization, so I made a list for him.'

'Good gracious, what else do you do?'

'I type and do the accounting. Chief's terrible at math. I'm good.'

'So I guessed.'

'My sister's even better. Loretta's a nurse over at Holy Cross and she just got into medical school.'

Within two minutes, Georgia was on the phone with Dr Emily Bryce, the Santa Fe coroner. She and Emily were quite close. They had met over another dead body a year or so ago. Odd circumstances yes, but the artist and the coroner found a bond and enjoyed each other's company.

Emily had an extension phone in her house from the coroner's office; she said people die all twenty-four hours, day or night.

'Emily, it's me, Georgia.'

'Oh, welcome back, dear, from the east. What's up?' There was a brief pause. 'Let me guess, you've got another stiff for me.'

'Yes, and the sheriff is out of town, and the police chief here in Taos where I am is locked up drunk in his cell.'

'Oh, that idiot Harold Bunker. Who's in charge?'

'Jesus – I mean Jessie.'

'Jessie the deputy?'

'Well, sort of, I guess.' She looked at Jessie. 'You a deputy?' she whispered.

Jessie shrugged. 'Guess so.'

'Well, I'll drive over,' said Emily. 'Who's the victim?'

'A Navajo woman about twenty-three or so. Meet me at the D.H. Lawrence house about two miles off the main road in San Cristobal.'

'Lawrence house? The chapel you were doing the stained-glass windows for?'

'Yes. Went down there this morning to see how the light came through at dawn. Needless to say, the aesthetics were somewhat marred by a bloody body. So much blood!'

'Head wound?'

'Yeah, nothing like a heavy rock to smash things up.' She paused. 'Poor thing's face is pulverized.'

'Oh my. You hold on, dear. I'll be there.'

'Can you bring anybody from the sheriff's office? You know Ryan is off at that conference in San Francisco. Any deputies around, like Joe Descheeni?'

'Yes, I just sent a report over to him yesterday. Aren't there any officers in Taos?'

'Well, as I said, the chief of police is in jail and so is his cousin Homer. Both drunk, apparently.'

'Well, I'll get right down there and pick up any spare cops at the station.'

'Thanks, Emily, and when you do get to the turnoff for the Lawrence house, follow the path down from where you see my car and you'll spot the chapel. I'll warn Frieda that you're coming.'

'Who's Frieda?'

'The widow of Lawrence.'

'Didn't you tell me that she's sort of a nutcase?'

'Mild nutcase, I think. But everyone got upset with her when she decided at the last minute to put her husband's ashes in a cement mixer.'

'Whaaat!'

'Long story. See you soon, Emily.'

They hung up, and Georgia turned to Jessie.

'So, Jessie, you want to go with me?'

He paused slightly. 'Just let me empty the chief's piss bucket.'

'Of course. Meet me at my car just out front.'

'Sure thing, miss.'

'Just call me Georgia.'

A few minutes later, he came out and got in the car. 'Had to get them both a cup of coffee and a doughnut. That usually sobers them up fast. I left the cell unlocked.'

'What's that you got there? Looks like a doctor's kit.'

'Crime kit.' He paused. 'You know – forensics.' He looked out the car window. 'Weird,' he murmured.

'What's weird?'

'Look at the moon still up there.'

'Lovely red color, isn't it?' Georgia offered.

'That's the point,' Jessie said. 'Blood Moon on the night of a murder.'

'It's called that? A Blood Moon?'

'Yes. Only happens during a full moon, when the sun fully shines on the surface of the moon. You see, Earth passes in between the moon and sun and cuts off the sunlight.'

'You're very observant.'

'I just like the sky – a lot,' he said softly. 'Because on the night of a Blood Moon, Earth partially blocks the sun, as I said, and the light waves are stretched out. So they look red. When this red light strikes the moon's surface, it also appears red.' He paused. 'Got it?'

'My, my,' whispered Georgia. 'I love that color red.'

'Just physics,' Jessie murmured.

Georgia could only think that she was glad the moon hadn't blocked the sun when she first got to the chapel, or she wouldn't have seen the radiance of the stained glass. At least she had that before she spied the body.

Frieda and Sybil were standing outside when Georgia drove up. She and Jessie got out of the car.

'This is the policeman?' Sybil trilled in her porcelain-teacup voice.

'Yes, he is!' Georgia shot her a fierce look. 'This is Jesus Yazzie, but you can call him Jessie.' She paused and gave Sybil a rather severe glance. 'Follow me, Jessie.' A look of sheer delight crossed the boy's face, and he gave a neat little bow to Frieda and Sybil.

Four minutes later, they stepped into the chapel. Unlike when Georgia had entered the chapel earlier, her gaze immediately fixed on the body.

'Poor Flora,' Jessie moaned softly.

'You know her well?' Georgia asked.

'She's a cousin, part of the Bitter Water clan, like me.' He paused for a moment. 'Poor Mateo. They were engaged to be married.' Jessie looked up at Georgia. 'This is terrible.'

'Yes, yes, it is,' Georgia whispered.

'More than terrible – be–be–' he stammered. Georgia watched him. 'Because he'll be the first suspect.'

Of course, thought Georgia, *because boyfriends are always the first suspects.*

'This the murder weapon?' he asked, pointing to the rock.

'I think so.'

He reached for the crime kit and took out a large spool of tape. He handed the tape and some ties to Georgia.

'What am I supposed to do with all this?' she asked.

'Mark the crime scene so no one will set foot in the chapel except police. Put it all around the chapel, but give it a wide berth and step carefully. We don't want to disturb any footprints. If you spot any, report to me, and I can make casts of them. In the meantime, I'm going to do a blood splatter pattern analysis.'

Georgia blinked. 'Jessie, may I ask how old you are?'

The boy's face suddenly crumpled. Georgia felt a surge of guilt – yes, guilt more than embarrassment. She began to stammer. 'It–it–it doesn't really matter, dear. I just wondered.'

'Well, I'm old for my age. Fifteen, but functionally I think I'm about fifty-three.'

Georgia smiled broadly. 'Well, then, you're not that much older than I am. I'm sure we'll make a good team.'

A broad, beautiful smile spread across Jessie's face.

While Georgia was tying the last of the crime tape, she heard voices coming down the path and looked up. It was Dr Emily Bryce with two deputies from the sheriff's office, Joseph Descheeni and Eddie Collins. Georgia tipped her head back.

'Yoo-hoo! Over here!' She then realized she was probably the only person at a crime scene who had ever yelled 'Yoo-hoo'.

'You already got a crime tape up, Miss O'Keeffe?' Joe Descheeni asked.

'Yes, the deputy from Taos brought it. He's inside doing a blood splatter pattern analysis.'

'Hmm,' Emily said. 'Usually, they leave that for me. Cops aren't trained. No offense, Joe.'

'This one is,' Georgia said in a low voice.

The three officers moved into the chapel.

'He's just a kid!' Georgia heard Collins exclaim.

Georgia chuckled to herself and got up to watch the scene inside.

She saw Jessie bent with a magnifying glass over the rock, the apparent murder weapon.

'It's interesting,' he said. 'We have a pattern that suggests the first impact was from blunt force. The rock there at the top of the victim's head was very effective and might have instantly killed her. The perpetrator was at close range, very close range. There is a classic drip pattern that happened after the first blow. I would say that the angle was almost ninety degrees – in short, directly over the face of the victim. There's a small pool of blood. Well, not so small. Head wounds are typically very bloody. One would have to assume that the victim was sleeping for the perpetrator to get this close to her.'

Georgia noticed that Emily's head was cocked, and she was not so much focused on the bloodstains as she was on Jessie.

'Young man,' she said in a soft voice, 'do you happen to be Jesus Yazzie?'

He looked up, and his eyes widened. 'Doctor Bryce? Doctor Emily Bryce?'

'Yes, and you're the young man who wrote to me two or three years ago about the rape case in San Pedro and the accuracy of buccal mucosa reagents in sexual assault kits.'

'Yeah, that's me. Did you think I was weird or something?'

'Not at all. But you said you were writing on behalf of Harold Bunker, the chief of the Taos police. I don't know how to put this, but it sounded like a somewhat sophisticated question for Harold. Who, as you must know, has some problems with alcohol.'

'Yep. I locked him up last night. That's a standing order from him to lock him and his cousin Homer up when they're drunk on the job. So that's why I'm here and not Harold or his cousin.'

'B–but . . .' Emily was stammering again. 'You certainly know chemistry, Jessie!' She paused. 'For a youngster.'

Oh, how Georgia was enjoying this, even though it was murder!

'Mentally, he's fifty-three,' she broke in.

'Can we change the subject?' Jessie asked.

'Well.' Emily sighed and continued. 'No sexual assault here, or I rather doubt it.'

Just then, Georgia recalled the heavy breathing, the moans of what she thought were pleasure and certainly not assault. Should she tell them this now? How would she explain it? *How can I, an old lady, be talking about not just love but sex?*

'Any idea, Doctor Bryce, as to time of death?' Descheeni asked.
The coroner shook her head.

'I can help you with that,' Georgia said.

'You can?' Jessie almost whispered the two words.

'You see, last night around seven o'clock, I was here.' She went
on to tell them about the sounds of lovemaking she heard and how
she turned back and decided to come this morning at sunrise. They
all stood gaping at her. 'You can probably find my footprints around
here. But they would have stopped at least fifteen feet from the
chapel.'

'No words? No conversation during the lovemaking?' Descheeni
asked.

'No . . . I mean, you know how it is . . .' Georgia's voice trailed
off.

Jessie, in the meantime, had turned redder than his hair. She
almost wanted to apologize to him. Poor boy. Was he trying to
imagine an old crone like herself making love? Even for a fifty-
three-year-old boy of fifteen, that would constitute the unthinkable.

Jessie now looked up and blurted out, 'The murder weapon is
interesting, though. This rock.' He was desperate to change the
subject from sex to geology – or anything, for that matter.

'What about the rock?' Descheeni asked.

'It didn't come from the immediate area.' Jessie replied. 'There's
no rock like that close to here. Whoever the murderer is, they imported
it. Maybe not from that far away. But there was some wheat grass
on it. Useless, however, for finding fingerprints. This rock is too
rough and porous. Doubt if you could get latents off it. You see, it's
a microcrystalline that consists of chert. Very dense, a kind of silica,
silicon dioxide.' He told them the chemical formula: SiO_2.

'OK, OK, but what about the wheat grass stuck on it?' Descheeni
asked.

'It doesn't grow at this altitude. Not too far away, but far enough
when you consider this rock must have been lugged up here.'

'But it's not that heavy, is it?' Collins asked. He started to pick
it up.

'No, put on gloves,' Jessie snapped.

'Oh, yeah, of course. Sorry about that.'

Emily and Georgia exchanged a quick glance. There was a glint
of mirth in both their eyes that was easily translated: *Guess the
young fellow knows what he's doing.*

Jessie was now bent over the rock, holding a flashgun in one hand and the camera with his other hand.

'So, who is the victim?' Descheeni asked.

'Flora Namingha, from the Sacred Water pueblo,' Georgia answered.

'What was she doing all the way over here?' Emily asked, looking at Georgia.

'She was commissioned to make the urn for Lawrence's ashes. Which she did. And now the pieces are all scattered about.'

'Don't touch them!' Jessie said. 'They'll be easy for fingerprints.'

'Of course, how stupid of me.' Georgia sighed. The highly polished black fragments would offer a perfect surface for finger-prints, but not for the colors that spilled across the earthen floor. Frieda had said that she was intending to use the urn for flowers since the ashes were now in the cement altar.

Georgia looked at the scattered fragments. They stood out against the pale earthen floor of the chapel, eating the colored light of the stained glass rather than reflecting it. The shattered urn seemed a testimony to the senselessness of murder. How did one make sense out of this? Murder always defied logic.

Jessie was now standing by her side, looking down at the frag-ments. He stooped down to look more closely.

'*Yah delah!*' He muttered the mild Navajo curse words.

'What is it?' Descheeni asked.

'Come over here. See that!' He pointed to the floor of the chapel about three feet from the base of the altar.

'Coyote teeth.' Descheeni's voice was low.

'Two incisors crossed,' Jessie whispered.

'Holy shit!' Descheeni gave a low gasp.

Georgia looked at Emily for interpretation, but Emily's lips were firmly clamped shut. Her eyes darted between Jessie and Descheeni.

'Skinwalker?' Jessie asked.

Descheeni inhaled sharply. 'Yeah, blame it on the witches.'

'Diversion tactic?' Emily spoke now.

Jessie was now looking between Dr Bryce and Descheeni.

Georgia knew that this was a Rubicon that the police out here often had to cross. Blame it on the supernatural evil, the Skinwalkers or witches that many Navajos believe in as opposed to just the regular, run-of-the-mill evil.

'Emily,' Georgia asked, 'how do you mean a diversion tactic?'

'I mean a white person trying to set up an Indian for committing the crime. Two coyote incisors crossed is not simply happenstance. Coyote is the chief troublemaker in Navajo stories. I don't have to tell you that, Joe.'

All eyes turned to Emily now.

'Possible, I suppose,' Descheeni said.

'Clever,' Georgia murmured.

SIX

Three hours later, alone in Spud's office, Georgia dialed the number that Ryan McCaffrey had given her at his hotel in San Francisco. There were three rings and then the sounds of some fumbling after the operator had connected her to his room.

'Georgia! That you?' He smiled, then quickly asked, 'Nothing wrong?'

'Not exactly.' Sitting in Spud's office with the receiver pressed to her ear, the gritty yet familiar sound of Ryan's voice washed over her.

'Oh, Ryan, you sound so, so wonderful.'

There was a beat before he replied, 'Georgia, is something wrong?' He knew her voice too well.

'Yes.' She paused for a few seconds. 'There's been a murder out here.'

She quickly explained what had happened. Ryan had to ask her to repeat a word or a sentence several times. 'Where exactly are you calling from, Georgia? I'm hearing a sort of buzzing noise every now and then.'

'I'm in Spud's office.'

'And who is Spud?'

'Uh, he's kind of the manager of Los Gallos.'

'Well, from my end, it sounds like you're talking through a sandstorm. Lot of grit.' *Or maybe it's tapped*, Ryan thought. He had just come from a session on wiretapping. Thomas Dewey, the special prosecutor of New York City, had given the main lecture. It focused on his 'wiremen', as they were called, who were experts at tapping into phone wires. There was a crackling noise that came and went. Ryan had just learned that this crackling was called 'swing'.

Georgia continued speaking. 'Joe Descheeni and Eddie Collins came down, along with Coroner Bryce, of course.'

'What about Harold Bunker? He's the chief over there in Taos.'

'He was – how shall I put it? – under the weather.'

Ryan sighed. 'Of course!'

'Well, there's an awfully smart youngster who works in that
office. Jesus Yazzie.'

'Yazzie,' Ryan repeated. 'Must be part of the Bitter Water clan
or the Shadow Mountain clan.' He sighed. 'Well, I get back in a
couple of days. Will you still be there?'

'Yes, they had to delay the memorial service for Lawrence because
of it.'

'Because of the murder?'

'Yes. You see, the body was found in the chapel.'

'Not Lawrence's body?'

'No, no, he died years ago.'

'Yeah, that's what I thought.'

How could she explain this to Ryan without sounding absolutely
nuts? She took a deep breath. 'His ashes were brought back here
to be put in an urn in the chapel. An urn made by the murder victim,
who was a potter. But then Frieda, Lawrence's widow, threw the
ashes in a cement mixer.'

'What?'

'Yeah. It upset a lot of folks. They liked to imagine his ashes
floating over the Kiowa hills.'

Ryan groaned. 'Oh, these artistic types!' he muttered.

Georgia laughed. 'You mean, like me.'

There was another sound on the line that was not a crackling one
but a sort of huff, as if someone were trying to suppress a laugh.

'That you, Ryan?'

'Me what?'

'You laughing.'

'No, not me. When have I ever laughed at you?'

'Often,' she replied. 'Better go. Goodnight, dear. See you soon.'

'Love you, Georgia.'

'Love you, dear.' They hung up. Her hand lingered on the receiver.

What was she going to do? She loved them both – Ryan and
Stieglitz. Did she feel guilty? Not really. Look at Stieglitz, after all.
He had Dorothy Norman, at least for now, and before Dorothy it was
the cook at Lake George and before that . . . Well, she had quit
paying attention. But still, they had history, a kind of thickness that
was not scar tissue in their relationship, which was not to be scorned
or dismissed. But experiences – good experiences, and the respect
as artists that they both had for each other.

With Ryan, there was very little history, but it was as if they had packed a lifetime of . . . of . . . Her mind searched for the word. She couldn't think of the right one, but it was there. There was something else, something that defied history, a baffling sensibility that drew them so close, inescapably close. She realized suddenly that it was as if Ryan were oxygen for her, the air she breathed, and he brought his own kind of incandescent light. As artists, she and Stieglitz were really just manipulators of light. Ryan needed to manipulate nothing. He *was* light. And she needed both these men in her life.

She set down the phone. There was a light knock on the door.

'Georgia, you done with your call?'

'Sure, Spud. Come on in.'

Spud entered, nattily dressed in a pale suit and a bright aquamarine tie.

She looked up from the phone. 'I suppose everyone's talking about the murder?' She paused. 'Now what's that sound I hear out there?'

'Rhumba music. Wallis Simpson. She decided to lighten the mood and is teaching everyone this latest dance from South America, the rhumba.'

'How thoughtful of her.' Georgia sneered. 'I think I'll refrain.'

She peeked around the corner and saw a tall, extremely handsome young man dancing with Sybil Hatch.

'I recruited Cowboy to dance with the wallflowers.'

'Good idea. Sybil seems to be melting under his gaze.'

'Who wouldn't?' Spud giggled.

'Now, Spud!'

'What, you think he's too young for me?'

'I'd never say that,' Georgia countered.

'No, you'd never say it, but you'd think it.'

'So, you're a mind reader now?'

He sighed. 'I guess I'm just so obvious. No one could ever read your mind, Georgia.'

'I'll take that as a compliment.'

Georgia surveyed the group through the half-open door of Spud's office. Dr Ellington was just entering, and Wallis, dressed somewhat exotically in a tight black sheath with a red rose tucked in the plunging neckline, was just accosting him as the music started again and urged him toward the dance floor with Mabel and Tony and a couple from New York.

'Follow me, Georgia, before the music stops.'

'I don't think I'm a rhumba type, Spud.'

'What type is that?'

'Not my type.'

Seconds later, the music had stopped, as had the dancers, Sybil and Cowboy right in front of Spud and Georgia. Cowboy was part of the staff at Los Gallos. He matched horses with guests for riding and organized pack trips. Georgia considered him a living piece of western ranch ambiance. The perfect accoutrement: a handsome cowboy, with white crinkly lines radiating from the corners of his eyes and a handsomely cut jaw. Part Navajo, he had a wonderful bronze cast to his skin. His eyes were actually an enigmatic gray-blue.

'Next dance, Miss O'Keeffe?' Cowboy asked.

'Well, if you insist.'

The music had changed. It was no longer the slow-quick-quick four-beat dance pattern of the rhumba but slower, more of a swing beat. It was easier to think and talk.

'So, Miss O'Keeffe, been a while since you spent time here.'

'Indeed. But as you know, the chapel brought me here.'

'Yes, and the windows are going to be so gorrrrrrgeous!'

'It's hard for me to think about them now since the tragedy.'

Cowboy's eyes seemed to darken. 'Horrible, absolutely horrible.'

'Did you know Flora?'

'Ah, yes. We go to the same church. We had our first communion together.'

'Why, I didn't know you were from here.'

'From the time I was five years old. My father was Paiute. But my mother left him when he got snapped up by the Mormons over in Utah. No way was she having part of that crazy religion. She came back to her people here.'

Georgia looked up at him. His complexion reminded her of the reddish earth around the Pedernal that she had painted so often at the Ghost Ranch. Apparently, people were always telling him that he should be in the movies.

'So, Flora was a nice girl and a talented potter. What would anyone have against her?' Georgia sighed. 'So sad.'

'The best girl.' His eyes were looking far off. 'It's just so hard for me to imagine who would want to kill her?'

When the music stopped and the dance ended, Georgia looked around and caught sight of Jessie at the bar mixing drinks.

'What are you doing here, Jessie?'

'Standing in for Raphael.'

'He's sick?'

Jessie sighed. 'He's Flora's uncle.'

'Oh dear.'

'Yeah.'

'I guess Harold is sober now?' Georgia asked.

'Oh yeah.'

'You told him about the murder.'

'Sure. He's over at Mateo's studio questioning him right now.'

'Oh no!' But then Georgia remembered that, of course, Mateo would be a suspect. The boyfriend always is, as Jessie had already said. 'I've got to go over there right now.'

'That's probably not a good idea, Miss O'Keeffe.'

'But I worked with Mateo on the stained-glass window design for the chapel. I know him. He couldn't possibly . . . I know him . . .' Her voice dwindled away. How many others had said this about a murder suspect? She knew him how? As one artist knows another. They had planned those windows together. They had sent sketches of designs back and forth across the country. But did that make her privy to his deepest thoughts, his secrets, his potential for violence? Caravaggio was one of the greatest Renaissance painters but was also a violent, horrible person. He was once arrested for throwing a plate of artichokes at a waiter, then it was carrying a sword without a permit and next it was murder. Such was the arc of his violence.

Nevertheless, she was determined to go to Mateo's studio on the Old Adobe Road. As she made her way out of the Big House, she could hear Cowboy announcing that he was going to lead a trail ride the next day for anyone who wanted to go and to please meet at the stable.

It was at least a forty-five-minute drive to Mateo's, but as far as Georgia was concerned, he had to know that there was someone on his side. She simply did not believe he was a murderer. But when she was a half-mile from the studio, she saw the police chief driving past, and in the back seat was Mateo, his head bowed. She honked and swerved sharply. The police car pulled over.

Harold Bunker rolled down the car window. 'Are you crazy, lady?'

'No, but you've got the wrong man.'

'Now, how would you know that?' Harold, a large man, was stuffed behind the wheel of the car. She could smell the booze on him from two feet away. He was partially bald, and it looked as if he had somewhat artfully arranged the few strands of hair he had left on top over his head. There was also a Band-Aid on his head that the strands didn't cover.

'Sorry about your head,' Georgia said.

'My head?' He put his hand to his scalp. 'Oh, that.'

She was buying herself time to answer what she considered an impertinent question. How could she assert he had the wrong man?

'Yeah, it looks like it got banged up.'

'What do you care about my head?'

'Because . . . because . . . I just do.'

Harold chuckled and looked over toward the police officer in the passenger seat. 'Did you hear that, Homer – she just does?' He inhaled deeply. His ample belly slipped over his belt buckle. 'Now, let me tell you something, young lady.'

'I am anything but a young lady. I daresay I'm probably older than you are.'

'OK, let me tell you, *old* lady. I don't want to have to arrest you for obstructing justice.'

'But on what grounds are you arresting him?'

'A condom.'

'A condom in a chapel? Wouldn't you call this a rush to judgment?'

'Not just in a chapel. In her – the victim. The coroner over in Santa Fe called us this afternoon.'

'Emily? Emily Bryce?'

'You know her?'

'Yes, she's a dear friend.'

A sob came from the car. She saw Mateo hunched over. His shoulders were shaking.

'Look.' Georgia sighed. 'I'm sorry I confronted you. I know you have a job to do.'

'Thank you, ma'am. Now, will you let us get on our way?'

'But just one more thing.'

Harold shook his head wearily. 'All right, what is it now?'

'You see, I am a good friend of Mateo here. He and I were working together on the stained-glass window for the Lawrence chapel.'

'Are you that famous artist from out east?'

'I'm an artist, and yes, I'm from the east. Not sure how famous I am.'

'Oh, yes you are!' Harold said and pointed an accusatory finger. 'Isn't she, Homer?'

'If you say so, Chief.'

Georgia leaned in the car window a little bit farther. 'Would you let me go back to the station with you and allow me talk to him a bit?'

'Now, why should we do that? Just because you're an artist and he's an artist? You're not his lawyer.'

'True, but I was talking to Sheriff McCaffrey over in Santa Fe.'

'You know the sheriff?'

'Yes, very well, and I called him this evening and he suggested . . .'

Harold and Homer leaned toward each other. Georgia stood back from the car, and they whispered. Then Harold turned toward Mateo in the back seat with cuffs on his hands and ankles.

'How you feel about this, Mateo? Wanna talk to this lady?'

'Yes, sir. I do.'

'Good!' Georgia said. 'I'll follow you back.'

SEVEN

'I would never kill Flora, Miss O'Keeffe. We were in love. So in love.'

'Then it *was* your condom that the coroner found.'

'Yes, yes. She sleeps with no one else. We wanted to get married. She was going to go home that night. She'd left her car near that arroyo just before you turned into Mrs Lawrence's place.'

Georgia now recalled that she had seen a car there when she had driven over to check the glass in the chapel and then again when she left. She hadn't even wondered why it was still there.

Apparently, no one else had either. But then again, cars broke down a lot in the desert – broken axels, radiators run out of water.

'So you left before Flora?'

'Yes. She wanted to take a nap. Her house is crazy with babies and noise, and an insane grandma who has dementia and is yelling all the time. If she tries to escape to her studio, they often interrupt her to come and babysit for the granny or one of the little ones.' He was quiet for several seconds, then spoke. 'It can be hard, Miss O'Keeffe. To be an artist in a family like that. You know. She never got much solitude.'

Georgia sighed. 'Look, I'll talk to Sheriff McCaffrey over in Santa Fe. This comes under his jurisdiction. He might be able to help in some way.'

'Still hard, Miss O'Keeffe.'

It bothered her that he was now calling her Miss O'Keeffe. For two years, they had been calling each other by their first names. It was as if the ground had shifted beneath them.

'Hard? In what way, Mateo?'

He looked straight into her eyes. 'The law is different for white folk than it is for Indians.'

So now she was white folk and he was Indian, and neither was an artist?

It was after midnight when Georgia got back to Los Gallos. She had just turned off the light in her car at the lodge and was reflecting on what Mateo had told her. It had been Mateo and Flora she had heard making love in the chapel that night. But he had left before she had, and she must have fallen asleep. So she was murdered as she slept, caught entirely by surprise. Georgia tried to imagine that rock smashing down on her face. If the first blow hadn't killed her, it had certainly been enough to stun her for any subsequent blows, which there definitely had been.

Georgia decided to walk toward the new, smaller courtyard on the west wing of the house – the Spirit Courtyard, someone had called it. It was supposed to have a lovely petroglyph inscribed on a large rock that Mabel had insisted could not be moved lest it disturb the spirits beneath the incised drawing.

As she walked through the arched entrance, a shadow sprinted across the splash of moonlight on the ground and then leaped over the large petroglyph rock. At first, she thought it was some large exotic bird, for the edges of the shadow appeared to be feathered. But now she realized, except for those feathers, the figure was human and nude. 'Oh! Oh! I am so sorry. I didn't mean to interrupt.'

'No, not all the spirits called for you. I called for you.'

Oh my God, thought Georgia. It was Dorcas Moore, stark naked and walking toward her. Georgia recalled that she had said to Spud the night before that every evening Dorcas seemed to show up more scantily clad in carefully draped diaphanous scarves. And now here she was in only feathers, and not so strategically placed. Was this part of what Georgia had overheard her explaining to Dr Ellington as karmic analysis.

'Please join me,' she said in a soft voice.

'For what?' Georgia gasped.

'It is the spiral dance. The sacred dance of the transition of the soul from the eternal struggle to the straight line of harmony. To the gathering of cosmic harmony.' Whenever anyone said 'cosmic' to Georgia, it was like fingernails on a blackboard.

'But why are you doing this?'

'For the transition of her soul.'

'Whose soul?'

'The girl who was murdered.' She was standing directly in front of Georgia.

'Flora? Flora Namingha?'

'Is that her name?'

'Yes, yes.' Georgia was aghast. There was nothing sacred about her dance. If anything, it was befouling, literally be-fowling. She began to laugh.

'And why are you . . . adorned . . . in chicken feathers?' She pointed directly to her pelvis and the chicken feathers.

'To give the soul wings, of course. Hence, I have attached these feathers to my sub chakras to aid not myself but the lost soul of Flora.'

Georgia burst into hysterical laughter. *But you didn't even know her name!* she wanted to scream. In her mind, Georgia had a picture of feathers coming back tagged, *Addressee unknown*.

'Are you laughing?'

Oh, Jesus Christ, Georgia thought. She was almost tempted to call Stieglitz to tell him about this. A new kind of Fluffy. Dorcas's face contorted into a scowl of absolute horror.

'Are you making fun of the spirits in this courtyard?'

Georgia glanced around the walled terrace. Chicken figurines did in fact top the walls, and the place was called Los Gallos. She just didn't expect anybody to take it to this extreme. There was also a slightly bitter aroma. She had a hunch it was from crushed peyote buttons.

'No . . . not of you, my dear. After all, Mabel did name her house Los Gallos.' She was about to tell her to take no offense, but what else could this insane woman take it as? She was not going to apologize. One did not apologize for idiocy dressed up in what they considered the raiment of the sacred. What was it that Mark Twain had said? 'In the first place, God made idiots. That was for practice.' She turned and walked out of the Spirit Courtyard as the antic shadow continued her feathered dance.

Now what? she thought as she exited the courtyard and spied a figure climbing out of a window. The night seemed to abound with spirits. Los Gallos should put out a *No Vacancy* sign. There was enough nuttiness already.

The figure turned, and a light from the corner of the house revealed the face of Dr Ellington. And wasn't that Wallis's room? What was he doing crawling out of her bedroom window at this hour? This could not be a midnight dalliance, could it? What about the prince? The royal family was in such a tizzy about the possibility of his marrying a divorced commoner.

The whispers about the couple had begun a year before. Now, here was Wallis already cheating on the man who might have to give up the throne for her. How had she and the doctor rhumbaed their way to bed so quickly? Georgia stood in the shadows and observed. She saw the doctor open the front door of the building and a light flick on in the Big Room. Another light switched on over the bar.

She wasn't sure how she could enter at this late hour without encountering him. She was tired and wanted to get a few hours of sleep in before she got up. It had been a long day.

She walked confidently into the lobby.

Dr Ellington was sitting in one of the leather armchairs, peering contemplatively into his glass. He looked up.

'Up early or late?' he asked.

'Yes, I suppose that does depend on your point of view. I stayed up late to watch the moon. It's a Blood Moon these nights, you know.'

'No, I didn't know that,' he replied as he rose to refresh his glass.

I didn't either, Georgia thought, until Jessie had told her and she had fallen in love with that luminous yet earthy red color that seemed to almost vibrate in the night sky.

He turned from the bar. 'Can I get you something, too?'

'No, it has been a long day.'

'Yes, death does that, doesn't it?' he said, raising an eyebrow.

She was trying to figure out exactly what he meant by that remark.

'Do sit down for a moment and have a nightcap with me.' He patted the couch as one might when inviting a small dog to hop up next to them. 'They've postponed the memorial for Lorenzo, you know.'

'Yes, I heard that.' She cocked her head and stared at him. What is this fellow up to? Is this sympathy or a sneaky way to make a pass? Hadn't she just seen him crawling out of Wallis Simpson's bedroom window? A new kind of house call by a doctor.

'I've had a long day, Doctor Ellington.'

'Please, just call me Bernard.'

'Well, as I said, it's been a long day, Bernard. Goodnight.'

She headed for her own bedroom, vowing to ask Spud the next morning if she could move into the Pink House – plumbing or no plumbing.

At sparrow's first fart, as Ansel Adams used to say on their camping trips, Georgia was up. She made her way to Spud's casita behind the Big House. He was an early riser, so she didn't worry about waking him.

The door opened just as she raised her fist to knock.

'Got your bucket?' He smiled.

'I can get one in a flash.'

'No need, they fixed it yesterday, late afternoon. Wanna have a cup of coffee?'

'Sure.' She debated whether she should tell Spud about the doctor's lively nightlife. She decided not to, but she did tell him about Mateo.

'Oh my God, that boy wouldn't hurt a flea. I don't believe it for one second.'

'I don't either. And as for those two loonies of law enforcement – Harold and Homer – I doubt their IQs add up to fifty.'

'Where the heck is Ryan McCaffrey, the sheriff over in Santa Fe? He's a great guy,' Spud asked.

'Yes, two officers from Santa Fe have already been over, but the sheriff himself is at a police conference in San Francisco.'

'Well, let me get the keys to my car and I'll help you move your stuff to the Pink House.'

'That's so kind of you, Spud. You know I don't do well with all those people flooding in for the memorial service.'

'It's been delayed a couple of days, as you must have heard by now.' Spud sighed. 'It's going to be odd, with New Mexico's most famous glassmaker, Mateo Chee, locked up for murder.'

Georgia looked off into the mid-distance. 'You know, I never even noticed the body or the blood when I first walked into the chapel. I just saw the light – the gorgeous colors of dawn light pouring through the stained glass. Strange, isn't it, how beauty can turn so quickly hideous?'

Spud reached out and gave her shoulder a squeeze.

As they were walking up to the main house to fetch her suitcase, a delivery van with a picture of a large bright flower on its side drove through the gates.

'Powell's Petals!' Spud exclaimed. 'All the way from Albuquerque. Now, what is that all about?'

'Somebody must have sent flowers for the memorial service,' Georgia said.

They were quickly disabused of that idea as a young fellow stepped out of the van.

'Got a delivery for a Miss Wallis Simpson. She here?'

'She's staying here,' Spud answered, 'but I doubt she's up yet.'

The young man reached into the back of the truck, took out a long white box and handed it to Spud. 'Cut two inches off the stems and put them in a vase of cold water and some ice cubes and they'll do OK. Keep them in a shady corner.'

'Thank you, young man,' Spud said, digging into his pocket and coming out with a fifty-cent piece. He tossed it to the driver.

'Well, thank you, sir. Thank you. That's mighty fine of you.'

'Long drive,' Spud said and took the flowers. Georgia followed him into the kitchen.

Tony Luhan was up already, helping the cook with breakfast.

'My, look at those!' he exclaimed as Spud removed the lid of the box to reveal at least a dozen red carnations.

Red carnations in the desert, Georgia thought, *stick out like a sore thumb.*

'Yep,' Spud said. 'For Mrs Simpson.'

'I don't think Maudie is up yet. Poor girl. Mrs Simpson works her to death,' Tony said.

'Who's Maudie, Tony?' Georgia asked.

'Mrs Simpson's lady's maid. Treats her like *chąą'.*' It was the Navajo word for 'shit'. 'Who do you think sent them?'

'The prince, most likely,' Spud said.

'Oh, the guy who's supposed to be the next king but can't marry her because she's been married already?' Tony asked.

'That's the guy,' Georgia said. 'He must have sent them.'

'There's a card,' Tony said. 'Should we read it?'

'No, Tony!' both Georgia and Spud said at once.

'Not polite,' Spud said.

'She's not polite,' said Tony. 'I can tell you that for certain – the way she treats Maudie, and she was flirting around with Doctor Ellington. Mabel thinks Mrs Simpson is beautiful. I don't see it.'

'Why in heaven does Mabel think she's beautiful?' Georgia said.

'Because she's skinny and Mabel's fat. She envies any woman who weighs less than she does. I told Mabel, climbing into bed with that bag of bones would be like sleeping with rocks.'

'Watch your step there, Tony. I'm skinny.'

'Not like that! You've got some padding on you.'

'Well, let me tend to those flowers.' Georgia took the bouquet to the sink and began cutting the stems. A small white envelope drifted to the floor.

'Ah-ha!' Tony exclaimed. 'It fell right at my feet.' He stooped down.

'Tony, no!' Georgia exclaimed.

'Hey, I can't even read it. It's not in English.' He went over to Georgia at the sink.

Georgia's brow wrinkled as she glanced at the card. 'How strange.'

'What is it?' Spud asked.

'Let me look closer,' Georgia said and peered over Spud's shoulder. 'I think it's German, and I think the prince speaks German fluently. So maybe that's their language for love notes?'

Spud offered. 'Not sure, but put it back, Tony. Last thing I want to do is be the object of that woman's wrath.'

But Georgia thought she might ask Alfred about this. She had planned to call him today. Now would be good. With the time difference, it was close to noon back east.

Fifteen minutes later, she was in Spud's office with the phone to her ear. Thank God Stieglitz was still in New York and not at Lake George, where there would have been a dozen relatives and one never knew who would answer the phone.

There were just two rings. 'Alfred here.'

'We have a Miss O'Keeffe on the line for you, sir,' she heard the operator in Albuquerque say.

'My darling girl!' he exclaimed. 'My Fluffy.' *Oh dear*, she thought. Well, that meant Dorothy wasn't around. 'Little Man misses Fluffy.' *Oh God*, if she were given to blushing, she would have been fire-engine red by now.

'Well, I miss you, too. Did I tell you who's staying here?'

'Ansel?'

'No, Virginia just had a baby.'

'Who, then?'

'Wallis, as in Wallis Simpson.'

'Oh God, that idiot prince's girlfriend. What a whore!'

'That's not nice to say, Alfred.'

'Well, I think she is. I heard she learned all her sexual tricks in a Shanghai brothel.'

'You heard that, did you?' Georgia couldn't help but wonder what kind of tricks Dorothy had shown him. Was she perhaps wearing feathers now? Prancing around Stieglitz's studio in the altogether. No, more like swimming naked in Lake George with him. Georgia did that with Stieglitz, too. Of course, it was April now, so the lake might still be frozen.

This made her think about Ryan – how she would love to swim nude with Ryan. Of course, not many places out here in the desert. But how comfy his body would be against hers compared to Stieglitz's.

'Yep, so what's up?'

'Well, a lavish bouquet of carnations arrived for Mrs Simpson this morning.'

'Now you want carnations?' Stieglitz laughed.

'Does that sound like me? Come on, Alfred.'

'OK, so what about the carnations?'

'There was a note enclosed.'

'And you read it?'

'It fell out, so it was hard to avoid, or not to notice that it was written in German.'

'The plot thickens.' Stieglitz laughed softly.

'I need you to translate. There are just two words that stump me. The note reads *'Für meine ewige Liebe und Königin.'* What does *ewige* mean and *Königin*?'

'Eternal is *ewige* – my eternal love. Like you and me. My queen. I guess he's already looking forward to becoming king and she'll be the queen.'

'Of course.' Georgia tried to tamp down the sarcasm in her voice. 'Why would the Prince of Wales write to her in German?'

'He's got a pile of German relatives and is said to be fluent in German himself. He's cozy with a lot of Hitler's crowd. Especially Axel Wenner-Gren.'

'Who's that?'

'Actually, not a German at all, but a Swedish millionaire who owns a luxurious yacht that they have been said to travel on. Wenner-Gren is not just close to Hitler but also Hermann Goering. Nice crowd. Was he the one who sent the flowers?'

'There was no name on the card. It wasn't signed.'

'Well, I wouldn't sign either, if I were German these days or close with Hitler. Which I am not. Born in Hoboken and proud of it!'

He was constantly reminding people of that, even though his parents were German and had moved back to Germany for Alfred's high school years, as they felt the education was superior there.

Now, however, there were rumors that his photographs were on Hitler's list of degenerate art.

'When are you heading back to Santa Fe?' he asked.

'Another week, maybe. I want to be here for Good Friday. I want to see the pilgrimage.'

'What pilgrimage?'

'It's a thing they do out here – an exercise in penitence, I guess one would describe it. People walk for miles with crosses strapped to their backs.'

'Sounds like fun.' He paused. 'Don't throw your back out, Fluffy.'

'Don't be ridiculous. I am only there as an observer, not a walker.'

'Are these the folks that flagellate themselves as they walk?'

'Some do.'

'Crazy!' He sighed. 'Sounds like you're having a wonderful time.'

Georgia laughed softly, *and to think I haven't even told him about the murder.* She then remembered Dorcas and the chakras.

'I have to tell you the craziest thing, dear.' She briefly relayed the naked feather dance she had witnessed.

Stieglitz gasped. 'She was what – clearing her tchotchkes?'

'No! Her chakras, not tchotchkes. Oh, you are a scream, Stieglitz.'

'Well, I'm glad you still find me entertaining.'

Not always, she was tempted to say, but she wouldn't go there.

EIGHT

M audie McPhee stood with her back to Wallis Simpson as she arranged the flowers. Her mistress had just returned from the lavatory, where she had burned the card. The ashes couldn't tell a story, but Maudie could. Without reading the note, she knew who sent them. But it was a dangerous game the stupid woman was playing, and there was no telling what she might do to her if Maudie breathed a word.

But she was desperate. She had to get out. Service was a tradition in her family. Her mother was in service to the prince's mother, Queen Mary, and her cousin was in the scullery at Balmoral and might wind up a parlor maid like her sister. Maudie would have given anything to serve in Buck House – or Balmoral or Windsor, for that matter. But working for the prince's forbidden girlfriend was all she was good for, apparently. And face it, she thought, even if he did become king and was allowed to marry this vile woman, what could she, Maudie McPhee, aspire to?

But this foreign place was so strange. Blistering sun, a vastness that made her feel like a speck in the universe. No nice English flowers, just prickly cactus sharper than any needle she'd ever been stuck by, and the snakes. Once she caught sight of three – three rattlers in one day. The clatter of those rattles was like a strange death knell. Jessie, the boy who sometimes worked in the kitchen, had told her that the only thing to do if bitten was to cut a cross in the wound and suck out the poison. Lovely country here, indeed!

She had never been lonelier in her life, and now, to top it all off, she might be 'in the way', as her mum would say. She shouldn't have let Rodney have *his* way the last night they were together, but she had. He promised her he would not let it happen. But now she realized that didn't mean it couldn't happen. And had she maybe subconsciously wanted it to happen, because if it had, maybe, well, maybe he would stay with her forever?

But what was she to do? She had tried drinking Epsom salts, as some girls had once talked about. It did no good except to make her throw up, narrowly missing a gown she was ironing for Mrs Simpson. Imagine that – vomiting on a Christian Dior gown.

Every night, she had bad dreams about the baby she was carrying, dreams of snakes slithering into the crib and piercing that tender skin with their fangs. If she could get out of here, could she somehow get back to England, to Rodney?

Rodney was in service at the most splendid manor house in England, Great Field Hall. He'd started when he was ten as a pantry boy, but then went into livery and proved that he had a way with horses and running a fine stable, which meant keeping the tack in order and the stables immaculate. Mrs Simpson and the prince had come over often in the course of the previous autumn. And, of course, that was where it happened. Maudie had been an assistant to the upstairs maid. And she made the fatal mistake of exquisitely mending a gown of Mrs Simpson's.

'Oh, to have such a skillful lady's maid, Leonora!' Wallis had exclaimed to Lady Bonsby, the lady of Great Field. And just like that, Leonora Bonsby gave Maudie to Wallis Simpson. Well, of course, who wouldn't? They expected that tramp, the Prince of Wales's lover, to become queen. What mid-level aristocrat – for that was what the Bonsbys were – mid-level – would not go to great extremes to curry favor with the future king's mistress? That's what it was like in service. One could get passed around. Maudie's parents were thrilled. Did anyone ask her if she wanted to go? No, of course not. She was handed over like a parcel to Wallis Simpson.

'Oi, me girl, you're on your way now!' her father boomed. But that's what bothered Maudie. On her way *where*, exactly? Her parents had such small hopes, such small dreams for her – small dreams that they considered quite grand. And now she was preggers, trapped in a foreign country with a vain, stupid woman.

Then she began to play the old game she had played as a child. She called it 'Would you rather?' Would you rather be in the desert with Wallis Simpson or, like her own pa, wind up in a foxhole in Verdun with poisonous gas filling your lungs? Would you rather be in an ocean chased by a shark or have a rattlesnake crawling into your bed at night? Oh, she could think of endless 'Would you rather?' questions, but it never eased her desperation, never resolved her predicament.

Then her mind spun off in another direction. Was her current situation a predicament or a dilemma? Not really a dilemma, she thought, because a dilemma implied that there was a choice, a solution, and that was not the same as a predicament, when one was simply stuck.

'I'm stuck,' she muttered. Back in England, she had tried some herbal remedies that girls used when they were 'delayed'. But they only made her miserably sick. She vomited for two days after ingesting the ground roots of black hellebore and pennyroyal.

She continued arranging the flowers. Carnations! Cheap. Or so said her sister Molly. And Molly would know. She worked for the Duchess of Glendower, who was considered the most elegant woman in London. Every season people raved about her taste, her clothing, her stunning mansions. Molly had told her she wouldn't have a carnation in her house. 'She'd make a bouquet of dandelions before having carnations.' Those were Molly's exact words.

'So shove these up your ass, Wallis Simpson,' Maudie murmured.

NINE

Cedric Barkley leaned in closer to the crypto machine. A cipher was coming through. There was a scattering of messages that covered everything from the crisis in Ethiopia with Mussolini to the health of King George. Room Forty of the cryptanalysis center at Century House at 100 Westminster Bridge Road, London, had served through the Great War as the very heart of the Secret Intelligence Service. Barkley looked at the coded message that had just come in.

'What the devil?' he muttered. He looked at his secretary. 'Marnie, get Fritz Freihoff on the line in DC.' He walked out of the crypto room down the hall to his own office.

Five minutes later, he was sitting at his desk and looking at the picture of his lovely wife, Melody. A light blinked on the phone, signaling that his call had gone through.

'Fritzy, my boy, what's going on?'

'Not much, a few gangsters on the loose. What else is new? How about you?'

'Not any gangsters. Just Pickles and the Lynx and a lot of shagging. Just got a notification that Pickles is in the desert. And the Lynx sent her a bouquet of carnations. Not the Lad.'

'Pickles?' Fritzy repeated. 'Ah, yes – *her*.' He had temporarily forgotten the code name for Wallis Simpson. And Lynx was Ribbentropp, who they'd had their eye on for years now. And 'the Lad' was the Prince of Wales.

'What desert?' Fritzy asked.

'Not Saudi Arabia. Your desert out in the Southwest. New Mexico. She received the customary bouquet of carnations with a note in which he addressed her as queen.' Barkley replied.

'Jumping the gun, wouldn't you say?'

'Just a bit.' He sighed wearily. 'But this supports the rumor that the Lad has made some sort of deal.'

'Indeed.'

'We're keeping an eye on it, but I just wanted to alert you.'

'There's apparently a lot of action going on out there. But we have a good team. You recall Wolf Boy?' Fritzy asked.

'The wire rat.' Wire rat was the name given to the team that installed the Hartley transmitter receivers in the Southwest. There was one 'Wolf Boy' who was particularly excellent and worked on the Ghost Ranch.

'We're moving him in closer. He's invaluable. Speaks German fluently now.'

TEN

'Oh dear,' muttered Wallis as she spied the letter on the bureau. *Guy*, she thought. *Guy Trundle*. How did he ever find out that she was here? He was utterly irresistible, especially in bed. What was resistible was that he was a salaried employee of the Ford Motor Company, the branch in London. He was 'well endowed', but not quite in the right way.

The prince was well endowed in the other way, but not quite enough – at least, not until he actually became king. She set the letter aside, then went through her drawer and found the letter that had reached her in New York before she came to Taos. She read it again. The prince seemed somewhat agitated about his finances. 'There could be, my darling, some financial uncertainties if worse came to worst.'

What did he mean, if worse came to worst? It left a range of possibilities. If, indeed, his father, King George, died – and according to the Prince of Wales, his father was on oxygen almost every day – that might not be long. But she gasped now when she reread it. How had she missed this P.S.? It was on the reverse side of the stationery. 'Mummy has been in constant talks with Lord Baldwin almost every day. And Lord Mountbatten.'

Lord Baldwin, the prime minister! Mountbatten! A dangerous configuration was assembling in Wallis's mind. Lord Baldwin, Queen Mary – who knew except for the prince and Joachim von Ribbentrop that she was here in this godforsaken land? And what are they talking about? Her, undoubtedly. What business was it of theirs? But even as the thought was forming in her head, she knew that was facile of her. It was their business because her lover was not just any lover but the heir to the crown.

Before she left, the prince had made some noises about MI5. He felt that his mail was being 'perused', as he put it. And his bills – or her bills, which he paid, from Dior and Schiaparelli. Well, everyone knew they were having an affair. Were all women associated with the royal family supposed to dress like Queen Mary, that pudgy drab woman encrusted with ugly jewels. She reminded Wallis of a cross between a Pug and a Schnauzer.

Oh, that lady was going to be trouble! But worse than Queen Mary was her daughter-in-law, the Duchess of York, married to the Prince of Wales's brother, second in line for the throne if anything happened to David, as he was called by his family. This was *not* going to happen. No, not ever. She hadn't come this far to have it all blow up in her face.

They were not going to have to depend on any royal allowance if events transpired the way she had hoped and David had dreamed. War was coming, maybe not right now or next year or the next, but soon enough. That was what Ribbentrop had said. And when it did, David would become a Gauleiter and Wallis a queen. *Gauleiter* was a German word that Ribbentrop had introduced her to, and she had become most fond of it. It meant the governor of a German district. If there was war and Germany won, Ribbentrop had told her that Hitler planned to make the Prince of Wales the King of England! Yes, England and the British Isles would be theirs as well as the rest of the Commonwealth – Canada, India, all the rest!

She and the Prince of Wales were not going to lose – not their home, not their title, not their throne and not their crowns. 'It can all be arranged,' Ribbentrop said as he rolled over, his phallus erect and beckoning as she slid down his belly, her mouth salivating, that last night they were together. Talk about having her cake and eating it, too. He was a great lover and seemed to appreciate certain specialties that she had learned in a Shanghai brothel.

She now took the most recent letter from David that was waiting for her when she arrived at Los Gallos.

> *Darling, I apologize for taking so long to respond to your last letter. My valet had to use the Royal Smelling Salts to revive me. Her crown? You want to try on Mummy's crown? Yes, I am sure that would be no problem at all. Of course, she would first have to consent to being on the same continent as you, but I am sure that can be arranged. But crowns aren't all they are made out to be. They're very heavy, quite cumbersome and, even in the most formal of clothing, one tends to look 'overdressed' in a crown.*
>
> *I am, as you know, determined to marry you. You shall wear that crown. Would you die for me, my darling?*
>
> *Lovingly, David.*

She took out a sheet of paper and began to reply to his note.

> *My dearest,*
> *You asked if I would die for you. Need you ask? Really?*
> *David, my dear, I would kill for you.*

There was a knock on her door.

'Yes?'

Dr Bernard Ellington opened the door and stuck his head in. 'You didn't hear the cocktail bell?'

'Oh, goodness me, miss the tolling of such a bell!'

She folded the letter she had just begun and slipped it into the English–German dictionary in her lingerie drawer, which she then locked.

ELEVEN

At the Santa Fe Police Department the following morning, Florence Gilbert had her Dictaphone on as she typed up a report that Ryan had dictated to be sent to the attorney general's office about the lackadaisical behavior of the public defender's office.

> *I find it reprehensible that Mateo Chee has been languishing in our jail for more than a week without having seen a public defender after being charged with the murder of Flora Namingha. The Bureau of Indian Affairs has been called up on this sort of thing already three times in the past year.*

A shadow was cast over her desk as she typed. She glanced up. A very peculiar-looking woman was standing before her. Florence's first reaction was that she was wearing a nightgown, for she was swathed in yards of filmy fabric. She was also wearing a wreath of desert marigolds on her head.

'What can I do for you?' Florence asked.

'I'm here to see Mateo Chee.'

'Are you on the list of approved visitors?'

'Since when is there a list of approved visitors?'

'Since he was brought in here by Harold Bunker, police chief in Taos, and Sheriff McCaffrey locked him up.' That was a teensy little lie, as it had really been Joe Descheeni who had locked him up when the sheriff was in San Francisco.

'Well, I am neither a police chief nor a sheriff.'

No kidding, thought Florence. 'Then I'm afraid you're out of luck.'

'Oh no!' gasped the woman. At that moment, Eddie Collins came in the door.

'What's up, Flor—?' He did not get to the second syllable of her name.

'This lady wants to visit the prisoner and she's not on the list.'

'You haven't even asked me my name. I'm Dorcas Moore.'

'Well, better look up her name, then, Florence.' Collins could not peel his eyes from the woman who stood a foot from him. He could swear that he saw her nipples through her outfit.

Florence brought out a folder. She made a big deal of putting on her spectacles, then she licked her index finger. 'Now, let's see here. This list isn't very long – nope. No Dorcas Moore on it.'

'That's impossible. I posed for him. I slept with him.'

Florence's eyebrows took a hike up to her very high hairline. Collins stifled a laugh.

'It was the Native American Crafts festival in New York,' Dorcas continued.

'Oh, mercy,' Florence said in a weak voice. Then she stood up. 'I don't care where this sexual act occurred, Miss Moore. You are not on the list.'

'Hang on,' Collins said. 'Hang on a minute, Florence. If I take her into the jail wing and let her see him and stay with them at the prescribed distance of ten feet, I think it's OK.'

'How do you know she's not carrying a weapon? You'd have to pat her down, Eddie.'

'No one needs to pat me down!' Dorcas pulled one little string around her waist, and at least five yards of filmy fabric dropped to the floor. She was standing almost nude in her panties and a sheer camisole. She twirled around and faced Collins. 'I'm all yours, sweetheart.'

He blanched and turned to Florence. 'Uh, er, you better come with me, Florence.'

Dorcas turned to Florence and smiled. 'I'm not dangerous, Florence.' She paused and then winked. 'You're really not my type.'

Florence turned bright red. Collins swore her little topknot did a spin on the crown of her head. For some reason, he remembered the officer training book and the regulations when accompanying a visitor to a prison cell.

'Uh, two officers of the law must accompany a visitor into the incarceration wing of the police station. The visit can last no more than ten minutes.

'All right, Miss Moore, Florence and I shall be on either side of you. You cannot stand any closer than ten feet to the cell. All your comments will be recorded. Florence, bring your Dictaphone.'

By some miracle, Florence had pulled herself together. She was all business as she unplugged the Dictaphone. Together, the three of them walked down the west wing of the jail.

'Mateo!' Dorcas wailed and dropped to her knees. 'My darling Mateo.'

Mateo looked up. Confusion swam in his dark eyes.

'Dorcas? What the hell?'

'Mateo, just one night, but you are in my dreams forever. I know that your true love was—'

'You know nothing about my true love. Nothing whatsoever.'

'I know it wasn't—'

'Get out of here!'

Florence and Eddie picked her up, one on each elbow, and carried her out of the incarceration wing through the front office and out to the sidewalk.

'Stay here with her, Eddie. I'll get her clothes,' Florence said.

At that moment, Spud Johnson dashed into the police station. 'What's going on here?'

'Oh, Spud darling!' Dorcas squealed.

'I saw you stagger in here five minutes ago,' said Spud.

'Stagger?' she gasped.

'Yes, stagger, Dorcas.'

'Why are you following me?'

'I'll take care of this,' Spud said quickly, turning to Collins.

Dorcas looked down at her feet, which were more covered than the rest of her, and mumbled something.

'Dorcas, you've been smoking that stuff from Las Cruces, haven't you?'

'Oh, Spud, you worry too much.'

'How did you get here? I hope you didn't drive?'

'No, Pedro brought me.'

'Pedro from the pueblo?'

'He admires me deeply.'

'I bet he does,' Spud muttered.

He was going to have to talk with Mabel when he got back. Dorcas was getting loonier every year. He knew about her fling with Mateo. Mateo had had many flings before he and Flora got together. Mabel had asked him to keep an eye on Dorcas. It seemed to Spud that there was more to keep an eye on than usual.

TWELVE

I t felt good to be back in the Pink House. Outside the walls of Los Gallos, the views were especially thrilling for Georgia. She had a better perspective of the sky and the surrounding landscape. The world seemed finer up here – wider, emptier. There was more time to think without the constant banter of the guests. And right at this moment, she was thinking that there was something that she had missed at the scene of the crime. She had been there, after all, in the half-light of the dawn, and even after the sun rose and Joe and Sergeant Collins had come, there were shadows that crisscrossed the chapel. She wanted to look at the crime scene again, but not only that. One question had dogged Georgia's mind. How had the car – and the perpetrator must have come by car, or maybe horse – gotten to the chapel? Not by the normal way of the Old Kiowa Road, then pulling up to Frieda's house and walking down the path. Was there another road by which someone could approach? Another pathway?

She looked out the broad window of the Pink House. The landscape unfolded before her. It was so different here than where she had been born and raised – Sun Prairie, Wisconsin. The land back in Sun Prairie was farmland. It stretched forever with precious few distractions. No mountains, no mesas or rocks sculpted by millennia of wind and rain. The landscape was spare and bereft of detail. Endless fields of wheat and grain that were distinguished only by what had been plowed and what had been seeded. There was the skyline, and it was never interrupted by a hill or crest. There was a hypnotic calmness to the land as compared to the Southwest. It had layers of geological history – an almost tangible history of the earth. She had often found relics of this past turbulent history – a shark's tooth, a mastodon bone. All this confirming what she had been told as a child: that once there were dinosaurs across this desert land; once there was a prehistoric sea through which giant fish swam. Her whole family laughed raucously when she blurted out, 'And I missed it!'

But when she came to the Southwest for the first time, she knew she hadn't missed it entirely. There were traces of this primeval world all around her. She fell in love with bones and rocks. She found dinosaur teeth from millions of years ago and petroglyphs from a thousand years ago. She was in a time of lost seas and the splinters of asteroids. A timelessness began to creep into every cell of her body.

But now, as she gazed out the window of the Pink House, she knew she had missed something in the chapel where Flora was murdered. She remembered one of Stieglitz's favorite quotes from Albert Einstein, whom he worshiped. It was about the notion of time. The only reason for time is so that everything doesn't happen at once. 'A practical man!' Stieglitz had exclaimed. 'Very practical for a theoretical physicist!'

Well, for Georgia, living in this place where eras overlapped with such ease and grace, a condition that she reveled in, she knew now that she needed to go back to the chapel. Everything cannot happen all at once – even murder. This indeed was a universal truth.

In another hour, the heat would be blistering. Better to go now. Siesta time here. In half an hour, both the town of Taos and the pueblo would be thick with sleep. Yes, a dense, almost magical sleep that would settle upon the landscape as if a spell had been cast in some sort of fairy tale. Now would be the time to go.

Twenty minutes later, Georgia turned off the Old Taos Road a half-mile before the Kiowa Road. If there was a back way into the Lawrence ranch, it might be this way. It was rough going, but she hadn't really lost her bearings. There was an old morada, one of the chapels of the Penitentes brothers, long abandoned, but the cross still stood. She could see that it bent slightly westward at an angle. The angle was different when compared to the view one had from the Lawrence ranch. But it served as a sort of compass in Georgia's head. It was as if a needle in her brain were swinging. She squinted her eyes and imagined the course she might pursue to get to the Lawrence chapel from this angle. Maybe this was how the murderer approached, easily bypassing the main house of the Lawrences. She pulled over to the side, climbed out of the Model A, and began to walk down the rutted road in a southeasterly direction.

She had been walking less than five minutes when she found the possible beginning of a path that turned down a steep embankment. She began to descend. She had not gone far when she saw that smack in the middle of the path was a neatly coiled rattlesnake. She stopped and gripped her snake stick.

'Well, *hombre*, this is not your usual time of day. Whatcha doin' out at midday? You going to move or what? Awfully bright for you out here, isn't it?' She looked at the vertical slits in the jade-green eyes. The snake began to uncoil. It was beautiful to watch. There was something almost hypnotic about the diamond designs of its skin. The beautiful shifting geometry slid into ever-changing patterns as the diamonds stretched and contracted when the reptile began to move across the path. '*Au revoir*,' Georgia said softly. The sagebrush trembled in a light wind.

She continued down the path. 'Ah-ha!' she whispered to herself five minutes later as she caught a glimpse of the chapel through a thicket of aspen trees. She stood still. She was approaching the chapel from the northeast, so only part of the stained-glass window was visible. It was the piece of glass with the pink iris. The petals of an iris, any iris, had always intrigued her. The way they folded back upon each other was almost like a dance, a ballet configuration. Even from this angle, Mateo had done a masterful job of translating her painting on to glass. He had succeeded in capturing the mystery at the very center of the iris that showed the veins of a contrasting color that burst from its throat.

That mystery of a flower unfurling seemed to have transmuted into the mystery of the death that lurked at the center of this chapel and now possessed Georgia. She knew the murderer couldn't be Mateo.

She approached the chapel slowly. She had brought an evidence bag of sorts with her. She wasn't sure exactly what evidence she thought she might find. It just seemed like the proper thing to do. A landscape artist did not bound into a field without tools. She supposed it was presumptuous to call herself a police detective; nevertheless, she should be prepared.

It was her old knitting bag that she used for collecting interesting rocks or the rattles she cut off aggressive snakes when she killed them. She found the rattles infinitely beautiful, and she kept them in bowls around her house back at the Ghost Ranch. She felt a bit silly now as she stood in the chapel in the puddles of color that fell through the two windows at high noon.

The smell of the concrete had dissipated, and the light had shifted, of course, as the sun outside moved in small increments across the sky. This in itself captivated her. She sat down on the earthen floor and watched the patches of light. A rose-colored patch was edging toward the corner of the altar. It was the corner where she had picked up several fragments of the broken urn that Flora had made for Lawrence's ashes. But now she noticed something different. The corner of the altar had been disturbed just a little. It looked as if the formwork surrounding the base of the altar on that corner had been pushed up slightly as the cement had set. It did not match the other corners. She walked over and crouched low. Indeed, it appeared as if some of the wet concrete had squeezed out from beneath the form. Someone had taken the trouble to scrape it off the dirt floor. She ran her hand over the surface of the floor and felt some gritty particles. She looked at her hand. The earthen floor left reddish dust on her palm, but there were a few gray specks of dried cement.

She sat cross-legged on the floor and rested her elbows on her knees. She had to think. First, she had found an alternate route to the chapel that avoided being seen by Frieda, and it was off the Old Taos Road, not the Kiowa Road. Therefore, the killer might be someone who knew the region fairly well. Second, the time frame could be narrowed, as Georgia figured the cement had been poured around mid-afternoon, perhaps just a few hours before she had arrived to see the sunset light coming through the stained glass and heard Mateo and Flora making love. She had also heard Frieda and Sybil arguing. So Mateo and Flora had arrived very soon after the concrete was poured. It was a 'quickie'. Georgia smiled to herself. She recalled what Alfred called 'quickies' in the shanty at Lake George when they succeeded in sneaking off from the absolute lather of weekend guests to make love. She supposed he was doing that now with Dorothy Norman.

The killer, Georgia reflected, must have come sometime after, say, seven thirty in the evening, when the cement would still be wet. And it would have been almost dark. The killer also must have been someone who knew the territory if he found that back way to the chapel. But what would his motive have been? Was Flora's death an unintended consequence of some other objective? If so, what was the primary objective? And who carried a rock of that size? Why not a knife or a gun? There could be myriad weapons that would have been much more transportable than an eight-pound rock. Surely the intention hadn't been to steal the ashes. There was no way to do that after they had been entombed in concrete.

Georgia was uncertain how long she had been sitting there, but as the shadows began to lengthen, she scraped up some of the concrete grits from the floor and put them in her evidence bag. She poked with her little finger beneath the base of the form boards. She could feel more grit. Taking a hairpin from her bun, she prodded a bit more beneath the board and found a somewhat larger piece of loose concrete about the size of a marble. She dropped it in the evidence bag. She looked about. The light and the shadows had definitely changed in the chapel. It must be getting on toward two in the afternoon. She seldom wore a watch since she'd come out west. She prided herself on being able to tell the time by the sun or the moon. She liked the idea of becoming synchronous with the moon and the stars, the planets and the earth. She couldn't do this easily in New York. There was 'bad light', as she thought of it. It spoiled darkness, and there was never enough sky, although her nighttime paintings of the city were in their own way satisfying. She had committed to darkness in those paintings, not just darkness but blackness as a foil for skyscrapers and the city. Only then did the cityscape come alive for her. Only then had she made her truce with darkness.

Finally, Georgia rose from the earthen floor. Giving one last look at the pools of light spreading across the ground, she headed out the door of the chapel and began to walk toward her car. Then, instead of going to the exact spot where she had parked, she chose to walk farther for several feet to see if there were any signs of tire tracks where someone else might have pulled over to the side. She made her way slowly, peering down the whole time.

The first irregularity she noticed was a depression in the dirt. It was as if the road had been worn away. Wheels had spun on the right side of the car, but there were no tire treads. The grass on the edge had been flattened – not just flattened but gouged. If it hadn't rained, there might have been tire tracks. She walked around to the other side of where a car might have parked – the left side. The ground here was less disturbed. She looked down. Something caught her eye against the reddish dirt of the road – a gray flattish fragment. Georgia in her decades as a pedestrian in cities had stepped in enough dog shit or coyote shit to recognize the signs of having to scrape one's foot off. The difference here was the color – gray. She held the fragment to her nose. Odorless. This was not dog shit; it was cement that had now hardened. Georgia could imagine the person approaching the car door and realizing that he had tracked the wet or damp concrete up to the car. She could picture him opening the car door, sitting on the seat and scraping it off the sole of his shoe. *Had any gotten into the car?* Georgia wondered.

She drove back to Taos and pulled through the gates of Los Gallos. A rather spiffy-looking roadster was stopped in front of the entry. A young woman opened the door and jumped out of the front seat. Lady Sybil Hatch ran toward the car. 'Bunny! And Eldon! Here at last!'

'Oh my God,' muttered Georgia. Sybil's daughter was called Bunny, as in Bunny Hatch. Did they not know that rabbits were kept in hutches? This was a bit too close for comfort in Georgia's mind. From the passenger side, a slender young man in a cream-colored suit and a boater hat stepped out. *The Great Gatsby?* Georgia mused.

What was the world coming to out here? The young woman looked like anything but a bunny. She was tall but substantially built, broad of shoulders and hips. Her hair tumbled to her shoulders in a froth of blond curls. When she turned so Georgia could see her face, she looked like a rather overgrown Shirley Temple. Complete with dimples. This must be the daughter engaged to the rich American. She now recalled that she had also heard that the daughter was involved with a gallery in London that specialized in primitive art, or, as Sybil corrected, Outsider Art. 'It's not simply cave paintings – it's "crafts" and "Outsider Art". There's nothing primitive about it.' She then added, 'As a matter of fact, Mabel was inspired to start her New York show at the Armory because of my daughter's gallery.'

The mother and daughter now raced toward each other and embraced.

'Darling Mummy.'

'You're here! Here at last! Little Bunster.'

Oh, for crying out loud! I might throw up, thought Georgia.

'Well, I don't want to say thank heavens for the delay of Lorenzo's memorial, given the tragedy, but my train was delayed in Washington, and then in Chicago, where I was supposed to transfer, there was a blizzard – imagine, a blizzard in April!'

'But where did you get this adorable roadster?'

'A gift from Eldon.' She turned and blew a kiss to the handsome young man. 'His father had it shipped out here from Chicago and to Santa Fe, where I picked it up.'

'How generous!'

'Indeed, Mummy.' She paused. 'And the delay of the service was because someone was actually murdered?'

'Yes, very sad. The body was discovered in the chapel.'

'Who was it?'

'A local girl.' Sybil said this so dismissively that Georgia felt slightly bilious. How offhand the privileged were.

'Who found the body?'

'Georgia – Georgia O'Keeffe.'

'Who's she?'

'You know, dear, the painter. She's quite famous. You haven't heard of her?'

'No, I don't know the name. I don't keep up with the contemporary art scene at all.'

Keep up with an art scene. The words seemed odd to Georgia. It suggested a runaway train or perhaps a stampede of paintings roaring across a vast terrain.

'There she is now! Georgia! Come over and meet my daughter, Bunny.'

'Not right now, Sybil. I'm a mess. Have to get ready for dinner. See you for cocktails.'

THIRTEEN

The Big Room at Los Gallos was packed. More locals had been recruited to help serve. Jessie was walking around with trays of hors d'oeuvres. Wallis Simpson was holding court, as it were, in one corner.

'So, the Prince of Wales's girlfriend is here to mourn as well, I see,' a voice whispered behind Georgia.

'Ansel, I can't believe it!' Georgia wheeled about and embraced him. 'I didn't think you could get away – what with a newborn and all.'

'Little Annie is doing fine.'

'You staying here?'

'Are you joking?' He opened his eyes wide, and a generous smile creased his face. Even though his nose appeared to take a slight left turn, his face was handsome. When he was just four years old, the San Francisco earthquake had tossed him to the ground, fracturing his nose badly. Over the years, the hair on his head had thinned, but his beard had thickened.

'You brought Waldorf?' Waldorf was Ansel's tent for camping out.

'Waldorf is still going. A few more patches, that's all.'

'Don't tell me the patch I sewed on six years ago failed?'

'No, that patch is fine. Just a few more added. You know I bought that tent on my fifteenth birthday!'

'So you're staying in it tonight?'

'Yes, out by the morada. I want to be here for Good Friday – the pilgrimage. The real reason that I'm coming, however, is Mary Austin. Before she died last year—'

'Mary, the author you worked with for your Taos Pueblo book?'

Ansel nodded. 'I promised her that I would take pictures before she died and I'd slip them into the next printing. And there is to be a second printing soon.

'Oh dear,' Georgia said and closed her eyes. A phrase of Mary's echoed in her mind: *The true desert breeds its own kind, each in a particular habitat, the frontage of a hill, the structure of the soil determines the plant.* Mary Austin was definitely her own kind, Georgia thought. She looked about. *Own kind.* What did that really mean? She glimpsed Dorcas Moore, who was excessively animated as she talked with Tony Luhan. What kind was her kind, for God's sake? All she could think about was chickens! And then there was the doctor, Bernard Ellington, in conversation with Lorna Charles, a gallery owner from New York who was a close friend of Mabel's.

'I have a great view of the procession from my window. I'm staying up at the Pink House. But that's the distant view as they approach. I'll most likely go out and try a closer perspective.'

'Looking forward to seeing the stained-glass work you designed for the Lawrence chapel.'

Georgia sighed. 'Yes, and you heard about the murder, of course. I don't believe for one moment it was Mateo.'

'Mateo the glass artist? They arrested him?'

Georgia nodded.

Ansel shook his head. 'That doesn't sound right at all.'

'It's not. I've never been surer of anything in my life.' She paused. 'What evidence do they have?'

'Not much that I can tell. Mateo and the girl were lovers.'

'Lovers' quarrel?' Ansel asked.

Georgia shook her head. 'I wouldn't really know. They planned to marry. Both fine artists. She was a potter.'

'Oh, my goodness, there's Eldon Burke.' Ansel lifted his chin and nodded across the room as he glimpsed the young man wearing a pale, cream-colored double-breasted blazer with tan pants and a very bold but narrow plaid tie with a small knot. He was lean with an angular jaw but a somewhat blunt nose. The nose looked as if it had wandered into the wrong face. He had what Georgia thought of as a Florida tan. No one had a tan like that this time of year except people who went to Florida for the winter.

'You know him?' Georgia asked. 'I just saw him for the first time today.'

'Ah, my dear, you've missed too many years out here. He's Bunny Hatch's boyfriend. He's come out a couple of times in the past few years. I'm told that the narrow ties with a small knot are now in fashion, thanks to the Prince of Wales.'

'Well, aren't you a fount of fashion knowledge!' Georgia said.

'And would you believe it, Bunny is now talking to the apple of the Prince of Wales's eye?'

'Hardly an apple! That scrawny thing?' Georgia muttered.

'Indeed. Wallis Simpson.'

Georgia gave a sigh, and they continued to look at the two women.

'You know, Ansel, don't hold this against me, but I find it diffi-cult to take anyone with a name like Bunny Hatch seriously.'

Ansel gave a deep chuckle.

Mabel was now making her way through the crowd, clapping her hands above her head to draw people's attention. She was wearing a white turban that reminded Georgia of a giant mushroom or perhaps a marshmallow. A young boy, the nephew of a friend of Georgia's, had once told her that marshmallows had been invented by the Egyptians two thousand years ago. She looked it up and he was correct. This is what she loved about children. Their endless curiosity into – dare she say – concrete things like marshmallows. None of this spiritual mumbo-jumbo – cosmic harmony rot.

Now she remembered the earnestness of the little fellow. Peter was his name. He was about eight years old. He had been standing in front of a painting of hers at Stieglitz's gallery, admiring the clouds. 'Like stretched marshmallows,' he said softly.

'Really!' Georgia exclaimed.

'Yeah,' the boy replied. 'You can do that when you roast them slowly – stretch them out like kind of a stringy cloud.'

'Yes, you're so right. I remember that from when I was a girl.' She laughed. 'That was long ago, of course.'

'Not as long ago as when marshmallows were invented.'

'Really now? Are you sure?'

'Yes.' The little boy inhaled deeply and brushed back his auburn bangs. 'No one realizes that marshmallows are a very ancient food. Invented by the Egyptians more than two thousand years ago, most likely during the reign of the Pharaoh Hatshepsut.'

And so they had continued talking. Another tidbit she had learned from this child was that if you were ever chased by an alligator, one should run in a zigzag path. They can't catch you. Kids were so willing to share arcane bits of information. There was no pretense, just truth really. To think that she might have been able to have had hundreds of conversations like that one with her own child if Stieglitz had not insisted on an abortion.

Meanwhile, Stieglitz himself, who had been standing not three feet away from her as she conversed with this eight-year-old, was

talking to some preeminent art critic about how 'women feel the
world differently than a man feels it . . . That a woman receives
the world through her womb. That is the seat of her deepest feeling.
Mind comes second.'

She had wanted to turn around and slug Stieglitz, but instead she
had crouched down and whispered to the little boy, 'Tell me more,
Peter. How can I protect myself from wild beasts?'

'Well, lions are another story,' he went on.

Every time she thought she had gotten over the abortion, that
vision of a child who never was would come back to haunt her,
peek around a door of her mind, so to speak, and say, *Remember
me. Remember me, the unborn one.* Sometimes she even felt a
phantom cramping of her womb expelling the fetus. And sometimes
it was as if the little ghost fetus loomed on the edge of her dreams.
The gender was never quite clear, but he or she was there, always.
And her profound anger with Stieglitz would swell like a tidal wave
within her.

'Quiet, please! Quiet!' Mabel was clapping louder, but the conversation continued. 'Jessie, get me the gong,' she ordered.

Jessie rushed back with the Tibetan cymbals she had purchased
on her last grand tour.

A crashing noise reverberated through the Big Room. The cocktail chatter instantly evaporated.

'Excellent,' she exclaimed. 'And if you are very good, I shall
perform for you later the Tibetan Cham dance, the dance of
compassion, but now I'd like to welcome you all to honor
the passing of our dear David Herbert Lawrence, or Lorenzo, as
we knew him. We shall meet tomorrow morning at the chapel where
his ashes are now interred.' She pressed her thin lips together in a
near grimace as she said 'interred'. Georgia wondered if Mabel
could restrain herself from giving her own opinion. The last word
anyone would ever use with Mabel was 'restraint'. But Tony was
standing beside her, and she saw him give her hand a squeeze.
'However, we also have something happy to celebrate tonight, and
that is the engagement of Bunny – daughter of our dear friend
and long-time visitor to Los Gallos, Sybil Hatch – to Eldon Burke.'
Clapping broke out and Eldon pressed Bunny's hand to his lips.
Bunny blushed. 'So, to the future Mr and Mrs Burke, let us raise
a glass!'

There was a wave of 'Hear, hear' as people raised their glasses.

Ansel leaned over to Georgia's ear. 'So, a name change. How does that suit you?'

'Bunny Burke – somewhat alliterative, don't you think?'

Upstairs, as she usually did during the cocktail hour, Maudie went about freshening up her lady's room. The first thing she always did was take a hairpin from her own hair to pick the very pickable lock of the drawer where Mrs Simpson kept her lingerie. It was humiliating enough to have to wash the woman's underthings, but she was strictly forbidden to open this drawer. Maudie, however, had learned to pick locks as a small child from her brother Alfie. And what she had found in this drawer, in the English–German dictionary, was priceless. Letters from the Prince of Wales as well as her other lovers, sales slips that she was obviously hiding from the prince until she guessed he could pay them. He was on some sort of allowance that came in once a month. Mrs Simpson tried to space out the bills, and on this night Maudie found an unfinished letter that she had started apparently just before the cocktail bell rang.

> *My dearest,*
> *You asked if I would die for you. Need you ask? Really?*
> *David, my dear, I would kill for you. And don't worry about*
> *your mother's reaction to me. I am sure after she gets to know*
> *me, we shall have a great fondness for each other . . .*

A chill ran through Maudie.

FOURTEEN

'Where do I go, Spud?' Georgia asked as they all filed into the large dining room with the two long tables.

'Right over there, dear – between Ansel and Eldon.' She pulled out a chair and seated herself.

'I don't believe I've had the pleasure, Miss O'Keeffe, of meeting you on my previous visits,' said Eldon Burke.

'No, it's been a while. But I understand you have been here on a few occasions in the past couple of years.'

'Yes, Bunny is responsible. Ironic, isn't it – a girl from England introducing me to the American Wild West?'

'Well, this is my first time back here in almost five years, but I must admit your name rang a bell for me.'

'I think I might be able to refresh your memory.' He paused and gave a quick smile. His deep green eyes twinkled. 'Shell painting.'

'Oh! You bought the shell painting!'

'My father, Eldon senior – or Chance, as he is called. It was for our house in Palm Beach. It would fit, don't you think?'

A year ago, when that painting sold, it had broken the record as the highest price ever for a painting by a living artist in America. But Eldon's response startled Georgia. It would fit. Fit what? Did people buy paintings the way they buy clothes?

'I suppose so,' she said hesitantly. 'But I've never seen your house.'

'Beachfront.'

In her own mind, she had a sudden picture of sand and tide running through the house.

'And you know that delicate pink of the inside of the conch shell? Mummy had the couches recovered to match it.'

'How . . . how . . . how very clever.' Georgia felt lost in this conversation. She turned to Ansel. 'Ansel, did you hear that?'

'Hear what?'

'This fellow, Eldon Burke – his mother recovered the couches in their Palm Beach house to match the shell painting I did.'

Ansel blinked rapidly. 'Uh, how curious.' Then he smiled broadly.

'Well, I suppose that leaves me out as I photograph almost exclusively in black and white, even with this new invention of Kodak's color film.'

'Oh, don't worry, sir, we have a number of your black-and-white photos in Mummy and Dad's Chicago apartment.'

'Ah!' exclaimed Georgia. 'Perfect place. "Hog Butcher, for the World, Tool Maker, Stacker of Wheat."'

Ansel guffawed, but Eldon appeared totally confused.

'Carl Sandburg, my dear.' Georgia clapped her hands together gleefully. 'The poem "Chicago".'

'Oh, yes!' Eldon smiled broadly, but it was clear from the blank look in his eyes that he had never heard of the poem or even the poet.

My, my, thought Georgia, *Bunny has bagged herself a winner.* She looked around the tables. She wondered if anyone in this room had known Flora? Would anyone care that a lovely young artist had been murdered? She felt so apart from this crowd. She wished Ryan were here. Talk about a fish out of water – that would be Ryan with this crowd. But he would have liked Ansel. He knew him a bit.

'Pardon me, ma'am.' A girl with a soft British accent leaned over to clear the salad plates.

'Ah, you must be Maudie?'

'Yes,' she replied softly. Her face suddenly turned a pale green. She dropped the salad plate with a clatter and clutched her stomach. 'Oh, oh, oh!' She gasped and vomited over the new plate she had just set down with the second course. Clapping her hands to her mouth, she fled the dining room.

Wallis gave a little shriek. Mabel stood up, frozen for a moment.

Georgia had already flown from the table in the wake of Maudie. She found the girl in the kitchen, hanging over the sink.

'Now, now!' Georgia said. 'Let me help you.'

'Oh, ma'am, I didn't mean to do it. I really didn't.'

'Of course you didn't! No one means to throw up.'

'Now, now.' Mabel was on the other side of Maudie. 'Don't worry, dear.'

'This is inexcusable!' a voice behind Georgia hissed. She knew exactly who it was. It took all of her courage not to turn around and slug her.

'Can I be of help?' Bernard Ellington had now joined the others crowding around the sink.

Wallis was still fuming. 'You can't get away with this kind of behavior.'

'What in God's name are you talking about, Wallis?' the doctor gasped.

'Vomiting in public.'

'Wallis, get out!' he said in a voice that had more than an edge of danger to it. This surprised Georgia. Ironically, the edge in his voice suggested to her that he must know Wallis Simpson better than she had realized. Did they have some history together?

An immediate fondness for the doctor sprung up in Georgia.

'Yes, get out,' Georgia reiterated.

'Can I help here?' Cowboy was immediately by Maudie's side. 'Out of the way, ma'am.' He scowled at Wallis Simpson. Then, almost lifting Maudie up, he guided her away from the kitchen and to a chair. Georgia and Mabel followed closely behind.

'Here you go, Maudie, my dear,' Cowboy said as he gently set her down on the chair. His large, rough hands patted the top of her head.

'Is she all right?' It was Eldon. His eyes weren't on Maudie but on Cowboy as he tenderly wiped her face with a damp cloth. 'Marcus, she OK?'

'Yeah. She's going to be fine,' he muttered.

'Now, Maudie,' Mabel said, 'let Jessie here fix you a cup of tea, and I'll bring another damp cloth to wipe up your blouse.'

'That will be good,' Cowboy said and stood back a step.

Georgia watched as Mabel kneeled with the damp cloth and began wiping Maudie's blouse and gently around her mouth.

'I can't stand her, ma'am,' said Maudie.

'Me neither,' Mabel muttered.

Spud had just arrived. 'Maudie, dear, I'll walk you back to your quarters.'

'But, sir, I have to lay out Mrs Simpson's nightgown and undo her bun and brush out her hair.'

'Maudie!' Mabel said sharply. 'Mrs Simpson is a big girl. She can do this herself. Now, you go along with Spud.'

Spud extended his hand toward the girl. She took it and got up. Putting an arm around her waist, he led her out of the kitchen.

Georgia knew she should go back to the dinner table, but she didn't really have the heart to do so. She thought of the people in the dining room. With the exception of Ansel, for the most part they did not appeal to her. Some were artists, yes, but many were hangers-on, aspiring artists.

She glanced into the dining room and saw Dorcas and Wallis sitting next to each other in a tête-à-tête. In Georgia's mind, the specter of feathers still hovered around the woman. The candlelight cast a flawless, waxy sheen on both their faces. But the oddest effect was their eyes: not closed, not open, but as if their eyes were part of a death mask, with no seam visible of an eyelid or eyelashes, just a bulge – a bulge of emptiness.

Georgia was tired. She had forgotten how exhausting it could be at Mabel's. All the people, all the talk, the thinly veiled competition. A real prize for an artist at Los Gallos was to come away with an introduction to an agent or gallery owner. She remembered the last time she was here: at least three people wanted introductions to Stieglitz when they went back to New York. She had her stock answer ready: 'I can't tell Alfred anything. Stieglitz does what he wants to do.'

It struck her now that one of the few people who would not be seeking to advance his career was Dr Bernard Ellington. He seemed to fit in nicely. He was a jolly sort and a good conversationalist, but still she wondered why he was here. Perhaps he was or had been a doctor for Mabel or Tony. She suddenly liked him better when she realized this. But had he really been trying to make a pass at her the other night? Not only that, but she had seen him that same night crawling out of Wallis Simpson's window!

And now she saw Bunny and Wallis with their heads together in what appeared to be an intense and intimate conversation.

'Oh, you must see this, Mummy!' Bunny suddenly cried out to her mother, who at that moment was standing by Georgia's elbow and about to take her seat at the table.

'Come, Georgia, let's go see what my little Bunny is plotting with the next queen of the empire.'

'You don't think that's really going to happen? Mrs Simpson and the Prince of Wales?' Georgia asked.

'I wouldn't put it beyond her. I wouldn't put much beyond this gilded whore.'

'Why, Sybil!' Georgia said in only slightly mocking surprise. Sybil Hatch was a royalist to the bitter end, and she could be bitter.

'What is it, sweetheart?' Sybil said, coming up to her daughter and putting a motherly arm around her waist.

Bunny's luxurious curls fell to one side of her face as she had loosened her hair comb.

'Mrs Simpson . . .' she began.

'Oh, just call me Wallis, dear.'

Bunny seemed to glow at this invitation to intimacy. 'Wallis and I have the same hair comb.' She looked up at Wallis, who was loosening her own hair. 'Except hers is diamonds and mine is mere Bakelite with some sparkly chips. But both butterfly wings.' She giggled. 'I lost the other one. It must be somewhere – not sure where.'

'Well, we can put an end to that.' Eldon came up to the three-some on his way to resume his own seat. 'My future wife should not wear plastic. I'll have a talk with my mother's jeweler, Harry Winston.'

Georgia felt a tinge of nausea rising in her gut, and she nodded to the group. 'Been a long day. I think I'll head off to bed.' She picked up her shawl from where she had been sitting.

'So nice meeting you, Mrs O'Keeffe,' Bunny said.

'It's Miss O'Keeffe,' Georgia corrected.

'But aren't you married to that Jewish man you mentioned the other evening?' Wallis asked.

Georgia was stunned for a moment. 'Yes, I am married to Alfred Stieglitz, a photographer in addition to being a Jew. I am his wife. But I am a painter. Georgia O'Keeffe.' She then inhaled. 'I actually feel that I am a very religious person, but I am not part of a religion. I suppose at best I might be a Buddhist.'

'How exotic,' Wallis murmured.

'Exotic?' Georgia was dumbfounded. 'It's not something I wear.'

She excused herself and walked out quickly. She needed to get to bed. She was wondering how she might survive the next few days, but she wanted to. Buddhist or agnostic, she was determined to see the pilgrimage on Good Friday.

Back at the Pink House, she began to undress but stopped abruptly when she realized how beautiful the evening was – blue, a dark, dark blue that was almost black but pricked with glittering stars. And like a thin dark veil of the Catholic Church, the shadow of a cross of the nearby morada, the meeting house of the Penitentes, spread across the ground. Had it been Good Friday, hundreds of

Penitentes would have walked the distance from San Cristobal, many from as far as Santa Fe, bearing crosses and some flagellating themselves with coarse ropes. She had to paint that cross right now, with the flickering stars behind it as she stood half naked and mildly chilly in the darkness of her own bedroom. The light was perfect for painting the morada. It would be perfect for a few more hours until the darkness began to be chased out by the new day. She must not waste it. So she painted until two in the morning, and as she finally went to bed, she imagined the morning dawning bright as the sun came through the stained glass of the chapel windows. Then they would truly show. It occurred to her that she might be said to live in a prism, or perhaps she was a prism, an odd living prism through which light refracted. *Funny idea*, she chuckled to herself before dropping off to sleep.

It was still late when Jessie made his way across the patio and through the gates of Los Gallos. He was tired and the question was, should he go home – a five-mile walk to his family's hogan out beyond Calle Valverde? He might prefer sleeping at the police station, a much shorter distance. Mateo Chee had already been taken over to the county jail in Santa Fe.

Fifteen minutes later, Jessie arrived at the station. He felt a soft touch on his hand as he inserted his key in the lock. He yelped and jumped.

'Oh, sorry, I didn't mean to scare you.'

'What the hell?' Jessie blurted.

'Sorry, really sorry.' It was the guest from Los Gallos, the one whose engagement had been announced to the Bunny lady. There was the shadow of a slight smile. 'I just . . . just . . . find you very . . . very . . .'

Fucking mariposa! Jessie thought as the man leaned over to kiss him. 'Get out of my way!' Jessie shoved him. The man fell to the ground and looked up pathetically.

'You don't understand,' Eldon pleaded.

'I goddamn well understand!' Jessie unlocked the door, stepped through and then slammed it. He heard a sob outside and went to the window. The man was still crumpled on the ground. Jessie watched as slowly he picked himself up and began to walk off.

There were a lot of queers in Taos, but nobody had ever approached him before. Spud was as queer as they come, but he was always a gentleman – a perfect gentleman. Jessie thought of himself as an almost virgin. He recalled now the profoundly embarrassing moment at the chapel with Dr Bryce and the two officers from Santa Fe. When Georgia had told them about the sounds of lovemaking in the chapel, Jessie had the agonizing realization that he was the only virgin in the group. It was mortifying. Shortly after that, to correct the situation, he'd gone over to Los Burros with his older cousin to the Desert Lily. But it didn't quite work. He came off before he could get his *pito* into the girl. But he was going again in a few days or so, just before Good Friday – not Easter! Valentine had been the whore's name, and she was very patient. He was getting hard now just thinking about her. *Don't you dare*, he muttered in Navajo.

He went to the window again and saw that the man who was Bunny Hatch's fiancé was gone. *Some fiancé!* he thought. He needed to distract himself. He remembered that Miss O'Keeffe had dropped off an evidence bag. She wanted him to look at some concrete fragments that she had found near where a car had parked. He hadn't even logged them in yet, so he went to the locker where the evidence was kept. He was glad that the chief had not signed off on it and sent it all directly over to Santa Fe. This was really their case. It had happened in their county. Yes, they had more sophisticated forensics over there, but Jessie had finally persuaded Harold to get some more equipment. The body, of course, had to go to Santa Fe. They didn't have a morgue in Taos. He took out the bag and spread the small fragments on a clean tray. It drove him nuts how Homer and Harold treated evidence. They never wore rubber gloves. If measurement was involved, they almost never recorded it accurately. They handled everything roughly, and if Homer was smoking, he inevitably let ash fall on to or into the evidence.

Now he looked at these fragments of cement. Some had what appeared to be dried mud on them, others not. There had been blood on the rock that served as the murder weapon and on the ground where some had puddled. The coroner, Emily Bryce, had collected scrapings from the rock and the ground and had sent back her report with the blood analysis. The actual cause of death was called 'significant blunt trauma caused by several blows to the head resulting in multiple skull fractures, bleeding across both sides of the brain'. 'Significant blunt trauma', Jessie reflected, must be similar to someone who had fallen from a building several stories high or had an eight-pound rock smashed on their head, which was exactly what had happened. He had weighed the rock when he got it back to the police station.

He could picture Flora sleeping soundly on her side. The rock, when it was first dropped, would have hit the side of her skull and the right temporal lobe. She perhaps rolled on to her back, so her face was up, fully exposed, and the perpetrator of the crime began to smash the rock into her face. Her nose was completely pulverized.

Head wounds bleed profusely. That was one of the first things Jessie had learned in the book that had become his bible for clinical analysis and autopsy findings in crime. As far as he could tell, there was no blood on these fragments of dried cement that Miss O'Keeffe had found, but the fragments were still interesting. He decided to get out the microscope that he had convinced the police chief to buy and use it to look at one of the smaller fragments.

There was something there that caught his attention. He turned the magnification on the objective lens to the highest point. What he saw was interesting: a seed of some sort. He went back to the crime locker and got out the evidence bag that contained the random debris from the murder weapon itself. There were the few blades of wheat grass that had been stuck to the rock. With tweezers, he put them on a glass plate and slid it under the lens of the microscope. 'A seed, that's what I'm seeing,' Jessie whispered to himself. A seed from the wheat grass stalk on the rock and one on the fragment of the hardened cement. 'It's embedded!'

He closed his eyes and began to imagine the path of the rock and the seed from a stalk of wheat grass. So now he knew that the rock and the seed had originated in the same place, and eventually that seed had wound up where Miss O'Keeffe had found evidence of a car stuck perhaps in the mud where it had been parked. But the seed was now separated from the rock it had traveled on. The rock had been left behind in the chapel with a stalk of wheat grass stuck to it. In short, the seed had drifted off the stalk into the wet cement and then traveled back with the murderer to the parked car. It must have stuck to the murderer's shoe when he left the scene of the crime with a clot of the cement stuck to his sole. The driver then scraped the clot off the shoe where it had eventually hardened with the seed embedded. In Jessie's mind, this confirmed that Miss O'Keeffe was right. The murderer had descended to the chapel by way of the Old Taos Road, not the Kiowa Road.

FIFTEEN

Maudie lay in bed thinking. Her nausea had subsided. They had all been so kind and caring about her when she had become ill. Spud had even offered to sit with her until she fell asleep. Miss O'Keeffe was so motherly, and Maudie didn't think she had any children of her own. Nor did Mrs Luhan and her husband, Tony. So why did she have to be stuck with Mrs Simpson, the old bitch? She wondered if she should try to run away again. If she could get to Los Burros, she knew there was a bus that came there. Then she could get to Santa Fe, take a train to Chicago and then get to New York. She had just enough money to get steerage passage to Southampton, England, and then to Rodney!

Would he be mad about the baby? She didn't think so. He was so kind and gentle. He had ten brothers and sisters. He must be accustomed to babies – or maybe he was sick of them? She shut her eyes tight. She couldn't think this way. The main thing was to get away – away from the old bitch, away from this desert. There were a few nice people – Miss O'Keeffe, Jessie, Mr Johnson. Mrs Luhan had enough money to send her back and forth across the Atlantic ten times without batting an eyelash. But dare she ask? Her husband, Tony, was very nice. He was very handsome, too, with his long braids often intertwined with silver threads as they were tonight. She was amazed when she learned that he could barely read and not write at all. But he was still very smart.

She thought back to that night more than a week ago when she tried to run away. It had all been fine when she left, but within an hour it was pouring rain. She stood out on the Old Taos Road. There had only been a single car in forty-five minutes. It had slowed down, and she thought it was going to stop. It almost did, but then it suddenly sped up, spraying dirt – well, actually mud – as it drove away. She sighed and began walking back to Los Gallos. *A muddy chicken I am!* she thought then as she rinsed her skirt and blouse in the sink. There had been something gritty in the mud as it swirled down the sink. She had run the water another minute to get rid of the rest of it.

*   *   *

More than two thousand miles to the east, Chance Burke leaned back in his easy chair at Arenas Doradas, his Palm Beach mansion. He stared at the Georgia O'Keeffe painting his wife had bought almost two years before. The highest price ever for a painting by a living American artist. When Eleanor had heard that their son was going to Los Gallos and that Georgia O'Keeffe would be there, she was desperate to go herself.

'We can't invite ourselves there, El. Mrs Luhan has to know you,' her husband replied from behind his newspaper.

'But she should know us because we paid more than any living human being for that painting.'

'Living human being who has made lots of money, but that doesn't qualify, honey.'

'Don't be coarse, Chance.'

'In the privacy of my own home, I can be as coarse as I want to be.'

Never deterred, Eleanor persisted. 'And, dear, Eldon says that Lady Sybil might announce his and Bunny's engagement.'

Chance put down his paper and rolled his eyes.

'What are you rolling your eyes for?'

Chance merely grunted. He would not say what he had long suspected: his son, Eldon Charles Burke, was a goddamn fairy. He had put detectives on him in New York, where he had first met this Bunny Hatch – Hatch or Hutch? He could never remember. How stupid to call a child Bunny if your last name was Hutch or even Hatch. In any case, while Eldon was screwing the Rabbit, as he thought of her, he was also having a high old time with Jimmy Donahue, the heir to the Woolworth fortune, in New York, visiting the pansy clubs, where men in drag performed and danced with patrons – many in drag themselves. Chance was appalled when he saw the picture of his son in one of his mother's Dior gowns dancing cheek to cheek with Jimmy Donahue. He had never told Eleanor. Had she even missed the gown?

But now he was getting reports back from Blackie, the private detective he had sent out to Taos, that apparently Eldon was up to fruiting around again. Who would have thought that out there in the desert there would have been so many fruits?

'Who?' he had asked Blackie.

'Cowboy,' the detective had replied.

'Cowboys do that? Who's he screwing, John Wayne?'

'No, Mr Burke, the fella is called Cowboy. That's his name. And Eldon seems attracted to him. Or at least was when he was last out there.'

'What's his real name?'

'I don't have a confirmation on that yet. He works in the ranch part of Los Gallos and fixes the guests up with horses and takes them riding.'

'Except, of course, for my son. Who's riding who out there?'

At that moment, Eleanor had come in. 'Who's riding *whom*, Chance?'

Her husband blanched. Had she heard everything? No. He set the phone down, not waiting for an answer, hoping she had been distracted by his grammatical error. 'Ah, you Wellesley girls, always the grammarians.'

'Not such a bad error, darling.' She leaned down and kissed his balding head. 'Not as bad as when you say "ain't".'

Chance blanched. 'Cowboys say "ain't", don't they?'

'I suppose so. Why?'

'Oh, nothing. Just thinking.'

And he was thinking. Thinking he had to put an end to this. The Rabbit seemed nice enough. He expected she was marrying Eldon for his money. But that was OK if Eldon could just get it up enough to produce a baby. He wanted an heir – a nice, rugged, real little boy, not any cowboy heir.

'Cowboy,' he muttered. 'Who calls themselves "Cowboy"?'

SIXTEEN

After painting most of the night, Georgia awoke to a drear morning with a light drizzle that hung like a mantel now over the cross on the morada. In the early afternoon of this same day, the funeral for Flora was supposed to take place. Georgia was happy for this, as she would not have to attend the luncheon on the patio following the memorial celebration in the chapel. She had originally planned to return to Santa Fe and the Ghost Ranch the following day, but she changed her mind. In just another few days, it would be Good Friday, and Ryan had telegraphed that he would not be back as soon as he had previously thought. Ansel had gotten her very interested in seeing the procession, and she had picked out a few perspectives for viewing – one quite close to the morada, others up in the hills looking down at the trail of the Penitentes. People from all over embarked on this journey during Holy Week, walking great distances in pursuit of miracles and to pray. Some would wear cassocks and carry large crosses. Some shouldered figures of their patron saints. And many carried artificial flowers to decorate the shrines and the graves of their families. Georgia had a penchant for artificial silk flowers. But artificial or not, flowers, like religion, had something dark at their centers in her mind.

Although her modest wardrobe had several black garments, Georgia had an unwritten rule of not wearing black to funerals. So she chose a cream-colored dress and thought it would be fitting to wear the lovely pendant that Mateo had made for her, a tiny replica of the stained-glass east window with the pale pink iris that seemed to bend toward the rising sun. She began to prepare for the memorial service.

Two hours later, Georgia was standing in the small chapel. It was crammed. Outside, a dismal light drizzle fell. There was not a scrap of refracted light from Mateo's stained-glass windows. *He should be here*, Georgia thought. *He no more killed that girl than the man in the moon.* She couldn't wait until Ryan got back. He had to look

into this. The only competent person in the Taos police department
was a fifteen-year-old boy who barely shaved.

There were no chairs, and Georgia had declined a position in the
front row. She felt an incredible sadness wash over her with an
undercurrent of anger. She recalled that sinking red moon, teetering
on the edge of the fading darkness on the morning she discovered
the body. Her view from the rear of the chapel now was mostly the
backs of people's heads. To her left, in her own row, she could
observe Bunny Hatch and her mother. Bunny's face was rigid and
devoid of any human expression. Sybil's head was bowed, and she
seemed to be chewing on her bottom lip. Bunny's fiancé looked a
little green around the edges, as if he had had a hard night.

Bunny turned to give a slight smile to Georgia. Her face suddenly
twitched as she caught sight of the pendant hanging from Georgia's
neck. She blinked several times and stared at it so fiercely that
Georgia felt compelled to whisper, 'Is something the matter?'

'Oh no, not at all, just admiring your pendant.'

'Yes, Mateo made it for me when he completed the windows. I
did the design of the stained glass in here.'

'Lovely,' she said softly as she nodded solemnly.

Martin Secker, Lawrence's publisher, was beginning the eulogy.

'In *Apocalypse*, the very last book Lorenzo wrote shortly before
his death, there is this sentence: "We ought to dance with rapture
that we might be alive . . . and part of the living, incarnate cosmos."
Yes, let us think about that rapturous dance of life.'

All that's fine, Georgia thought, *but what if you're cut down like
Flora in the middle of all this rapture, as she was just after making
love to Mateo – what then?*

Did anybody sitting here even know Flora, or care about her if
they did know her? Tony Luhan must have known her. He was now
standing next to Mabel. They both seemed enveloped in grief, but
was any of it for Flora? Mabel in her own way had been in love
with Lorenzo. She had moved heaven and earth to get him to come
to Taos the first time with the gift of a house and land. He prolonged
her agony by coming by way of western Australia. It took him years
to finally arrive and claim his gift.

Another gentleman now came up to the front to speak. He was
impeccably dressed in a style of men's jacket not seen since the
Great War, a morning suit with a curved asymmetrical tailcoat
in the style of Prince Albert, Edward VII. The king had been

notoriously fat, and it was suggested that this cut disguised his enormous posterior. But this man, one Casimir Westcott, was painfully thin. Unknown to most of those gathered, one could sense the mystification his presence provoked. It seemed to saturate the room. He spent several seconds casting his eyes around the assembled mourners before speaking a word.

'Yes, I can tell you are all wondering, who is this man?' He leaned forward and gave a warm smile. 'Well, I don't mean to disappoint you. Or, for that matter, alarm you, but I am – was – well, frankly, continue to be David's – or rather Lorenzo's, as you call him – solicitor.

'I know! I feel you all wincing at the very thought. I think more negative things have been said or written about lawyers than any other profession. And the leader of that pack, of course, is Charles Dickens. Indeed, he should be sued for *Bleak House* and his insinuations, nay, outright diatribes against my kind. Slanderous, I would say!'

This evoked some mild laughter, and Georgia had to admit she was enjoying this fellow. 'One of the less virulent statements about lawyers is that lawyers spend their professional careers shoveling smoke. Well, I now want to tell you about some smoke that I am shoveling for my dear departed friend, David Herbert Lawrence. And the smoke is billowing right here in America, where the book *Lady Chatterley's Lover* is being condemned as unpublishable because of its lewdness.

'But worse than that, if it would be published, these self-appointed guardians of America's want to sanitize it.' An audible gasp rolled through the audience. 'They are terrified of thinking that American readers would be exposed to these salacious thoughts. That some grand infection would seep into the country. We here know it is all "smoke" for it obfuscates the true beauty, the elegance of this book.

'But why? Why would this book be attacked? This is why: the very notion of an upper-class woman consorting with a gamekeeper goes against the protectors of morals and the upper classes. Now I would argue that if the lord of the manor were having sex with a servant girl, it would cause no problems. But this is what is happening now in America. They are using smoke and mirrors to distort some of the greatest writing in this century. So, I am going to fight this tooth and nail from distant shores. I promise you that on my love and friendship for our beloved David I shall do this.'

The audience burst into applause. Frieda wiped tears from her eyes. She rose from her chair to embrace Casimir Westcott.

Then she turned to the east-facing window and raised her middle finger. '*Fick dich, Amerika!*' She spat out the words. Dozens of middle fingers shot into the air. '*Fick dich, Amerika!*'

Frieda now placed a gentian violet atop the altar. Then, touching her trembling fingers lightly to the surface of the altar, she began to speak.

'When Lawrence first found a gentian, a big single blue one, I remember feeling as if he had a strange communion with it, as if that violet yielded up its blueness, its very essence, to him. Everything he met had the newness of a creation.'

Frieda's words breathed a lovely and gentle spirit into that chapel. It was almost as if the splendid stained glass began to shine and reflect on its own during this sunless day. This was the calm after the storm of the previous speaker. Both were needed.

Georgia left the chapel to go look for violets. She would take them to the service for Flora, which was to take place the same afternoon. She knew there were some about to bloom near the Pink House. She had promised Jessie that she would drive him to the service. Jessie had told her that he and Flora were related, both part of the Bitter Water clan. She had never been to an Indian funeral. She imagined it would be quite different.

SEVENTEEN

'Jessie, what's that on your face?' Georgia asked as she followed his directions toward the Blue Cliffs.

'Ashes – mourning custom.'

'And your hair. You chopped it off.'

'That, too. Part of the custom.'

'Should I have ashes on my face?'

'No, only relatives do it.'

'What about these?' Georgia held up the bouquet of gentian she had picked behind the Pink House.

'Nice,' Jessie said.

'It's OK, then?'

'What do you mean OK?'

'I don't know the customs. I don't want to offend anybody.'

'No, why would you ever think that?' Jessie was silent for a while as they drove out. After about five minutes, he said, 'You know, our customs are a little different from white folks'. So, we're heading out now toward the Blue Cliffs for the service. You know them – the cliffs?'

'No.'

'They're off the road to Fort Defiance. They took her body up there.'

'That's far from where she lived.'

'That's the point. They don't want the *chindi* to find her or come close to the relatives. And those cliffs face west and are to the north of where she lived. Hard to find footprints on those cliffs. They wrapped her body and will leave her there. And now we'll go to the bottom of those cliffs and in our own way pray – but do not mention her name. We believe that it slows her journey to the next world.'

Georgia could not help thinking of Dorcas Moore's disgusting performance in the Spirit Courtyard, which had made that journey a travesty.

Jessie didn't speak for a while. As the Blue Cliffs came into view, Georgia saw half a dozen figures.

'Those are the sweepers,' Jessie said.

'Sweepers?'

'They sweep the footprints away from the men who have carried her up there so she can't follow them back to her hogan or the chapel where she was murdered. Because she was murdered, they have to be extra careful.' He paused. 'Remember, Miss O'Keeffe, don't say her name. We never say the name of the person during the burial. Bad luck.'

'But these are OK?' She nodded to the blue gentian violets.

'Oh yes, you can just scatter them around. Or leave the jar with the water by a rock. Sure.'

By the time they got to the sweepers, they saw several other cars behind a bluff and about fifty mourners.

'I see Father Donald over there. He's standing by Cowboy,' Georgia said.

'Yes,' Jessie replied. 'Father Donald is a good guy. He understands the Navajo ways and she went to his church.'

'And so did Cowboy, I understand.'

'Yes, I'm pretty sure that Cowboy was one of her carriers.'

'Carriers? Pallbearers?'

'Yes.' He nodded.

'What if there hadn't been any cliffs?'

'Trees – they often take the dead to high trees on a board that is wrapped tight with blankets.'

They continued for another minute or two in silence.

'Pull over here,' Jessie said.

The people had now assembled in a small grove of cottonwood trees.

Cowboy came up to Georgia and tipped his hat. 'Those are pretty, Miss O'Keeffe,' he offered, looking at the gentian. 'I can take them up there to the cliffs for you after the service.'

'Oh, that's nice of you to offer. But you don't have to do that, Cowboy.'

'I don't have to, Miss O'Keeffe, but I want to. You know, from one artist to another.'

Georgia looked at Cowboy. Her eyes filled with tears. 'That's so lovely, Cowboy.'

'No problem, ma'am.'

The ceremony was about to begin. Georgia noticed a small girl, perhaps eight years old, standing by Father Donald. Two tracks of tears ran down her ash-covered face. The priest had a hand on her head. She was hunched over like a little old lady, as if she were carrying a lifetime of grief on her shoulders. A woman went over to her and gently led her away from the priest, who was about to begin the service. The resemblance was clear, and Georgia could see that this must be Flora's younger sister.

The service itself lasted just a quarter of an hour.

Georgia stayed behind with Jessie and watched Cowboy walk up the narrow path from the cliff base with the bouquet of flowers in his hand. It was an image that would stick with her for as long as she lived but one that she would never paint.

'I need some gas,' Georgia said as they were driving back to Taos.

'A cousin of mine has a gas station a mile or so up the road.'

'Good.' The image of Cowboy walking up the path with the gentian was still vivid in her mind. Then she thought of Mateo languishing in the jail in Santa Fe. She couldn't wait until Ryan got back. He'd know a good lawyer.

'*Yá'át'ééh!*' Jessie said as they drove up to the gas station. A lanky fellow came out from the garage, where a car was up on the lift.

'*Yá'át'ééh!*' the man replied.

'Whatcha up to?'

'Got a new car.'

'How'd you manage that?' Jessie asked. 'Oh, by the way this is my friend Miss Georgia O'Keeffe. Miss O'Keeffe, this is Jonno. Jonno Yazzie.'

'Hello there,' Georgia said.

'Wait, I'll show you how I managed it. Or maybe didn't manage it,' Jonno replied to Jessie and smiled broadly.

'And what's that stuff in your hair. You going gray?'

'No.' Jonno dug his hand into his pocket. 'See this?'

He brought out a small lump. 'At first, I thought that it was just sand in the throttle. But then I found a whole lump of this. There's a hole in the floor of this junker near the accelerator. Some of it got in my hair too when I was under the car. Instant gray hair.'

Jessie gave a low whistle. 'Seen this before?'

Georgia was leaning over and said, 'Good gracious! It can't be.'

'But it is, Miss O'Keeffe. The car up on that lift was out on the Old Taos Road.' Jessie leaned closer for a better look.

'What are you two talking about?' Jonno asked.

'Murder.' Georgia and Jessie both said at once.

'Why don't you two come in and have a Coke and tell me about this.'

The three of them sat at a small table next to the car on the lift and sipped their Cokes while Jessie explained about the connection to Flora's murder.

Jonno, a big, husky fellow in his early thirties, looked up at the car.

'You telling me that the person who drove this car might be the murderer of Flora?' He spoke softly, his voice drenched in disbelief. 'I mean, this woman seemed so nice and said she couldn't wait for me to fix the car, but if I drove her all the way to Albuquerque, she could catch a bus and go see her poor ailing mother who was dying and she'd leave the car for me.'

'You mean she didn't want it back?' Jessie asked.

'She said she didn't need it. It had been nothing but trouble since she bought it. If I could fix it, it could be mine. She was fed up with it breaking down all the time.'

'White girl, eh?' Jessie asked.

'Yeah.'

'What did she look like?' Georgia asked.

'Black hair. Medium size, you know. Just kind of normal-looking. Nothing special. She was wearing sunglasses even though the sun was hardly up.'

'Any kind of accent?' Georgia asked.

'All white folk sound the same to me.'

Jessie looked up at the car on the lift. 'Well, Jonno, looks like this could be a key piece of evidence.'

'How do you figure that?'

Jessie explained about the altar and the ashes mixed in the cement. Jonno shook his head slightly. Georgia could almost read his mind: *You white people are so weird!* He picked up the small lump of concrete, peering at it and turning it around. 'You mean some of this fellow's ashes – the writer fellow – could be in this?'

'Maybe,' Jessie replied. 'The microscope at police headquarters isn't powerful enough.'

'They have a better microscope at the coroner's office in Santa Fe,' Georgia offered. 'But we don't need to know whose ashes are in that lump. We know that.'

'Too bad we can't get fingerprints off this lump,' Jessic said.

'All you'll get is Jonno's here and mine from the lumps I brought into the office,' Georgia replied.

Jessie looked up at the car. He sighed. 'What we really need to do is lower that car and go over it with a fine-tooth comb for more evidence. No telling what the woman left behind.'

'Not much. She only carried a small suitcase and her pocketbook.'

'You have a telephone here, don't you, Jonno?' Jessie asked.

'Sure thing.'

'I better call the chief and have him and Homer get out here with a crime kit and plenty of black powder. There could be latents all over it.' He paused and turned to Jonno. 'Yours too, of course.'

'Latent what?'

'Fingerprints – hidden fingerprints. A car surface is ideal. Hard, smooth metal.'

The crime kit was delivered twenty minutes later. Jessie decided that both Harold and Homer were most likely too drunk to drive back to the station and that he would drive them back in the police car.

'Without a license?' Georgia asked. 'Shouldn't I drive?'

'No such thing as a driver's license out here, Miss O'Keeffe,' Jessie replied.

When he returned, he handed Georgia a paintbrush from the crime kit.

'You should be good at this.'

'Don't count on it,' she replied.

'I'll demonstrate. But first I'll get your prints and Jonno's so we can establish a key.'

'A key?' Jonno asked.

'Yeah. See, we have to eliminate ours from any others we might gather.' They were standing outside the car. 'Put your fingers from each hand on these ink pads. All five,' he said.

'Good,' he said a few minutes later. 'Now we have a key. We'll be able to eliminate ours and get to work on the car.' He took out what looked like a saltshaker of powder and sprinkled it on the dashboard, then brushed it lightly across the surface and the steering wheel.

'OK, look! Hundreds of prints are showing up.' He reached into the crime kit and took out a roll of tape. 'Now watch carefully while I lift these prints on the sticky side of this tape.' He paused and careful pressed the tape on the print. 'I'll look at these later with the loupe, which will magnify them so I can see the ridges.'

He and Georgia set to work lifting latents. 'You got it, Miss O'Keeffe?'

Georgia looked down at his long skinny fingers. 'Call me Georgia, dear. We're practically holding hands here.' She noticed a blush creeping up Jessie's neck.

'Harold and Homer would have really messed things up,' Jessie said. 'You have to be very careful lifting these latents,' he muttered while crawling over the interior of the car.

'Well, mine will be all over this car,' Jonno said.

'Doesn't matter. I'll just eliminate yours and see what we got left when I compare them to any of the others we got back at the office.'

'Did you get any off the murder weapon?' Georgia asked.

'No, impossible from the surface of that rock.'

Georgia was now carefully peeling up the tape from the driver's seat with the black powder. Placing the tape on a white index card, she wrote 'driver's seat of car'.

Five minutes later, Jessie announced that he felt they had enough latents.

'Now, give a description of the woman again, Jonno.'

'Well, kind of tall. Very black hair. Like Indian straight black hair. But no accent – not Navajo or Tewa. Just plain old white people accent.' He paused. 'She was big. Broad-shouldered.'

'Did she carry anything besides that small suitcase and her pocketbook?' Georgia asked.

'Not that I saw.'

Georgia stood now with her hands on her hips. She squinted to the north.

'What are those shacks way over there?' she asked.

'Just some abandoned hogans off the Old Santa Ana Road,' Jonno replied. 'Kids go over there and chew peyote, smoke marijuana – that kind of stuff. But they stopped that a while back.'

'Why's that?' Georgia asked.

'Skinwalkers.' Jessie's words were barely audible. His voice tightened with anxiety.

'Oh,' Georgia said softly. She knew it was something that she as a white person shouldn't poke her nose into. Ryan had became skittish when she once asked him about the Skinwalker stories. And she now remembered the two coyote teeth found at the chapel amid the fragments of Flora's broken pottery. It was hard for her to reconcile superstition with Jessie's keen, insightful mind. She wasn't even going to try.

With the crime kit packed up, Georgia and Jessie thanked Jonno for all his help. Georgia headed toward her car and Jessie to the cop car.

She turned toward Jessie. 'So, you don't want to go out there to the hogans with me, do you?'

'Uh, not really.'

'What if I go and you stay in the police car? It's not that far out of the way.'

Jessie pressed his lips together. 'No, it's not. I–I . . . Well, you can do what you want to, Miss O'Keeffe.'

'I want to. Maybe because I'm white they won't bother me.'

Jessie shrugged and said nothing. His eyes would not meet hers.

'I'll follow you. Or you follow me; I know a more direct route.'

'Thanks, Jessie.'

Ten minutes later, the road they had turned on petered out and they were bouncing along as it became even rougher. Georgia stopped the car and leaned out the window. The place was certainly abandoned. Trash blew aimlessly around the cluster of hogans. A wheelbarrow was overturned. There was a small pile of what appeared to be bedsprings. By all appearances, this spot boldly declared its abandonment. Georgia couldn't help but wonder why. Were there really Skinwalkers? Did only the brave and the stoned gather to smoke peyote and not be bothered too much? The view beyond the trash was beautiful as the land dipped into the Questa basin, known for its geological wonders that yielded everything from quartz to turquoise and topaz.

She stepped out of the car. 'I guess we could go gem hunting in the basin,' she said.

'Overrated, I think,' Jessie said, leaning out the window of the police car.

'Really?'

'Yes, mostly rock for whetstones – you know, knife-sharpening tools.'

'But what if you found diamonds?'

'Industrial diamonds are worth crap. Oh, sorry, ma'am, didn't mean to swear.'

'Quite all right, dear,' Georgia said, climbing out of the Model A. She turned to Jessie. 'Wait here, I won't be long.'

'Miss O'Keeffe, you sure about this?'

'Jessie, I'm never sure about anything. If I had to be sure, I'd never have become a painter.' She reached over the seat and grabbed her snake stick.

The hoodoos, those thin spires of rock formed by erosion and wind, rose to teetering heights. They made Georgia think of a ghostly choir. A pale white moon hung in the sky like a glaucous eye. There were in all four hogans close to each other. She had entered two so far, but now, standing in the third as she leaned on her snake stick, she immediately noticed a difference. It was neat, immaculate and so unlike the rest of the encampment. The floor had been swept. There was no trace of peyote buttons. No discarded marijuana water pipes. Not even ashes in the fire pit. There was no stovepipe going through the open hole in the ceiling. But there was a faintly odd scent – a scent that one would not associate with the high desert. She was uncertain how to describe it – slightly woodsy, perhaps.

The hogan itself was six-sided as opposed to the eight-sided others. It had been occupied. That was Georgia's gut instinct. This hogan had been so thoroughly cleaned that it might as well be a total erasure of any life that had been lived here.

Georgia stood in a corner where two of the six walls met and a broom was propped. A perfect circle of blue sky floated above the fire pit, casting the only light other than that from the doorway. Georgia inhaled sharply as she saw a slim shadow creep across the floor. She stood as rigid as the broomstick as the shadow lengthened.

'Miss O'Keeffe?'

'Oh, Jesus!' She gasped. 'I mean, Jessie, it's you.'

'I didn't mean to scare you. But I didn't like the idea of you going alone into these hogans.'

'Because of the Skinwalkers?'

Jessie just shrugged.

'Did you see the other hogans?' he asked.

'Just one. It was a mess. This one, as you can see, is hardly a mess. Very neat.'

'I think this was a weaver's hogan.'

'How can you tell?'

'The shed outside – that was for the loom.'

'You knew the weaver?'

'No, but my mom did. She died a while ago. Malinda Chee.'

'Like Mateo Chee?'

'Yeah, probably a cousin.' He paused. 'A lot of the Chees are very artistic. Yazzies, too. Silversmiths mostly.'

'That's interesting,' Georgia said softly. Despite its immaculate appearance, she felt a kinship with this place. What a view the weaver Malinda Chee had from where she must have sat at her loom. They went outside and stood where the loom most likely had been, facing west. She could imagine Malinda sitting there, sending the shuttle of the weft thread through the warp. Pushing on the foot pedals of the loom to raise or lower the shafts, the frame that holds the warp. There was still snow capping the mountains from the winter.

Jessie was now beside her and said, 'To the left over there is Blue Lake. There's a pilgrimage there in August.'

'Not Christian?'

'Definitely not,' he said. 'It is where the spirit of the Pueblo god lives. We go to pray and worship the sky, the stars, the moon, the clouds, the air – whatever the gods have given. It is the source of all life for the Puebloans.'

'Yes, I've heard of Blue Lake.'

Jessie leaned over her shoulder and pointed. 'Over there you can see Punto Rojo. The pilgrimage route on Good Friday goes right by it.'

'But everything else is such a mess. Why would the weaver live here?'

'It wasn't always this way.'

'Really?'

Jessie nodded.

'What happened?'

'I'm not sure. Some might have thought Malinda Chee was a witch. I don't know. But after she died, the others left. Thought the ground was haunted. And then kids started coming here to smoke, to drink. Not near town or anyplace where they could get caught.'

'Thunderheads forming over there.' She was looking toward the north, Arizona. 'But look at the tops of them reflecting the sun. So beautiful.'

'Ice crystals,' Jessie said.

This land is absolutely magical! Georgia thought. *Simply magical.* She inhaled deeply, but still there was that lingering scent. So out of place. Something had happened here, and it wasn't just kids chewing peyote or smoking marijuana.

Two hours later, Jessie walked into the police station and found Homer and Harold well into their cups. He sighed. It was still worth asking.

'Hey, chief, did the report on the latents from the murder ever come back from Santa Fe?'

Harold looked at him dumbly. 'What?'

'The Flora Namingha murder up at the Lawrence place.'

Harold scratched his head. 'Oh, that one?'

Jessie sighed. *That one?* It wasn't as though they had a murder here every day.

'Yes, that one – Flora Namingha.'

Homer yawned. 'As I recall, there were latents all over that chapel.'

'How can you recall? You weren't even there – neither one of you. You were both locked up at your own request.'

'Oh, that's right,' Harold said. 'Thanks for reminding us.'

Jessie sighed. He now walked over to the evidence drawer to add the clumps of cement that Miss O'Keeffe had collected. Dried cement was not exactly an ideal material for collecting fingerprints unless it was wet when the person's fingers touched it. His eyes fell upon something else: a shiny black fragment – a piece of the fractured vase that Flora had made for Mr Lawrence's ashes. How had this been left behind from the rest of the evidence the Santa Fe cops had taken? Then he remembered that Miss O'Keeffe had picked it up, put it in her pocket and delivered it to him a day or so later. He had forgotten all about it.

Putting on rubber gloves, Jessie carefully lifted the fragment from the file. He hoped that not too many hands aside from Flora's had touched it. How would it compare with the latents they had taken off the car at Jonno's garage?

He now took another look at a print he had taken from the steering wheel. When examining fingerprints, one establishes a key. In this case, the key print was Jonno's, for he had handled the car. So Jessie had taken his first. All the other latents would be compared to Jonno's. There were not that many others from the car. But one set did have a distinctive pattern.

'Arches!' Jessie murmured under his breath. Less than five percent of all fingerprints had this tent-shaped pattern. 'Not ulnar loops or whorls, but arches.'

This was a first for Jessie. The shiny black fragment that had been fired in cow dung, then smoked to impregnate the clay with carbon, clearly showed an arched marking, 'tenting' up, as it were, amidst the other more common patterns. And this evidence had come directly from the chapel, not the car, not any wet cement or concrete chunks. He had taken Miss O'Keeffe's fingerprints and those of the investigative officer Descheeni. The fingerprints of Collins and the coroner Dr Bryce as well as Flora's were already on file, and none had arches. These would be distinctive. These would possibly belong to the murderer.

'Henry, where are you?' Jessie murmured to himself as he scanned the shelf of books on the wall above the evidence examining table. 'Ahh, there you are!' He reached for his *Classification and Uses of Finger Prints*, written by Edward Henry, the Inspector General of Police in Bengal, India.

EIGHTEEN

Eleanor Burke was sitting in front of her dressing-room mirror in Palm Beach. They certainly had come a long way from Chance's bootlegging days – which, as Eleanor rationalized, wasn't exactly bootlegging. He just owned the fleet of small boats that slid down the foggy Canadian coast and unloaded in Maine. Then there was that tiny speck of Jewish blood in her veins. No one questioned her and Chance's admission to the Everglades Club, especially after Chance's contribution to the new hospital. But now he was on the phone with one of those lowlifes from his past, someone named Buzzy, or maybe Bugsy, who had something to do with smuggling Scotch during Prohibition. But more important, he had arranged for their daughter Amy's abortion.

It always made Eleanor nervous when she happened upon Chance making a call to this Buzzy or Bugsy fellow.

'You're out there?' Chance said. 'Well, get it done.'

Out where? Not Chicago, Eleanor wondered. 'Out there' sounded west to her rather than east – far west, not Chicago. Eldon was out there, too, announcing his engagement to Bunny Hatch, the daughter of Lady Sybil Hatch. Though her official title was 'the Dowager Countess', as she was the widow of the late Lord Hatch, the owner of Stonebridge. However, the property was a mess and would require immense infusions of cash from Chance Burke.

Eleanor dabbed some powder on her nose and emerged from her dressing room. She dared not ask specifically why he was on the phone. Chance hated it if he thought she was listening in on phone conversations.

'Who was that?' She feigned ignorance.

'Nothing, darling.'

She was sure it was something and gave him a flirtatious little smile.

He smiled back. 'Come here, honeybunch. Whatcha got under that? I can see your titties.'

'Oh, Chance.' She sighed.

'Come on, a quickie.' He opened his dressing gown. 'You want me to put a black tie on this?'

Eleanor giggled. She did a little prancing dance toward the erect penis and climbed on top of him.

As he thrust into her, he wondered how that idiot son of theirs could be a pansy.

'Oh, Chance!' she gasped.

Eleanor had no idea about Eldon's proclivities. Chance would die before telling her. He couldn't imagine how she didn't suspect. But she didn't.

NINETEEN

'Here's where she's staying, Ryan.' Tony Luhan opened the door of the Pink House. 'Hope the bed's comfortable.' He gave his cousin a wink.

'Enough of that, Tony,' Ryan chuckled.

'What brings you here?'

'Missing Georgia.'

'And the murder?'

'Well, that, too. I know Mateo Chee. He's a good kid. I'm not buying this lovers' quarrel rot.'

'Doesn't sound right to me, either,' Tony said.

'Do you know where Georgia went?'

'I think she actually went to Flora's funeral. It's today.' He paused and looked around. 'Oh, and by the way, there's a vase right there on the bureau for the flowers you brought.'

'Good.'

'That was nice of you.'

'She's a nice lady.'

'Yes, I am!' Georgia said as she stepped through the door. 'Ryan, what in the world? Why are you here?'

'Well,' Tony said. 'I'll be leaving now.' He gave Ryan another wink.

'Because I missed you,' Ryan replied.

She looked at him narrowly. Not that she didn't believe him, but she sensed there was something more. 'Let me get these flowers in water before they wilt and then . . .'

'To bed. Be quick about it, as I might wilt, too.' He had begun stripping off his shirt.

She sneaked a look. She liked the spume of gray hair that lifted from his chest. It reminded her of the spindrift that blew from the crest of waves. How big he was. Massive, compared to Stieglitz, but with a bit of a belly on him.

When Georgia first met Ryan, she was somewhat confused – the Irish name but most definitely a Pueblo face. Or, she would soon learn, not just Pueblo but a Navajo face. He had wide, high cheekbones.

His eyes sloped slightly, but they were not black or brown like those of most Indians out here, but an enigmatic blue that in the course of a day could change from a midnight blue to gray to baby blue. His salt-and-pepper hair was thick and brushed straight back. Tall, slender in the hips, he was irresistible. And best of all, he was so comfy to cuddle up to. He was insulated, had a thickness to him that steadied her – yes, *steadied* was the only word she could think of. Sometimes the noise of her ideas – ideas for paintings, or music she had been moved by, or really anything – seemed to rattle around within her as if looking for a place to roost. She needed balance and steadiness. Ryan gave her that.

Half an hour later, as they both lay in bed, Georgia turned to him.

'OK, why are you here, handsome?'

'You. I missed you.'

'I accept that, but why else?' She rolled over on top of him and spread her legs. 'I'll ask you after round two.'

Now on her back, she stared into the darkness and sighed. 'Time just seems to fly with you.'

'OK,' Ryan said. 'I can't exactly say, but I can tell you it has nothing to do with Flora Namingha's murder.' He paused. 'I'll leave that to you.'

'Oh, thank you. How do you know I'm doing anything about that murder?'

'Just a wild guess.' He chuckled. 'How long are you planning on staying out here?'

'Through Good Friday,' she replied.

'Got religion or something?'

'Never religion, but I'm an ardent ritualist. I've never seen the Penitentes making their pilgrimage to a shrine.' She climbed out of bed and led him to the window that looked out on the morada. The stars were just coming out and hanging over the building just as they were the first night she began the painting. 'See that!'

'Yes, beautiful.'

'I've been painting it all week. Now it's only a few days until Good Friday. I want to see it in daylight as the faithful make their way.'

'Are you going to paint them?' he asked.

'Never! It would be intrusive.' She hesitated. 'I just want to see the circle completed.'

Ryan was not sure what she meant by this comment, but he didn't ask. There were many times when Georgia just seemed to dissolve into the cryptic maze of her own mind.

She took him over to the easel to look at the painting in progress. They stood in front of it, still nude with their arms around each other's waists. Ryan whispered in her ear as he looked at the starry night of the painting and the shadow of the cross spreading over the land. 'There's a proverb, not Navajo or Tewa but Serbian.'

'What is it?' Georgia asked.

'Be humble, for you are made of earth. Be noble, for you are made of stars.'

Tears filled Georgia's eyes. This was why she loved this man, this dear, dear man.

But she sensed for the first time that he was holding something back. It was certainly not like Stieglitz holding back on his latest liaison: *A petite affair, Georgia. It means nothing.* This was not an affair, and it meant something. Then again, didn't she hold back from him? Did she share with him every little detail as the idea for a painting began to form in her mind? There are people, people who are involved in the most intimate and intense love, who hold back. They do not share all, reveal all. There was, however, a large, impenetrable part of Ryan's mind that she had never experienced before. She found it disturbing. She guessed she would have to live with it. The question was, could she?

TWENTY

That evening's cocktail hour, which Georgia was hoping to avoid, Ryan insisted on attending. Georgia promised to come down a bit later.

It was another dance night. Not the rhumba but the cha-cha-cha this time. The instructor was Cowboy. When she got there, the dancing was still going on. Catching sight of Ryan steering Wallis Simpson around the floor, she tried not to gasp. Cowboy was dancing with Mabel. He navigated toward Georgia.

'You're next, sweetie,' Mabel called out.

'It's not like I'm a wallflower, Mabel.'

'Cowboy is a divine partner.'

'Yes, I am, ma'am.' He flashed a dazzling white smile. He could be a movie star, Georgia thought. He probably would be. Some Hollywood type would come out here and discover him. Cowboy movie stars were the rage these days – John Wayne, Gene Autry, Roy Rogers – but none of them was a real cowboy, at least not in Georgia's mind.

Bunny and Eldon were dancing, and the doctor was with Sybil. They actually made a nice pair.

Eldon and Bunny managed to collide with Georgia and Cowboy twice. Each time, Bunny gave an awful scowl.

Jessie, standing on the sidelines, looked especially grim. The third time Eldon bumped into Cowboy and Georgia, he muttered sotto voce, 'I beg your pardon!'

'He ain't begging nobody's pardon,' Cowboy muttered. At that moment, the doctor cut in.

'May I dance with the greatest woman painter in America?'

Georgia gave him a pained expression.

'What's the matter?'

'So, who is the man painter that is better than I am?'

'Oh dear, *mea culpa.*'

'Apologizing in Latin doesn't help,' she snapped but gave a bit of a smile. 'Insensitive of me,' the doctor replied.

'It's a common habit of men to look through a bifurcated lens and possibly miss one half the world.'

'So best painter ever – how would that do?'

'Don't overcompensate for your error. I wouldn't necessarily go that far. Just a simple recognition that both sexes exist. Let others decide the rest. Speaking of which, I need a break.'

'All right. I think I'll ask Miss Maudie for a dance.'

'Oh my, that would be interesting. Mrs Simpson might get her feathers ruffled about that.'

'She treats that girl miserably.'

'You care?' She wasn't sure she believed him – even if he was a doctor.

'Of course I care.' He looked at Georgia stunned, but there was a flicker of something else in his very attractive blue eyes. Was it alarm?

She sat down next to Cowboy and began to watch Ryan and Wallis cha-cha-cha-ing.

'Scrawny thing, ain't she? Mrs Simpson.'

'No scrawnier than I am.'

'I'm not just talking about her body. Her mind. "Skinny mean", as my mother used to say. You saw how she treated Maudie that night she got sick – like dirt, I tell you.'

The dancing stopped, and Cowboy excused himself for the rest of the evening. She saw Ryan sidle up to Eldon with a drink in his hand. What in the world would he have in common with Eldon Burke? She chastised herself immediately. *It's a cocktail party, you fool. You're acting like a jealous teenager at a prom.* Ryan could talk to anybody he wanted to, and it didn't mean he was hiding things from her. He wasn't trying to horn in on her turf – her crime turf. His own officers, Descheeni and Collins, were handling the case from Santa Fe. Mateo was already locked up there. Why could she not accept that Ryan was here to see her? To make love to her. This was not a business trip for him. It was a romantic interlude after a long conference in San Francisco before getting back to work as usual in Santa Fe. Why could she not simply accept this? He hadn't even asked her anything about the murder. He didn't need to ask, as the case was officially being handled by his own department. Yet she was haunted by a suspicion that he was not telling her the entire truth. She looked up and saw him dancing with Bunny. She was surprised by how graceful he was. She had expected him for some reason to have two left feet.

'Why make that face, Georgia?' Tony said as he came up to her.

'What face?'

'A kind of scowl, like you're fretting.'

'No, no, not at all. I'm just noticing that your cousin there is a very good dancer.'

'Ryan?'

'Yes.'

'His late wife Mattie taught him. She was a great dancer. She taught him a lot.'

Something collapsed in Georgia. She was angry with herself. How small, how petty she was being.

'Wish I'd known Mattie. I really do.'

'She was a wonderful woman. She was the librarian in Santa Fe, but they had met in high school,' Tony said. 'Come on, get up. Let's dance.'

Ryan had glanced over as she took to the dance floor with his cousin. He knew exactly what she was thinking and had to berate himself for closing off this part of his mind from her. Mattie, of course, had been used to it. 'The undiscussable', she had called it. She never asked questions. Nor did Georgia, but in this instance, she was – what should he say? – readable. She oozed suspicion. 'Oozed' – a word Ryan could never dream of using with Georgia. She did not ooze. But she was oozing now.

When the dance finished, Georgia made her way toward Mabel, Sybil, Bunny and Frieda.

Frieda embraced her extravagantly. 'How can I ever thank you enough? Such a beautiful design for the windows! How could I have done it without you?'

'And how could I have done it without Mateo?'

'Ah, poor Mateo,' Mabel said. 'I don't for one second think he murdered that girl.'

'Nor do I.' Bunny and Sybil spoke at once.

Another woman, Lorna Charles, had drifted over to the group. 'Did you know him, Bunny, you being in primitive art?'

'Glassmaking is hardly what one would call primitive art – and by the way, no one uses that term. Sometimes it is called Raw Art.' She sniffed, and her nose, which was very pink, reminded Georgia of the minuscule quivers of a rabbit's nose as it nibbled.

'Raw?' Georgia said. 'Raw as opposed to well done?'

'Oh, what a hoot you are Georgia!' Bunny exclaimed. 'No, more like naïve. My gallery specializes in it. It's also called naïve art or self-taught.'

Georgia couldn't help but wonder what the difference between naïve and self-taught art was exactly.

'And do you specialize in anything within this genre?' she asked.

'Yes, we are especially focused on Bengali art and their masks, which are magnificent. The masks are used in their traditional dance, called the Purulia Chhau dance.'

'It must be a fascinating gallery. I myself am quite interested in weaving – *diyogis*.' Lorna was definitely anxious to show off her knowledge, as she used the Navajo term for rug, *diyogi*. 'I'm especially fond of Elsie Chee's work. Her rugs are exquisite.'

'I believe, if I am not mistaken, Elsie didn't weave rugs but blankets,' Bunny corrected.

Georgia was darting her eyes between the two women. This was becoming like a tennis match of Outsider Art knowledge.

'Oh, I must have her confused with her sister, Malinda Chee.'

'Possibly,' Bunny answered vaguely.

'Malinda lived out on the Old Santa Ana Road, didn't she?' Lorna said.

'I really don't know. She's been dead for years now.'

'Not that long really?' Lorna countered. The volley continued, and Georgia remained silent, trying to anticipate where the ball would land next.

'Yes, really,' Bunny said almost sharply and turned to walk away.

Sybil was obviously a bit taken aback by her daughter's abrupt departure, as were Lorna and Georgia. She drifted away from the conversation and headed toward the bar for another glass of wine.

Georgia now turned to Lorna. 'You said that Malinda Chee lived out on the Old Santa Ana Road?'

'Yes, I went there once when she was still alive. I wanted to see her blankets. She was a master weaver. But I do remember her hogan – a six-sided one with a shed-like affair outside for her loom. She had a stunning view of the Sangre Cristo mountains from her loom. There are references to them in all of her weavings. Along with the Four Sacred Mountains, of course. She was not just a master weaver but a master dyer as well. She could capture the color of those mountains in any season.'

Spud came up to Georgia and Lorna. 'Sorry to interrupt, ladies, but Georgia, there's a phone call for you.'

'Me? Oh dear.' She hoped it wasn't anything with Alfred. He'd had a bit of a digestive problem. Most likely an ulcer. At least not stomach cancer – Alfred tended to jump to the worst possible conclusions.

It was not Alfred but the coroner in Santa Fe.

'Hello, Georgia, Emily here. Don't mean to disturb you, but something interesting has come up in regard to the Namingha murder.' The soft lilt of a Cork accent came through the phone.

'Oh my goodness, Emily, I didn't expect to hear from you. I thought you had that all wrapped up. I went to the burial ceremony just yesterday. Well, they call it a burial, but it wasn't that exactly. So, what's going on?'

'It's rather odd, dear. But we extracted some hair from beneath the victim's fingernails and in her teeth.'

'Yes,' Georgia said softly.

'Forgive the pun, but it looks like a bit of a – dare I say – tangle went on there. Aside from scratches, the hair did not match the victim's hair when we got it.'

'What do you mean?'

'In a nutshell, it wasn't human hair.'

'Well, what was it?'

'It was hair from an animal.'

'But a human killed her.'

'Yes, I don't doubt it for one minute. Smashed her head with that rock. But Flora fought back. She pulled on what she thought was hair, but it was a wig made from animal hair – you know, goats, sheep, maybe horsehair.'

'How can you tell?'

'Under a microscope, human hairs have club-shaped roots. But the hair we found under her fingernails and in her teeth had roots that were not club-shaped at all. Animal hair scales are overlapping, or what is called imbricate. Human hair scales are not.'

'How do you explain that?'

'Well, as I said, we have to assume that the murderer was wearing a wig. Most likely sheep – angora sheep, possibly mohair, you know.'

'Good gracious.'

'Yep, at first it looked just like the victim's hair. Same color and all. But you get it under that new microscope – God bless Mabel for donating the money for it – and well, it's a totally different ball game – or species. Not to make a pun here, but we all – you included – combed that crime scene and didn't find any wigs. So in spite of some hair found under Flora's fingernails and teeth, the murderer must have left with the wig intact.'

Georgia inhaled sharply. 'Emily, there's something else.'

'What's that?'

'We found what we think might have been the murderer's car. We checked it out for fingerprints. Maybe we missed some hairs but not an entire wig.'

'I doubt the killer would have discarded the wig after the murder.'

'Are we to assume that because whoever it was wore a wig, the murderer is a woman?' Georgia said.

'Not at all. But possibly we can assume that the person was not Indian, more likely a white person trying to have Indian-like hair.'

Hmm, Georgia thought. There was nothing as beautiful as the thick black hair of the Indians that fell down their shoulders like molten tar. She touched her own thin, graying hair that she twisted back into a knot that Stieglitz once said looked like a bagel. What a wordsmith that man was!

TWENTY-ONE

Neither Georgia nor Ryan slept well that night. It was past midnight, and they both lay in bed awake but feigning sleep. Should she have told Ryan about the call from Emily? For some reason, she didn't. He would find out sooner or later. After all, Emily had to report all this to his office. So, was the fact that she had withheld this information the first lie? But what was he not telling her? It was as if each of them were alone with their thoughts and yet they could not share them. It was a lonely place. Did he feel that way – lonely with his secrets?

The little she had hunched about Ryan's reasons for being here was that it must in some way be connected to the Feds. This often happened in New Mexico and the Southwest, as there was so much in the way of tribal lands that fell under the management of the federal government, and crime knows no borders, really. Ryan seemed to be one of the law enforcement officers first contacted in such cases. He had a history of working with the FBI, in particular with his good friend Lincoln Stone, a special agent and the first Negro to work for the agency. The Taos murder case was strictly local, so it was all in the bailiwick of that crack investigative team of Harold and Homer. But why was Ryan here? Not to learn to dance with Wallis Simpson. Georgia wouldn't pry, but she could think.

She looked over at Ryan. He appeared to be sleeping soundly except for some small twitches in his eyelids. What caused these twitches? Dreams? Anxieties? Subliminal thinking? Ryan claimed he had no anxieties. Once his wife died after a long and painful illness, fear left him, but his mind was always working, solving dilemmas that came up in either the ordinary or the more exotic aspects of his work when it crossed paths with the FBI or the SIS, the covert Secret Intelligence Service that often worked with the FBI. Usually, international crime was involved.

But why am I trying to solve his case? Georgia thought – still observing his twitching eyelids – *and not mine, the death of a lovely young woman*. It suddenly dawned on her. Could it be that the two cases were in some obscure way intertwined without either one of them realizing it? If so, Ryan had the edge, for he knew about the murder of Flora Namingha, and she knew nothing about the crime that had possibly brought him out to Taos.

She got out of bed and walked over to the painting of the morada on the starry night. Even in the dim light before dawn, she could tell that she did not have enough cobalt blue paint as a foil for the stars rising over the immense cross of the building. It was the starry night that had to be the foil, the night foil for the looming cross. 'Too dark,' she muttered. But every single tube of cobalt blue that she had brought with her had been squeezed dry.

It was six years earlier, in 1929, that she had painted her first black cross with stars. She had forgotten how this scene, although different, demanded so much cobalt blue. It was almost as if the painting were scolding her. *How could you forget! The stars don't shine, they look muddy against the black.* She'd have to drive into Taos and get some more paint.

She glanced over at Ryan. His eyelids twitched and then suddenly opened.

'What the hell are you doing?' he sputtered as he looked at Georgia, who stood naked in front of the painting.

'Looking at you. Trying to read your mind.'

'Not my dreams?'

'I have a feeling you don't dream.'

'How about my body?'

'It's holding up pretty well for an old man.'

'You think so, do you?'

'Yep.'

'Well, what do you want to know that's in my alleged mind, Georgia?'

'What you won't tell me about – why you are out here.'

'At least we got that straight,' he said and sat up.

She knew him too well. He'd just shut down the conversation.

'I have to go get some more paint in town, then I'm going to go over to the Sacred Water pueblo,' she said.

'Any particular reason?'

'Is this an "I'll show you mine if you show me yours" situation?'

'Why would you think that?'

Georgia laughed. 'Why not?' Then she patted his knee. 'Don't worry, it's not. I'm just going over there because that was where Flora Namingha lived.'

'I thought she was Navajo.'

'She was, but her father died when she was young, and her mother's second husband is a Hopi guy. She was a potter over there.'

'OK, good enough.'

'Good enough, but you won't tell me why you're here?'

'Nope.' But he leaned over and kissed her.

TWENTY-TWO

'Well, now, sir, the question is, do you want to kill or do you want to grab?' The storekeeper was addressing a customer.

'Kill. What else? I sure as hell don't want to keep it as a pet,' Bugsy said with a laugh.

'Then I would definitely suggest the long snake tongs with the Gilly Teen, they call it. Double blade action. Snaps the head right off a rattler.'

'That would fucking do it, wouldn't it?'

The door jingled as a new customer arrived.

'Watch your language, sir. Lady just came in.' He turned toward the door. 'Morning, Miss O'Keeffe.'

'Morning, Ed.'

'What can I do you for?'

'Two tubes cobalt blue. Ran out.'

'Sure thing, ma'am.'

'Is that Georgia O'Keeffe?' Bugsy whispered.

'Indeed it is, sir.'

'My goodness.' He immediately remembered the painting in Chance Burke's library. He turned around and nodded to her. He instantly felt ashamed of his coarse language. Yes, she was as skinny as a dried stick and pushing fifty, but she seemed almost luminous to Bugsy.

'Hello, ma'am.'

At that moment, Ed came back with the Gilly Teen. 'Here you go, sir.'

'So, you're going snake killing, are you?' Georgia asked.

'If I have to.'

'I just kill them with a pointy stick. Works fine and a lot cheaper.' She smiled quickly. 'Always worried I might cut off my toes by accident with that gadget.' She smiled again. 'I can be clumsy.'

For some reason, this simple statement scared the bejesus out of Bugsy. Because he sensed that she was not the least bit clumsy.

* * *

Georgia had decided to ask Jessie to accompany her to the Sacred Water pueblo.

'So, Miss O'Keeffe, what do you want to do out there?'

'Well, I thought maybe I could offer my condolences to Flora's mom, for one thing. And then, you know, just look around.'

'It's a popular place for tourists because of the pottery.'

'Well, I might buy some pottery.'

'And blankets and rugs, too,' Jessie added.

'Really? I thought those were just Navajo crafts.'

'Doesn't mean they can't be sold together. Sacred Water is becoming popular with the tourists. There's a very good shop there that has a lot of the Chee weavings.'

It took Georgia only five minutes to realize that the Sacred Water pueblo had become somewhat of a tourist trap. She and Jessie had gone their separate ways. After about ten minutes, Georgia had the sensation that someone was following her. She didn't want to turn around and make it obvious, but she did turn a corner into a small alleyway and dipped into a shadowed niche in an adobe wall. In less than a minute, a small child came into the alley.

Georgia stepped out and faced the child. The girl froze. It was the same girl she had seen at Flora's funeral. She clutched something in her hand. Georgia thought she might run away down the rest of the alley, but instead she ran straight for Georgia and nearly knocked her down. In a mixture of what sounded like Hopi and Navajo, the little girl attempted to shove something into Georgia's hands.

'Fix it! Fix everything.'

Georgia grabbed her, and the object dropped to the ground. The head of a small doll rolled off.

'Oh no,' the girl wailed and threw herself down on the pavement.

'Child! Child!' Georgia gasped. 'It's OK. I'll try to fix your doll.'

'You can't fix it. You broke it. It's a spirit doll. Everything is broken now and can't ever be fixed.'

'A spirit doll?'

At that moment, Jessie came up and began speaking to the little girl in the same mixture of Hopi and Navajo. By this time, she was sobbing inconsolably.

Jessie turned to Georgia. 'This is Flora's sister Elena. She says this is a spirit doll.'

'Yes, that's what she told me, but what is that?'

'I don't know. It's definitely not a Kachina doll,' Jessie replied.

'They only do good things. Given as gifts to women upon marriage and things like that – first babies.'

'Who gave this to you, Elena?' Georgia asked.

'A lady.'

'What lady?' Jessie asked and then repeated the question in Navajo.

'I don't know.'

'But why did she give this to you?' There was a long silence.

'Elena?' Jessie said softly. Still the girl said nothing. 'Is she here now in the pueblo.' Elena shook her head.

'Did she come here ever?' Jessie asked. Now Elena nodded her head.

'Why did she give the doll to you, dear?' Georgia asked, holding the small hand in her own.

'She . . . she said . . . it was a truth doll. And if I didn't tell the truth, someone would die.'

'And what did she ask you?' Georgia ventured.

'She asked me about Flora, and now Flora has died and it's all my fault, but I told the truth. And now everything is broken.'

Jessie inhaled deeply. 'What truth did you tell, Elena?' The girl tipped her head and looked up at the sky but kept her eyes shut tight. 'I told her that Flora and Mateo were in love.' She took another deep breath. 'And that was the truth, and now Flora is dead and Mateo is in jail, maybe forever. So she lied to me! I told the truth.'

'Who was this person?' Georgia asked.

'A white lady.'

'You sure?' Georgia asked. She held the headless doll in one hand. She glanced down at the head that had fallen off in the alley. If anything, it reminded her of a voodoo doll or possibly an African doll of some sort. It had none of the bright colors of a Kachina doll. The carving of the head was crude. The hair was a small ball of what appeared to be shredded wool. The body looked as if it was made from a cartridge case, and the dress was a gaudy, striped fabric. The doll was no more than six or seven inches in length.

'I don't want it anymore. It only brings bad luck. My sister is dead. Dead!' And she started to sob again.

Georgia took both of Elena's hands. 'Now, you listen to me, Elena. Nothing you did or didn't do caused your sister to die. That's just a bunch of hokum.' The word came back to her from her childhood in Wisconsin.

'Hokum?' Elena asked, opening her dark eyes wide.

'Nonsense – that's what hokum is.' Georgia paused. 'But if you could think of anything else about the person who gave this to you, it might be helpful.'

Elena shook her head slowly.

'Well, now, if you do think of something, get in touch with Jessie here or with me. My name is Georgia, Georgia O'Keeffe. I'm staying over at Mrs Luhan's place. You know where that is?'

She nodded her head.

'Good girl.' Georgia gave her shoulder a little squeeze. 'You miss your big sister, don't you?'

The child's dark eyes filled with tears.

Georgia reached out and hugged her. How good it felt to hug this child.

TWENTY-THREE

The following day, Ryan seemed more preoccupied than ever, and it wasn't with her. It was distracting to Georgia, and this irritated her – that she was distracted by a man and not her work! Time for work. Time to drive her dear Model A out into the desert and start to really paint again. In her mind, painting indoors, looking out of the window from the Pink House, although ideal for the morada painting, did not count as really painting. She often painted indoors in the shack at Lake George, but rarely here in New Mexico. Getting outside and painting would get her mind off Ryan.

Fifteen minutes later, she was in her Model A, the easel firmly strapped down in the rear of the car in the makeshift studio where she would seek shelter when the sun got too hot. Pure happiness seemed to fizz through her. *Desert champagne!* she thought as she drove out into wilder and wilder country. It was not that far from Mabel's house, in fact, but the terrain instantly turned feral. Roads seemed to dissolve, hogans vanished, as did any signs of people or civilization.

But what interested her were bones. She had found some extraordinarily good sun-bleached pelvic bones of cattle out in this direction some years before. The apertures in those bones always fascinated her. No one was exactly like the other in shape. Basically, of course, there was a triangular bone between the two hip bones of the sacrum. It was the two oval voids that interested her. Crouch down on the ground and the ovals framed a world, the land. Pick the structure up and tip it toward the sky and it framed the flawless blue of a cloudless day.

She realized a couple of years ago that she had always painted these skeletal remains white, often against the blue sky – like gigantic telescope lenses. But recently, she had departed from the white of the bone and what it could frame and began introducing color – shifting from red to orange to yellow. In her mind, it was a huge chromatic shift, like a new symphony coming to life with a stampede of new notes, a new scale of color and texture.

As if to greet her, when she rolled up a small hill, there was an absolutely gorgeous pelvis emerging from the ochre sand. What a serendipitous moment. She was right to drive out here today. The light still at a perfect low angle, the bones loomed surreally from the sand. If she could just hold down the sun for a few more minutes while she set up. *This is where I belong . . . I belong in my head*, she thought as she set up her easel. She wanted to catch the eastern light coming through the aperture of the pelvis.

She didn't see white now; she saw in her mind's eye a ring of fire glazing the oval shape, which she enhanced until it almost appeared as if a bloody egg were bristling forth with new life. The blood of new life. She painted through those early morning hours, then decided to move back into the studio in the rear of her car as the heat rose and the light cast a hideous glare over the landscape. Useless high-noon light. She unrolled a mattress over the front passenger and driver seat so she could catch a snooze. Midday offered the most uninteresting hours for a painter. All drama was leached out of the light.

She slept for maybe two hours. When she awakened, the colors outside were beginning to shift to the cooler end of the spectrum. The wind had shifted as well, and she thought she heard voices.

There was a slab of rock fifty feet or more from the Model A that dropped off into a shallow arroyo. The voices seemed to float up, but the words were indistinguishable. Sound could be distorted out here by the stone cliffs of canyons and even arroyos. She got out of the car and crawled closer. Two figures sat side by side with their backs to her, a man in a cowboy hat and a woman. She strained to hear the words. They weren't speaking English but German, she suddenly realized!

'*Wie weit ist es bis zum Bahnhof?*'

'*Keine Sorge. Ich kann Sie hinbringen, Vallis.*'

Vallis, as in Wallis?

What the hell was Wallis Simpson doing out here with a cowboy? A German cowboy? Was it Cowboy from Los Gallos? She couldn't get a good look at him, but there was something vaguely familiar in his voice, even when he spoke German. She flattened herself on to her belly and crept back toward the Model A. She had to get out of there.

As quietly as possible, she got back into her car. Putting it in second gear and then releasing the clutch, she rolled backward down the slope. She didn't turn on the engine until she was at the bottom of the hill.

Now, why was Wallis consorting with a German-speaking cowboy? A German cowboy? Was there such a thing?

TWENTY-FOUR

ood old Florence Gilbert, Ryan McCaffrey thought. A sheriff couldn't have a better secretary. She followed instructions to a T and was polite. Well, she was a little snippy with Georgia in the beginning, but she had warmed up. And she was intuitive and patient with the young rascals, as she called the deputies. She had telephoned Los Gallos and left a message: 'Tell Sheriff McCaffrey that the results came back on that case and it's positive.' This translated to 'call the Feds from a secure phone'. This meant going to look for a pay telephone out here in the middle of nowhere as the one into Los Gallos was indeed tapped as he had suspected when he had first called Georgia. But where the hell was he going to find a pay phone?

The only secure phone that Ryan knew about was one a mile or so out of Los Burros at a junction where there was a gas station. He had a mental map of all the pay phones in New Mexico. There were only twenty in the entire state – three in Albuquerque, one in Santa Fe, this one in Los Burros, with the others scattered about hither and yon.

Thirty minutes later, the gas station came into view. As he pulled in and stepped out of the car, a lanky fellow came out of the garage.

'What can I do you fer?' As skinny as a scarecrow, he hobbled out from behind a fuel tank.

Ryan didn't really need any gas but thought it only polite to ask. 'Can you fill her up?'

'Sure thing, mister.' He was a bent, elderly man and wore an old Navajo hat. His face corrugated with wrinkles reminded Ryan of the fractures in the desert lands around Chimayo. His hands were like rawhide. Missing several teeth and with a permanent squint in his left eye, this was a man as gnarled by time as a thousand-year redwood.

'I was wondering if I might use the pay phone there?' Ryan nodded toward the phone booth.

'It'll cost ya.'

'I know. It's a pay phone.'

'But you have to pay me, too. Another five cents.'

'You the government now?' Ryan chuckled as he dug into his pants pocket.

'Nope, just me – Felton Walker Howson the Third. But you can just call me Walk.'

Ryan dropped the coins into Walk's hand.

'Thank you. I suppose you think I don't do much to keep the phone booth in shape, but I do.'

'You do, do you?'

'Ya see, rats get in there and the occasional rattler. Wanna hear a funny story?'

'Sure, why not?' Ryan answered. It always paid to listen to these old codgers. Sometimes they said something that was valuable, although in the case he was working on, Ryan doubted it.

'Well, coupla weeks back a woman came in here. Went into the phone booth, and then I see her flying out, screaming like bloody murder, and then guess what?'

'What?'

'She flipped her lid – yes, indeed!'

'What do you mean?' Ryan asked. 'Literally flipped her head?'

'Not her head, her wig.'

'Wig!'

'Yep, she was wearing a goddamn wig. She goes into the booth, and a rat jumps out at her on her head. The rat and the wig both fly out of there together. Funniest thing you ever saw. The rat had it in its mouth, but dropped it soon enough right in the middle of the road. She dashed out and smacked the wig back on her head and skedaddled out of here. Never made her phone call.' He sighed and chuckled. 'Never seen anything like it in my life.'

'Well, that's a new one. You want to check the booth before I go in?'

'Naw, you can do it yourself. Just knock a few times after you open the door and anything in there will skedaddle out.'

Ryan did as he was told. Nothing skedaddled out. It didn't take long to reach his contact.

'Hello, friend,' Ryan said as he heard the familiar voice of Lincoln Stone at the Bureau – now, as of last year, called the Federal Bureau of Investigation. 'How you doing, buddy?'

'Fine, and you?'

'OK. All things considered, OK,' Ryan replied.

'Your fellow has arrived. Carrying a sniper rifle, Russian one. Must be well financed.'

'Any idea who the target is this time, Linc?' Ryan asked.

'Can't quite figure it out. I mean, the usual suspects don't fit this scene. Not bootleggers – Prohibition is over, and Scotch wouldn't be coming through San Francisco. Pretty Boy's been gone almost two years now,' Linc replied.

'Pretty Boy as in Pretty Boy Floyd?' Ryan asked. Pretty Boy was mostly into robbing banks. 'Not a lot of banks out here, Linc. Think harder.'

'I'm not even sure your Bugsy is after a mob guy.'

'He's not exactly "my" Bugsy, Linc. I wasn't expecting him to show up in New Mexico. Bugsy Siegel's been in Nevada. Everyone knows that. He's setting up a casino and looking for prostitutes to import. So you're telling me he might be in New Mexico doing a hit job for a major client.'

'Well, I'm telling you he is in New Mexico. Maybe it's something personal, Ryan.'

'So you have no idea who the client is?'

'No idea. But we traced the sniper rifle to him and now he's in New Mexico.'

'You got the goods on the rifle through Fritzy at SIS?'

'Of course. You think my boss has the skills of Fritzy? Dream on.'

'What else do you know about Bugsy?'

'Some talk about red tape for casinos in Las Vegas; he might try New Mexico.'

'Oh, for Crissake, and then the Bureau of Indian Affairs will get into the act. That will wreak havoc out here.' Ryan sighed. 'What else do you know about this Bugsy guy?'

'Not much. Dresses flashy, a Brooklyn accent.'

'What the hell is a Brooklyn accent?' Ryan asked.

'How should I know? I'm a black man from Georgia. But this guy's been into everything since Prohibition has been over – gambling, prostitution, loan sharking. Known for his proficiency with a gun and extremely violent. But we have tracked him to the region around Taos, as I told you before.'

'OK, I'll keep an eye out.'

He certainly wasn't at Los Gallos, Ryan thought. He'd stand out like a sore thumb. But seconds after he hung up, he had another thought. Call Fritzy – Fritz Freihoff himself – at SIS.

He had the number in his wallet and dialed the operator to connect him. Someone picked up within two rings.

'SIS,' a woman's voice answered. It sounded like Eileen, Fritzy's secretary.

'Uh, is this Eileen?'

'Yes, sir, it is.'

'Eileen, this is Sheriff McCaffrey from New Mexico.'

'Oh, yes, sir, bet you want to speak with Doctor Freihoff.'

'I do, indeed.'

Ten seconds later, Fritzy's thick accent came through the receiver. 'Ryan, my friend. How are you doing?'

'Well, a bit stumped.'

'What stumps you, my boy?'

'I'm out here on a "hybrid project".'

Fritzy laughed. 'Of course, breeding exotic crimes.'

'I hope I'm not breeding them. It's kind of local but with a touch of what could be federal.'

'Go on.'

'So, this fellow Bugsy Siegel. Got word he's out here with a sniper-style Russian rifle.'

'Oy vey!'

'Yeah, right, oy vey!'

Fritzy laughed. 'You speak Yiddish like an Indian.'

'Only part Indian.'

'OK, let's try this again,' Fritzy said. 'Oy . . . deep inhale. Very sharp exhale with a bit of a huff.' He giggled. 'OK, let's get to it. What have you and Bugsy got going on?'

'He's out here for something. Not sure what, but it's bad.'

'Always bad with Bugsy whenever he crosses state lines, especially with a Russian sniper rifle.' He paused. 'So, where are you staying?'

Ryan hesitated, as he knew that Fritzy was a childhood friend of Alfred Stieglitz and knew Georgia.

'Los Gallos,' Ryan replied.

'And why there?'

'Oh, just convenient. You know my cousin Tony Luhan is married to Mabel Dodge.'

'No kidding?'

'No kidding.'

'Well, keep this under your hat, Ryan, but one of ours is there, too.'

'Oh, Jesus Christ, you're the one who bugged the phones.'

'Hmm, possibly. Have you met Wallis Simpson?'

'Indeed, I was cha-cha-cha-ing with her last night.'

'You don't say.'

'No really.'

'Was Doctor Ellington jealous?'

'Doctor Ellington? Oh, yes, the doctor who's staying there. Seems like a nice chap.'

'He's our chap,' Fritzy said calmly.

'Whoa! Whatcha got going on out here?'

'Can't really say, but you remember the old gang.'

Ryan knew immediately what Fritzy was talking about. The Lutzen group, a ring of Nazi spies that had seeped into the country and was deemed capable of a lot of damage. But he dared not speak the name on any unsecured line.

'We're not finished with them yet. Seems like the Prince of Wales is quite fond of his German relatives,' said Fritzy.

'Jesus Christ!' The Lutzen Ring had been very active close to Santa Fe. And it was thanks to Georgia a year ago that they got on to them.

'No, oy vey!' Fritzy sighed, then added under his breath, 'Such an aggravation, these goddamn Nazis.'

TWENTY-FIVE

t was close to midnight when Ryan was convinced that Georgia was finally sound asleep. She was not a light sleeper, but it often took her a while to fall asleep. He had already arranged with Cowboy to take a horse from the stables out into the desert. He dressed as quietly as possible and slipped out of the bedroom.

Cowboy was waiting for him in the stables.

'I won't be long,' Ryan said.

'No problem, Sheriff.'

'And let's keep this between you and me.'

'Absolutely, sir.'

'As I said, I won't be long.'

Cowboy watched the sheriff on the pinto dissolve into the mist. He rode well for such a large man and was at ease on the pinto, whose patches now merged with the air, for the night was vaporous as it could sometimes turn in the early spring.

Ryan's destination was the Ojo Grande, a horseback riding trail near where Tomas Benally had said to meet him. Georgia would be fit to be tied if she knew Ryan was meeting with Tomas, a wrangler at the Ghost Ranch and an extremely smart fellow. She was quite close to Tomas's two sisters, Rosaria and Clara.

Tomas had made himself a valuable informer to the FBI and the SIS, the Signal Intelligence Service in Washington as well as the Secret Intelligence Service in London. To date, Tomas had installed at least fifty Hartley transmitter receivers and tracked down close to twenty suspected Nazi spies in the Southwest that belonged to the Lutzen Ring. And he was still not finished with them. If anything, the Lutzen Ring was spreading like a cancer and was now evolving into the German American Bund.

Tomas didn't just wrangle cattle. He had found a special satisfaction in the process of assembling the Hartley transmitter receivers – the coils of winding copper wire, the transformers, the large valves – all the parts, the guts of the radio. He had picked up the technical skills so quickly and learned how to build the receivers, rectifiers, and frequency meters within a matter of weeks. He loved the work the way he loved rodeo riding.

The Hartleys provided a covert listening device that could pick up signals from the German American Bund units, like the Lutzen, that were multiplying dramatically and pinpoint their exact locations. The Bund comprised American citizens of German descent. They were not just spies but dedicated to promoting a favorable view of Nazi Germany.

Ryan had planned to meet Tomas by a large petroglyph about a quarter mile in on the trail. The mist had cleared by the time he approached and heard Tomas's horse neigh softly. The stars cut the night, and a shooting one blasted across the blackness as if freed from its ancient path.

'What a night!' Ryan sighed. 'You know the First People legend of how the star seeds were shaken loose from the cottonwood when a storm came through?'

'Oh, yes, what Navajo kid doesn't know that one?'

'Imagine a tree giving birth to stars! What if it were a male tree? Could it still happen?' Ryan asked. 'Think about that.'

Tomas laughed. Sometimes the sheriff came up with the oddest thoughts. He suspected that was why he and Miss O'Keeffe got on so well. They were both outliers in the way they thought about the world.

Ryan sighed. 'So what have you got for me, Tomas?'

'Nothing good.'

'Lutzen Ring?'

'I doubt if they're actual members.'

'Who?'

'Wallis Simpson.'

'Well, well, or, as my Irish grandmother used to say, "Oh my stars and garters."'

'Thought you should know.'

'Thanks pal.' Ryan looked up at the sky, turned his horse and headed back to Los Gallos.

Tomas turned his horse in the opposite direction and headed toward the buried Hartley radio, HTR'37. He needed to check the battery. If it had died, well, that was good or, rather, explainable. But if not, this would be the third in a month, and that would indicate that someone had sabotaged the transmitter-receiver. He headed toward the site. Dismounting, he unpacked his tool kit and extracted a small trowel, his headphones, a voltage meter and a device that Tomas himself had designed that functioned as a radio compass. It could pinpoint the location of any enemy interference or listener that might be picking up the HTR's presence.

He had been working for less than ten minutes. His earphones relayed every signal tone from all the others in the region, and his ears were attuned to any outlier signature tones or bounce signals that would indicate interference from unwanted listeners. He had his own remarkable sound memory, an obviously overdeveloped part of his own brain. Now a voice infiltrated his head with frightening clarity.

'*Haben Sie gefunden was Sie suchen? Ich bin bereit einen Deal zu machen – einen sehr großzügigen Deal für Sie.*'

'*Wer sind Sie?*' Tomas felt the snub end of a revolver pressed to the base of his neck.

'Are you interested in a deal?' the man said.

'Possibly,' Tomas growled. 'But before I make a deal, I like to know who I'm dealing with.'

'Well, Wernher von Braun, for one. Are you impressed? Don't turn around. I shall come to you.'

Tomas felt the pressure of the gun vanish from the back of his neck as the man took steps around him. In the moonlight, he cast a long shadow. He was tall and slender and wore very thick glasses.

'So, what do you say?'

'Who's Wernher von Braun?' Tomas asked.

'Never heard of Wernher von Braun?' He tipped his head back to laugh.

Tomas knew that fifteen feet behind the man was a cliff. Dare he? As if to answer his question, at that very moment Pablo, the horse, broke wind explosively. The man turned his head. Tomas charged.

'*Guter Gott!*' the man screamed as he dropped into the night.

Breathing heavily, Tomas went to the side of the cliff. He saw the body crumpled below. He bent over and picked up the Beretta the man dropped before he fell. Gratefully, he looked at Pablo. 'Thanks, buddy,' *The fart that saved the world*, Tomas thought.

Forty-five minutes later, Ryan slipped back into the bedroom and undressed. He looked down at Georgia. She appeared so tantalizing, sleeping on her back with her long white hair streaming over her beautiful shoulders like water running in a brook. He climbed as quietly as possible into bed. Five minutes later, she turned over, still half asleep.

'I smell horse. Why do I smell horse?' she muttered. She turned over again, then went back to sleep, or whatever world she slept in, as he was unsure what one would call the sleep world of Georgia O'Keeffe.

TWENTY-SIX

'What are you moping about now, Maudie?' Wallis Simpson asked as she came into the room where Maudie was ironing the slacks she planned to wear to the cocktail hour tonight.

'Nothing, ma'am. You can try these on now.'

Wallis pulled off her dress and put on the slacks. Maudie kneeled to check the length, as she had shortened them.

'What's this?' Wallis said, frowning deeply. 'You did something to the zipper. It won't close at the top. You were just supposed to shorten the pants.'

'I didn't do anything to the waist.' Maudie swallowed. Dare she say it? 'Maybe you've gained a little weight?'

A darkness spread across Wallis's face with the force of a gathering storm. It did not faze Maudie in the least. In fact, it inspired her. She felt a hurricane force building within her own body.

'Actually, ma'am, you look a bit chubby to me.'

'I'm not chubby!' she screeched. And she kicked her foot with its spike heel at Maudie, who fell over and started bleeding from her forehead.

I have her now, Maudie thought. 'Pay for me to go back to England. Pay for me or I'll tell about your lover, Herr Ribbentrop, who sent the carnations. I'll tell everything. Your other affair with Guy Trundle, the car salesman, the emerald necklace that has yet to be paid for.'

'You wouldn't!' Wallis's face was like a diabolical mask, distorted with rage.

'Yes, I would! And I'd tell my aunt who works for Queen Mary, and her husband, Antony, who is a dresser for the king and . . .'

Wallis lifted her foot. The spike heel hovered above Maudie, and then, before she could move, Wallis brought her foot down squarely on Maudie's stomach. The stiletto heel sunk in. There was a spurt of blood, and Maudie felt a terrible cramping. Wallis took off the shoe and began to hit Maudie's head with it. But she stopped as she saw a puddle of blood forming on the floor beneath Maudie.

She scrambled away to flee the spreading pool. She reached for a cushion on a couch.

'You can't hide it!' Maudie smiled through her pain. 'You can't hide it now, bitch!'

Steps were heard racing up the stairs. Spud and Dr Ellington charged through the door. Maudie was drenched with blood, her eyes rolled back into her head.

'Just a little accident,' Wallis gasped. 'Maudie tripped pinning up the hem of my slacks.'

'Not a little accident,' the doctor said, kneeling by Maudie. 'Massive bleeding. We have to get her to a hospital.'

'Holy Cross Medical Center on the Weimer Road,' Spud said.

'We have to go now!' the doctor said as he picked Maudie up in his arms. By the time he got downstairs, he was drenched in the young girl's blood.

Wallis had followed them down the stairs, babbling.

'I was standing there so she could pin up the slacks and suddenly I felt faint and toppled over on her, apparently. Oh dear, I need a drink.'

Spud turned to her. 'You need to get out of here,' he said in a low, dangerous voice.

Two hours later, Ryan returned and walked into Los Gallos.

He was half relieved that Georgia hadn't come back yet. He wanted time to think. Mariel, one of the cleaning ladies, came out of Spud's office with a mop in hand. 'Just in time, sheriff. Phone call for you.'

'What happened here?' he asked as he looked at the wet floor.

'Accident,' Mariel replied softly. 'Maudie, Mrs Simpson's lady's maid. Not sure what, but a lot of blood. They took her to the hospital.'

'Oh dear,' he mumbled as he walked into Spud's office and picked up the phone. 'Fritzy twice in one day.'

'Just found out. That certain doctor staying where you are?'

'Yes, yes, the one you told me about earlier.'

'He's one of theirs.'

'Theirs? But you said "ours" less than an hour ago.'

'SIS has him in their crosshairs. Just found out.'

'Theirs? Crosshairs?' Ryan repeated. It could mean only one thing. 'He's a double agent, Fritzy?'

'You got it. Hooked into the Lutzen Ring.'

Ryan set down the phone. He took a deep breath and shut his eyes for a moment. When he walked out of the office, he saw Mariel and another employee of Mabel's still mopping the blood from the terra-cotta floor.

Things were turning strange too quickly. He knew that Georgia realized that he was not out in Taos just for a rendezvous with her, that he obviously had other business on his mind. They had been brought to this place at the same time by some odd quirk of fate but for separate reasons – or were they that separate? He couldn't imagine how his interests or purposes could cross paths with hers and the murder of Flora Namingha. And now this news from Fritzy that the good doctor, Bernard Ellington, was a double agent. Was there any chance that in some peculiar way there was in fact a convergence in their both being out here – the crime that was so consuming Georgia and Bugsy Siegel's presence in New Mexico?

He stretched out on the bed in their room, and just as he was beginning to doze off, he heard footsteps outside and a squeak as the door opened. Should he pretend to sleep or not? He rolled on to his side and made a slight snoring sound.

'Oh, you're awake,' Georgia said.

'Well, no, actually. I was just falling asleep.'

'No, you weren't. You never snore when you sleep on your side.'

'Oh.' No use trying to fool this woman ever. 'Well, I've got to tell you a funny story.'

'A funny story?' Georgia kicked off her shoes and plopped on the bed. She grabbed her left foot and began to massage it. 'My corns. Feels like they're on fire.'

'How romantic. Wanna fool around?'

'Uh, maybe.'

'Wanna hear my funny story?'

'Sure, funny stories are always a good lead into witty foreplay.'

'Doctor Freud, I presume.'

'Ha!' She laughed. 'Now, go ahead with your funny story.'

'I was heading toward Los Burros earlier today, and I stopped to make a pay telephone call at a gas station. The old codger who ran it was something of a character and he told me this story.' He continued. 'So when the rat came out of the phone booth, this lady flipped her lid, or actually her wig!'

'Wig!' Georgia exclaimed and jumped from the bed.

'Yes, wig? What's wrong with that?'

'McCaffrey, you and I have got some talking to do.'

'Oh, once again an "I'll show you mine if you show me yours situation"?'

'Most definitely, Sheriff.' She paused for a second. 'Foreplay!' she cackled.

Ryan shook his head. 'You're impossible, woman. What have you got?'

'A phone call from Emily Bryce about a wig.'

TWENTY-SEVEN

Maudie lay in the gathering darkness of the hospital room. She heard the door handle turn. She expected to see the nurse – Loretta Yazzie, Jessie's sister – or Dr Goldstein. The sleeve of a white coat appeared. Dr Goldstein. But not! A taller, more slender man.

'Oh, Doctor Ellington. You're still here?' Maudie asked.

'Just wanted to make one last check before I go,'

'That's very kind of you, but Doctor Goldstein and the nurse have just been here and say I'm doing nicely.'

'One can't be too careful when transfusing a patient. The pressure flow has to be just right.' He went to the side of the bed and read some gauges. 'Oh, indeed! I suspected this might happen.'

'Oh dear! Something wrong?'

'Not to worry, my dear.' He was squinting at a dial.

'Maybe you should turn on the light.'

'I wouldn't want to disturb you.' And in that moment, Maudie knew deep within her that something disturbing was about to occur.

'I have excellent night vision. I don't want to unsettle you.'

He gave a quick smile. Too quick, thought Maudie.

'I'll just open the shade over there and let the moonlight in. We'll make this adjustment by moonlight.' Again, the quick smile as he went to the window. A blade of moonlight came through. She saw him lift his hand slightly as if to wave at someone. She gazed at the shadows of his long fingers against the wall. She recalled going to the village once with her mum to see a shadow puppet dance. It was called Timba and the Ginger Man.

The doctor turned and walked back to the pole that held the transfusion bag. From the side pocket of his white coat, he took something out.

'What's that?' she asked. Her voice was trembling.

'Just a pressure bag to accelerate the rate of flow.'

'But . . . but shouldn't Doctor Goldstein do that?'

He bent over close to her ear, his eyes glittering in the darkness. Something odd was happening. His face began to blur. She felt a deathly coldness creeping through her body as if frost were forming in her veins.

'*Auf Wiedersehen, Schatzie,*' he whispered.

Jessie Yazzie stepped through the front door of the Desert Lily. The women were half clothed – one woman was actually dipping her enormous titty into a fellow's beer – but no one seemed to notice Jessie's arrival. A minute or so later, Lily swaggered out from behind a curtain and immediately spied him.

'Welcome, darling.' She was hanging on the arm of a smart-looking dude with spats and slicked-back hair.

'First time, eh?' said the slick man with a very funny accent. He slapped a ten-dollar bill into Lily's hand. 'Fix him up with a good ride, Lily.'

'I will. And remember me when you get to Vegas.'

'How could I ever forget you – those eyes, those boobies, that twat?'

Jessie almost fainted. All he wanted to do was fuck. A simple fuck. He didn't have the capability of talking like this slick dude. *Just a fuck.* He wanted to get it over with.

Half an hour later, he walked out of the brothel. Relief was the only feeling he experienced. Relief and just the teeniest bit of not exactly pride but perhaps accomplishment. One thing checked off his checklist of manliness. The next time he went to confession, he would not have to whisper through the screen of the confessional booth that he had masturbated. He could just say, *Father Donald, I did it. I really did it – with a girl! Not just a girl, a big woman with enormous titties. And I loved it. Hit me with it – one hundred Hail Marys, no problem.*

The phrases, the sentences he used in the past when he confessed to masturbating were ridiculous and tortured. *Father, I confess to the sin of being unchaste with myself* or *Father, I have fornicated with my own body.* There were countless code words he could use. The latest and stupidest sounding was 'Onan'. Even Father Donald said, 'Huh, boy?' When that word came out of Jessie's mouth, it sounded more like the name of a planet than anything else. He wanted to tell Father Donald to look it up. He had looked it up after finding it in an English novel and was surprised to see it had nothing to do with a planet. It was just another way of saying masturbation. It came from the Bible. Genesis, Chapter 38. Onan was the son of

Judah. 'And Onan knew that the seed should not be his; and it came
to pass, when he went in unto his brother's wife, that he spilled it
on the ground, lest that he should give seed to his brother's wife.'
Why do they have to say all that? Well, he, Jesus Joe Yazzie, had
spilled oceans of seed all over the place and just this one time into
this one lady with enormous breasts and, yes, a delightful pussy.
Her name was Bessie. She sucked him off, too, but she was missing
a couple of teeth and it didn't feel quite right.

He'd go to confession, but not right now – not until after Good
Friday. He'd feel like a total fraud if he went now. He wanted to
live in the splendor of this moment just a bit longer. Next Sunday
after Easter. He would still be suspended in this shimmering halo
of the light of Bessie for a bit longer. Just a bit.

He heard footsteps behind him and turned around to see the man
who had given Lily the ten-dollar bill.

'How'd you do, sonny? Bessie give you a good ride there?'

'Uh, yeah, yeah. Just fine.'

'So I want to ask you. Uh, I understand that you sometimes work
up there at Los Gallos, the Mabel Dodge Luhan place.'

'Yeah, yeah. I help out now and then.'

'There was a guy here the other night from there. A little light
in his loafers if you get what I mean.' He laughed. 'Guess I should
say light in his cowboy boots. Matter of fact, that's what they call
him.'

'What?'

'Cowboy. Good-looking son of a gun. You know him? He still
at Los Gallos?'

'Oh, yeah. He takes guests out on trail rides.'

'He still there?'

Still? Jessie was not just a sensitive listener but also a somewhat
analytical one. The word 'still' struck Jessie as odd. Cowboy had
always been in Taos and it seemed like forever at Los Gallos. He
could do anything – lead trail rides, fix plumbing, dance with lonely
ladies at the cocktail dances.

'Yeah, he's still there.'

'Now I hear there's this big march coming up on Good Friday.'

'Not a march – a pilgrimage, they call it, with the Penitentes –
but anybody can go.'

'You going?' the man asked.

Indians don't blush, but Jessie felt a blush creeping up in his neck. He thought of his pecker, his *aziz*, in Bessie's half-toothless mouth. He thought of himself riding, galloping on top of her, firm in her saddle, his dick firing off like the Fourth of July.

'Uh, maybe not this year. Not sure yet. Listen, I got to run.'

'Run where?'

'Back to the police station.'

'You a cop.'

'Not exactly.'

'But that's about five miles from here – you're a runner?'

'Sure. I'm Navajo.'

And he began running east into the pulsing red light of a new dawn.

A blade of light slashed across the Navajo blanket that Georgia and Ryan slept under. She watched as it slowly slid across the serrated woven diamond design, a classic motif in Navajo blankets.

The 'I'll show you mine if you show me yours' strategy of analyzing crimes hadn't worked as well as Georgia had hoped. Ryan was not really impressed by Georgia's theories about the killer wearing a wig. He just kept chuckling to himself about the lady flipping her wig in the phone booth when assailed by a rat. He could see no overlap with his own interests. He had at least admitted to her that he was out here on a federal case and had talked to Fritzy Freihoff at SIS. Georgia had actually introduced Ryan and Fritzy the previous summer when the Lutzen gang was burbling up around the Ghost Ranch. He owed her that.

As the light played across the blanket, for some reason it reminded Georgia of the pendant that Mateo had made for her. She got up and went to the drawer where she kept it and then climbed back into bed.

Dangling it over her head, she watched as the light coming from the window caught the surfaces of the pendant.

Georgia felt Ryan turn over. 'You awake?' she asked.

'Maybe. It depends.'

Georgia snorted. 'On what?'

'Not sure.' He yawned. 'You going to grill me on why I'm out here aside from my passion for you?'

'Maybe.'

'OK, I better get up. What do you have there?'

'The pendant that Mateo Chee made me that's based on the

stained-glass window design.' She sighed. 'It's so sad. He didn't kill Flora. I just know it.'

'Then you've got to prove it somehow.'

She rolled on to her side to look at Ryan. He was right, of course. She hadn't really been trying to prove it. She was just all hung up on the stupid wig. The wig in one sense proved nothing except that the person wanted a disguise to cover up their identity. But there could be many reasons to wear a wig. Perhaps the person was like her friend Esther from art school who suffered from a very rare condition, alopecia, that caused massive hair loss.

Had the police department ever gone to Mateo's home studio to find any clues? Only to arrest him. It was not surprising. Homer and Harold were the laziest law enforcement officers ever. She needed to get out to Mateo's house. There must be something that would help her, point her in the right direction. She'd try to track down Jessie to see if he would go with her.

She got up and quickly dressed. 'Catch you later,' she said as she gave Ryan a quick kiss goodbye, then raced to her Model A.

She switched on the ignition, then, pressing the fuel tap under the dashboard, she pulled the throttle on the steering column. She turned the silver knob in front of the passenger seat, then pushed the clutch all the way down while pushing the starter button on the floor. There was nothing but a weak hiccup. She tried again and again.

'Damn!' she swore.

She walked into Los Gallos. Spud greeted her at the door.

'Hello, Georgia.'

'Have you heard anything about Maudie?'

'Last I heard, which was last night, she was recovering well despite a lot of blood loss.'

'Doctor Ellington back?'

'Not yet.'

'Well, in any case, my car's broken down. Is Jessie around? I thought he might help me out.'

'No, he's not in yet, although this might be his day to work at the police station.'

Georgia sighed. 'Oh, did Wallis leave?'

'Not yet. She can't get a car.'

Georgia couldn't imagine anything worse than driving all the way to Albuquerque to deliver Wallis to the train station.

Ryan came into the courtyard.

'Thought you'd left.'

'Car won't start.'

'Let me have a look.' He tried for ten minutes.

'Could you take me and drop me off at the Old Adobe Road?'

'That's Mateo Chee's house studio?'

'Yes.'

'Well, that's in the opposite direction of where I'm going.'

'Where's that?'

'Can't say.'

'All right.' Georgia tried not to sound grumpy. She went inside and settled in a chair.

'Can I make you a cup of tea, Miss O'Keeffe?' Mariel, the young woman from Spud's office, came out.

'That would be lovely, dear. And where is everyone today?'

'Well,' she said, looking at her watch. 'It's still early. Just seven o'clock. But a lot of people are driving over to Santa Fe and some as far as Chimayo for all the Easter stuff. Much nicer here. Not as crowded.'

'Will you be part of the pilgrimage here?' Georgia asked.

'Yes, I really have to. My Aunt Ava would never speak to me again if I didn't. But we cheat a bit.'

'How does one cheat?'

'They take a car to Punto Rojo and walk from there. Just the last three miles at the junction between the road leading into Taos from Espanola and the one to Oja Caliente.'

'Sounds good to me.'

While Mariel went for the tea, a magazine caught Georgia's eye. *Outsider Art.* She began to page through it. There were several advertisements for galleries that dealt in Outsider Art. There was a small ad, less than a quarter of a page, for one called Inside Outside. Wasn't that the name of Bunny's gallery? Apparently, it was the go-to gallery in London for Navajo weavings as well as sub-Saharan African carvings and jewelry. Odd, she had stressed the Bengali art and not mentioned the Navajo or sub-Saharan art in the conversation the other evening.

Mabel came into the room. 'I can't believe it!'

'Believe what?'

'Doctor Ellington's left. No warning, nothing. He's been coming here for years. Never even said goodbye or anything. Somehow he came back and got his bag and just left!'

'But he went to the hospital with Maudie.'

'Yes, I know that. And now Wallis Simpson has upped and vanished. No goodbye, nothing. Not that I'm crying over that.'

'How did she get away?'

'Handsome fellow from Santa Fe, Navajo, picked her up.'

'Not Tomas?' Georgia asked.

'Yes, I believe that was his name. Tomas Benally. It was very odd. When she greeted him she said, "*Guten Tag.*" That's German.'

Georgia was stunned. Ryan had told her that Tomas was critical to the British SIS in picking up the Lutzen Ring spies. He had become fluent in German, of course, for he indeed listened to their secret communications constantly through the Hartley transmitter receivers that he had planted throughout the Southwest for British and American intelligence. That would be something that Ryan would be interested in. Then it dawned on her. Maybe that was why Ryan was out here and playing his cards so close to his chest.

Ryan had worked with Fritzy Freihoff at the SIS in Washington. Georgia and Stieglitz both knew Fritzy, Stieglitz from his childhood in New Jersey, Georgia through Stieglitz and her discoveries of the Lutzen Ring last year. Things were coming together in a most interesting way. This was a eureka moment if there ever was one – or maybe not, since Archimedes jumped out of his bathtub and ran down the street in ancient Greece, proclaiming, 'Eureka, the king's crown is not pure gold!'

TWENTY-EIGHT

oretta Yazzie walked down the corridor with her clipboard. She wanted to check on the young English girl. Girl? Woman? In any case, she had suffered a rather minor injury to her forehead but a terrible miscarriage. Transfusions, however, had brought her back quite nicely. There was a 'Do Not Disturb' sign on her door. Odd, thought Loretta, the chart showed that Hildy Lopez had just checked her.

At that moment, Hildy came down the corridor.

'Hildy, did you just check Miss McPhee?'

'No, I was coming to do it now.'

Loretta opened the door. 'Jesus Christ! Pull the alarm.' There was blood all over the floor. It seemed to Loretta as though she had stepped out of her own body. She picked up the blood bag and reinserted the needle in Maudie's arm.

'No pulse. No pulse.' Hildy gasped, then punched her in the chest and pressed the stethoscope to her ears.

Nurses and doctors rushed into the room. A bewhiskered doctor began to pump her chest violently. Then he bent over her and tried mouth-to-mouth resuscitation.

'Got a heartbeat, doctor,' Loretta exclaimed. 'One more now.'

He inhaled. 'I think we've got her back.' He looked at the pressure bag on the pole. 'Who put that on?' he roared.

Five minutes later, Maudie's color had returned. She blinked her eyes.

'What happened, Maudie, dear?' asked the doctor.

'I don't know, sir.'

'Who put this pressure bag on the transfusion bag?'

'Another doctor.'

'Another doctor? I'm confused.'

'Doctor Carter?' Loretta asked.

'No, Doctor Ellington,' Maudie replied weakly.

'Wait! Do you mean the doctor who brought you in here with Spud Johnson?'

'Yes.'

'But he's not a doctor here.'

'I know,' Maudie said weakly. 'I was so frightened. I tried to scream but I couldn't. It was as if I was paralyzed.'

The doctor turned to Loretta. 'Loretta, better call those two buffoons at the police station.'

'Yes, sir.'

Jules Goldstein had worked in this hospital for the last twenty years. In his entire medical career and earlier in Chicago, he had never seen anything like this. Why would someone try to kill this girl? He had to report this as a crime. It gave him the chills to think that there might be a murderer in this small, well-run hospital.

Loretta poked her head in. 'Both on their way.'

'Harold and Homer? Right?'

'Right.'

'Any chance your brother could come?'

'Not sure where he is at the moment.'

'Not in school, I guess.'

'Doubt it,' Loretta replied.

'Waste of time for him,' Dr Goldstein said. 'Keep an eye on her. I'll be back in ten minutes to check her again.'

He then left the room and turned down the corridor toward his office. Sitting down at his desk, he picked up the phone and called Los Gallos.

'Doctor Goldstein here. May I speak with Doctor Ellington?'

'Uh . . .' Mariel hesitated. 'Doctor Ellington seems to be gone.'

'Seems to be? What do you mean?'

'He's gone, sir, just gone.'

'Well, can I talk to Mabel?'

'Certainly, Doctor.'

'Hello,' Mabel said. 'It's you, Jules?'

'Yes. Where'd Ellington go?'

'No idea! I wish I knew. He's left. Just plain left. Someone must have picked him and his bag up. His room was completely empty.'

Jules Goldstein leaned back in his chair, removed his glasses and pinched the bridge of his nose with his thumb and forefinger. 'Oy vey,' he murmured softly. 'Someone has violated his Hippocratic Oath.' Then he knew: *Someone has attempted murder.*

Felton Walker Howson III peered at the twenty dollars that the slick-looking fellow in spats driving off in a beat-up truck had slipped him to tell him whether a fellow, mid-fifties, driving a Buick, had stopped here to make a call. If the car did stop here in the future, to please call the Desert Lily and leave a message for Ed Benjamin and confirm that such a car had been at his gas station. Word had come from Vegas to Bugsy that the county sheriff out here was on to him.

Walk had every intention of doing it. After all, who couldn't use twenty bucks during the Depression. He thought about it for two days. And was still thinking about it when the battered gray Buick turned into the gas station. He crumpled up the ten-dollar bills and stuffed them in his pocket, then, thinking again, took them out of his pocket, lit a match to them and watched them crinkle up in the flames. 'Gone,' he muttered and felt a weight lift from him.

So what if I'm forty-six days late for Ash Wednesday, Walk thought. Just two days until Good Friday. How could he do the pilgrimage with this on his mind? That guy was the devil himself. Such was his rationalization of burning up two crisp tens in a fire of his own making. As an added touch, he bent down and, taking some ashes in his fingers, he streaked them across his forehead. *I feel great!* he thought. He'd eat beans tonight, and if they made him fart, well, he'd light those, too. No one had ever accused Felton Walker Howson III of being rational.

'Ha!' he exclaimed as he looked out the window and watched the Buick's door open.

Ryan stepped out of the car. 'Hello, Walk!' he called out as he dug into his back pocket for his wallet.

'No need, sir. Free today. Having a sale on phone calls.'

'That's not necessary, Walk,' Ryan said.

'Yes, it is, sir, and no rats in there. I already checked this morning.' And then he thought, *The only rat was the one in spats!* He should be a poet.

'OK by me.' Ryan looked closer. 'Hey, Walk, you got some dirt on your forehead.'

'Not dirt, God's blessing.'

Ryan pressed his lips together. 'Umm-hmm.'

He turned toward the phone booth and entered the special number that Fritzy had given him. Fritzy picked up on the first ring.

The thick accent and only four words: 'Guess what, my friend.'

Ryan caught his breath. 'What?'

'We picked up the doc at the Mexican border last night.'

'Who picked him up?'

'Wolf Boy.' Ryan realized immediately: Wolf Boy was code name for Tomas Benally.

'Not only that, but Tomas drove back and got Pickles.'

Pickles, Ryan thought, the code name for Wallis Simpson. How she would hate that.

'Yes, her, but didn't arrest her. Maybe slept with her but didn't arrest her.'

'Why not?'

'She's too valuable. He drove her to the train station in Albuquerque, where she got a train east. We're going to let her run as far as she can.' Fritzy sighed. 'I don't joke about this kind of stuff. Might I remind you, doc out there is a double agent,' he snapped and hung up.

Ryan stared at the phone as if it were an instrument of betrayal. He instantly recalled the image of Georgia trying to cha-cha with Ellington. She had been chatting amiably with him. This was not just surprising but alarming. Why did agents turn like this? Money? Yes, of course, but there was something more. There was something that he had often thought about. There were certain people who were obsessed with being able to penetrate the most inner circles in all walks of life – social, political and, yes, intelligence oper-ations. They sought to belong to this elite group just beyond their own grasp where the power lay. They had no loyalty, no fealty, except to themselves and their boundless vanity and their own obsession with a mastery of power.

What was he dealing with? He wished that Georgia were here now. He knew she was irritated when he declined to take her over to Mateo Chee's house. More than irritated. She had, however, suppressed calling him a cranky old man. He loved it when she did that. He was yearning for her now. *Call me cranky, sweetheart, I'm in love with you.* He began humming the tune, making up his own words: *Let me call you cranky / I'm in love with you. / Let me hear you whisper / That you love me too. / Keep that cranky glow / In your eyes so true. / Let me call you cranky / I'm in love with you. / Stand with me through thick and thin / And we'll be cranky to the very end.*

TWENTY-NINE

Georgia was in Cowboy's car as they drove out to Mateo's house on the Old Adobe Road.

'This is very nice of you, Cowboy.'

'You can call me Marcus.'

'Marcus? That's your real name?'

'Yes, ma'am.'

'So why don't they call you that instead of Cowboy?'

'It was Mabel's idea. You know, because I wrangle the horses and take the guests out on trail rides. But I write poetry, too.' He chuckled. 'Guess they can only cram so many artists into Los Gallos.' He laughed. 'And my poetry might not be intellectual enough.'

'There are cowboy poets? Really!'

'Yep, that's what we call it, cowboy poetry. There are quite a few of us.'

'Well, my goodness. Could you recite some for me, Marcus?'

'Sure.' He coughed slightly and, keeping his eyes on the road, began.

> *Take off your boots.*
> *Shake off the sweat.*
> *It's time to lay back and have no regrets.*
> *You spent the day on the trail*
> *In the blistering sun.*
> *And now by the fire you've done your run.*
>
> *The cattle will lull you to sleep with their braying*
> *It's time to shut your eyes and start praying*
> *For before you know it, the sun will be up*
> *And you'll be grumbling, 'Aw shucks,*
> *Aw shucks.'*

'Oh, lovely,' Georgia responded as she thought, *Well, he isn't William Butler Yeats.* But she liked thinking of Marcus putting his head down on his saddle and looking up at the stars while the cattle brayed and he prayed. She turned to Marcus. 'Not bad, not bad at all, Cowboy – I mean, Marcus. Rather comforting.'

'Oh, call me anything you want.' He paused for a second and turned to look at Georgia. 'You can call me queer, if you like, or homo.'

Georgia wasn't exactly shocked. She certainly knew plenty of queer people in the art world, but it was something about the innocence with which he made this remark that touched her very deeply. She put out her hand and touched his right hand on the gearshift.

'Thank you,' she said softly.

Two minutes later, they pulled into the drive of Mateo's house.

'The door is probably locked,' Georgia said.

'Don't worry, I know where he keeps his extra key.' Cowboy saw the shocked look on her face. 'No, he didn't play both sides of the fence like I do. We weren't lovers. There's been some robberies in the area, so I told him to put a spare key in a loose brick in his rainwater catch to get into the house if something happens.'

Two minutes later, Marcus turned the lock, and they entered the front hall of Mateo's house. They passed through the living part into the studio by a passage from the kitchen. Everything seemed very neat and precise. There were two drafting tables, where he made the designs for his pieces. Georgia saw her designs for the chapel windows pinned to a bulletin board above the drafting tables. On one drafting table was a light box with a piece of graph paper, on to which he would transfer drawings to the glass panes. This was exactly how he had reproduced Georgia's watercolor designs. She turned on the light box to see what he had been working on most recently. She caught her breath as an elegant drawing of Flora's face appeared. He must have been midway through transferring the design. It appeared that he had been tracing it with a thick black marker, and it looked as if there were two pieces of pink and violet glass ready to place over the drawing.

'You see.' Georgia traced her finger over the drawing. 'He'll take that plate of glass, put it on top of the light box and with a scoring tool make the first lines on that piece of pink glass. Most likely, he'll then take the violet glass for another part of her face.' She inhaled softly. 'A stained-glass Madonna,' she whispered.

At just that moment, they heard a car pull in. They both froze.

'Oh, Jesus!' Cowboy said. Seconds later, the car gunned its engine. Wheels squeaked as it turned around and peeled out of the drive.

'Not the cops.' Cowboy exhaled.

'No, they wouldn't have left that quickly.'

'But who would?' Cowboy wondered aloud.

'I don't know,' Georgia muttered. But one thing she did know was that she wasn't done with this place.

Jessie Yazzie was agitated. He almost wished he had cut school that day. But as soon as he walked out, he saw his sister waiting for him.

She looked deathly pale.

'What's wrong? Ama Sani?'

'No, not Grandma. Something else.'

'What?'

'Maudie McPhee.'

'She died?'

'Almost.'

Jessie's sister explained about Maudie and the conclusion of the hospital that Dr Ellington was the last person who saw her. Dr Goldstein had now arranged for her to be guarded around the clock.

'Harold and Homer?' Jessie asked.

'Would you ask Harold and Homer to guard anybody?'

'No.'

'We're all taking our turns here at the hospital,' she said.

'I'll take a turn. I like Maudie a lot. I have to work the bar tonight at Los Gallos, but I could come in after.'

'I don't know, you look a little tired. What were you up to last night?'

'Nothing,' he said and shuffled his feet, refusing to meet his sister's gaze as he remembered his evening with Bessie. *Oh God, don't let me get a hard-on here.* 'I'm going over to Los Gallos now. I'll let them know I have to get off a bit early.'

When he walked into Los Gallos, the living room was empty except for Georgia, Ryan, Mabel and Tony in a tight huddle.

'They didn't leave together,' Mabel was saying. 'The doctor just plain left. Not sure how. A bit later, Mrs Simpson was outside with her ridiculous number of suitcases – Tony helped her.'

'Anything you can remember about the person who picked her up?' Georgia asked.

'Not much,' Tony replied.

'Uh, by the way, someone tried to kill Maudie,' Jessie broke in.

'What!' Mabel cried.

'How . . . Why . . . Who?' Georgia said.

Jessie took a deep breath. 'Doctor Ellington, most likely. My sister Loretta is a nurse at Holy Cross. They've set up a guard around the clock. I have to go over at six thirty this evening, right after working the bar, to help out.'

'Go whenever, Jessie!' Mabel said. 'I can't believe it. He's been coming here for years. You know, being a doctor and all, he had recommended patients to come to Taos who had asthma and then decided to come himself.'

Georgia looked at Ryan. One thought seemed to crackle through the air between them – the *Lutzen Ring*! There had been recent indications that Nazi groups similar to the Lutzen Ring were spreading in this country through a new organization called FoNG, Friends of New Germany. Ryan thought of what Fritzy had just told him about Tomas Benally being moved in closer. Closer to what? But why would Maudie be a victim of FoNG?

Georgia felt an avalanche of anxiety. It was as though she were caught in a whirlpool of growing uneasiness – worried for Maudie, worried for Jessie, who would be standing guard at her hospital room. Quite frankly, she was worried for the world! She imagined Bernard Ellington speeding off in a car, Wallis Simpson, the woman whose window she had spied him climbing out of, and then the carnations and the note, *Meine ewige Liebe*. And the cowboy speaking German. The pieces of a ghastly puzzle were vaguely coming together.

She imagined tentacles of evil spreading across the globe to this isolated desert where people came to indulge their ridiculous little fantasies of spiritual renewal or, in the recent terminology, psychic healing. She had heard one woman talking about the latest spiritual cocktail, peyote mixed with Ayahuasca tea: 'A spiritual enema,' the woman said. Georgia had set her Margarita back on the bar as she felt that she might vomit in a most unspiritual manner. She loved Mabel and Tony, but this was a Never Land every bit as much as Peter Pan's. There were a lot of Peter Pans here, with a Captain Hook and apparently a possible scattering of Nazis. Ellington, Wallis Simpson, the Prince of Wales, like the desert's trapdoor spiders, were crawling out of their burrows and passing through their silken doors to wreak havoc on the world.

THIRTY

Eleanor Burke stood trembling with excitement on the arm of her husband as they disembarked from their chauffeur-driven Rolls-Royce beneath the portico of Xanadu, the most opulent of all the Palm Beach mansions. This seemed to her the consummation of all her dreams, all she had ever wished for. Oh yes, that was the line from Hamlet: *A consummation devoutly to be wished.* But Hamlet was talking about death, not life. They'd seen the play in Chicago with John Gielgud as Hamlet, no less. Of course, Chance had dozed off by the second act, and she had to keep giving him a poke to stay awake.

Chance turned to her. 'What the hell are you wearing?'

'What do you mean? A gown, of course.'

'But that thing on it?'

'It's an Elsa Schiaparelli gown.'

'It has a lobster painted on it, for Crissake.'

'A lobster painted by Salvador Dalí.'

'Hope they don't mistake you for dinner. Throw you in a pot and boil you!' Chance guffawed raucously.

Eleanor would have told him to shut up, but at just that moment she spotted Wallis Simpson. She squeezed her husband's hand. 'Chance, over there!' She nodded to her left.

'What?'

'Wallis Simpson!'

'Well, thank God it's not that bastard Joe Kennedy.'

'Please, Chance!'

They were shepherded on to a terrace where waiters in silk caftans wearing turbans passed trays of glasses of champagne.

'Good Christ, is it Halloween?' Chance murmured. 'What the hell are these waiters dressed up as?'

'Servants in Xanadu, probably,' Eleanor whispered. Then she caught her breath. Wallis was walking toward her with a tight, thin-lipped smile.

'So, you are the distinguished Mrs Burke who bought the fabulous Dalí dress?'

Eleanor was almost overcome. She was nearly ready to rip it off and give it to the woman. Her eyes scanned Wallis's face. *Has she had a facelift or what?* Things were pulled rather tight, especially around the mouth. She had heard they made the incision behind the ears and then winched everything back and up.

'Well, that is so kind of you. The dress is a bit crazy but so much fun to wear.' She laughed softly. 'And when did you get here?'

'Three days ago.'

'Direct from England?'

'Oh no, I was visiting friends out in New Mexico.'

'My goodness, our son is out there now at Los Gallos.'

'Well, so was I,' exclaimed Mrs Simpson. 'Eldon Burke – is he your son?'

'Yes!'

'I cha-cha'd with him.'

'Oh!' Eleanor was almost trembling with joy. 'Did you hear that, Chance? Mrs Simpson was out at Los Gallos and danced with Eldon.'

'I was just admiring your wife's gown.'

'Well, I told her, Mrs Simpson, be careful or they might throw her in the pot and boil her up for the first course.'

Eleanor was mortified.

But at that moment, a turbaned waiter came up with a small silver tray.

'A telegram, Mr Burke.'

'Thank you.' Chance took the envelope and stepped a few feet away.

IN THE CROSSHAIRS.

Relief, thought Chance. Sometimes with your children there were no other options for protecting themselves against themselves.

On the same night, Bugsy Siegel was staying at a ramshackle cabin just outside Los Burros, imagining the twenty thousand dollars that would be coming his way with the assassination of the fellow who was screwing Chance Burke's son. He liked non-mob-associated jobs even if they were high-falutin' millionaires like Chance, who was anti-Semitic and probably flirted with Nazis and those Bund operations that were popping up through the FoNG. Yes, Bugsy himself was a fairly observant Jew despite being a mob hit man for other crime families. He remembered the night at the conference in

Atlantic City some years before where he and Meyer Lansky discussed a truce with the Capone gang. The conclusion was that the Yids and the Dagos would no longer fight each other.

It was right after that conference that he first met Chance in his Chicago mansion. 'But what about the Irish?' Chance had asked. He had wanted him to go after Joe Kennedy. Kennedy was rumored to be moving in on bootlegging in Canada and taking whisky across the border of the two French islands, St Pierre and Miquelon, off Nova Scotia. Chance had the routes between Canada and Minnesota, with Duluth being a major port of entry. If he could get the eastern ones, he would have sewn up a good part of the American–Canadian border. But it was not to be. Prohibition was over.

However, making a connection like Bugsy was pure gold. Chance liked Bugsy a lot. He had mentioned once to him how Eleanor worried about that teeny-weeny bit of Jewish blood, especially with their son about to marry a British heiress. Well, not an heiress exactly, but certainly aristocracy, complete with estate and a mother with a title but very little money. 'Not to offend, Bugsy, but can you keep quiet about the Jewish blood?' he said.

'No offense, Chance, none whatsoever. I'll make sure no one ever hears about it.'

At the time, they had been smoking very expensive Cuban cigars in Chance's sumptuous Chicago library. Chance pointed with the ash end of his cigar to a painting on the opposite wall. 'Ya' know how much that painting cost?'

'What is it?'

'Desert landscape. Very abstract. I bought it at ten Gs, now worth four times that.'

'Ya gotta be kidding me.'

'Nope.'

'Who painted it?'

'Georgia O'Keeffe. My wife is nuts for her.'

'I'd be nuts for her too if she can bring in that kind of money.'

'She might be kind of a dry fuck.' Chance laughed. 'Saw a picture of her once. She's pushing fifty. No boobs, skinny as a dried stick. Beef jerky, that's what she looks like.' Bugsy sighed and tipped his cigar ash into the ashtray. 'But hey, getting back to that little speck of blood, you wouldn't believe whose little speck I took care of recently?'

Chance leaned forward. 'Whose?'

'Actually, I can't say specifically because, as I told you when I first met you, my lips are sealed. Zippo!' He wiped his index finger across his mouth.

'I respect that, Bugs. I really do.'

'Look, all I can say is that Jew is a member of the royal family. It's a collateral cousin twice removed from George V.'

'You know this for a fact?'

'Not only do I know it, but I know the *mohel* who did the *bris* for this person's grandson.'

'*Mohel? Bris?*'

'You know.' He pointed to his crotch. 'Circumcision. The *mohel* is the guy who does the snipping.'

'Oh,' Chance replied and resisted crossing his legs.

And thus the deal was made, and Bugsy's last words to Chance Burke were: 'Not to worry, my friend. We'll take care of this fairy who's causing your son trouble.'

Chance reread the telegram and felt a profound relief. This was easier than the speck of Jewish blood in Eleanor's ancestry. It was just one person who needed to be done away with. One goddamn creep who was fucking his son.

THIRTY-ONE

That evening, Georgia couldn't sleep, or so she thought. But when she woke up, there was a note from Ryan: *Your car has been fixed, forgot to tell you. Needed a new spark plug or two.* Damn, this was irritating. Why hadn't he said where he was off to?

Fifteen minutes later, as she made her way across the patio to her car, she saw Lorna Charles with her arms crossed, staring at a just-departing car with Bunny Hatch and her fiancé, Eldon, at the wheel.

'Hello, there,' Georgia said as she walked up beside her. 'You look somewhat perplexed.'

'I actually am, Miss O'Keeffe.'

'No need for formalities – just call me Georgia.' *Or George*, she thought, suppressing a smile, as now Ryan had taken to calling her George on occasion. Somewhat better than Fluffy. She had never really objected to Alfred's nickname even though it was an anatomical reference. But now she thought it could be confused with a name for a pet rabbit, such as Bunny.

'And what perplexes you, Lorna?'

'Bunny Hatch.' She turned to Georgia now. 'Do you remember the brief conversation I had with Bunny about the Chee sisters and one being a rug weaver and the other a blanket weaver.'

'Yes, but not precisely.'

'Well, I had said that Malinda had lived out on the Old Santa Ana Road. And Bunny had replied she wouldn't know as she had died so many years ago. But that isn't so. I checked with my gallery agent, and she said that Malinda Chee died only two years ago, and we were outbid on a Malinda Chee blanket by none other than Bunny Hatch's gallery. She also confirmed that Malinda lived on the Old Santa Ana Road.' She paused and turned toward Georgia. 'Why would Bunny lie about when Malinda Chee had died?'

It was as if a darkness flowed through Georgia. 'I–I . . . can't imagine why,' she replied.

THIRTY-TWO

Often when Georgia drove in the desert, her imagination wandered freely, sifting images as silently as the softest winds stirring the sand. Sketches emerged. Music and shapes commingled, colors bled together, and now, almost inexplicably, she found herself driving out to the Old Santa Ana Road. She spied the twisted hoodoos or what some called tent rocks, the thin or sometimes squat spires of sedimentary rock that were formed by wind and weather. Under this light, those hoodoos looked like disfigured dwarves dancing a macabre dance beneath a threatening sky. The wind blew harder, screeching around the hoodoos, giving them hysterical voices, as if a ghostly choir had risen from the earth. But then the entire world turned red with swirling sand.

'Good Lord!' muttered Georgia. She pulled over to the side of the road and stopped the car. 'A monsoon.' She leaned forward. A shrill screaming enveloped everything. Then she saw an immense rolling sea of red sand hurtling toward her like an army of banshees. It seemed impossible. Monsoons – or haboobs, as they called them out here – supposedly only occurred during the summer. It was still April. She closed the windows tighter and pulled out a scarf to cover her mouth. She had heard that inhaling during these freakish events could smother people. The world turned completely red within a matter of seconds. There was nothing else. She was in the vortex of a desert storm. She was unsure how long she sat behind the wheel, but the change was sudden. There was a split second of silence, as if the whole desert were inhaling for its next blow. It came. A downpour of rain pummeled the car. A knobby bolt of lightning ricocheted across the sky. Witch's fingers, as Georgia's sister Claudia used to call such lightning.

Next there was a deafening crack, as if the whole world were splintering. Gusts of wind smacked the car as she turned down the rutted road and came to a halt. Jagged spears of lightning jabbed the air. She would not risk getting out of the car. The sparse cottonwoods crouched against the wind. The din of the rain on the car became deafening. Even if she wanted to get out, she most likely could not push the door open against that wind. She heard another car approaching and she pressed her face close to the window. It screeched to a halt and then backed up quickly, gunning its engine. Who else would be idiotic enough to be out here and not stop while this wild dust storm blew? She had been in one last summer. The racket the haboob made was deafening.

'Nothing lasts forever,' Georgia muttered to herself. And soon enough, the wind settled. The raindrops on the car body became louder. Last gasp, she thought of the desert kraken. The rain began to lessen. Soon it was nothing but a soft, almost soothing patter against the metal of the car. She climbed out of the car and looked about.

Crouched close to the ground, the hogans appeared untouched from the outside. However, other things had been scattered about helter-skelter, including the shed where Malinda Chee had had her loom. As she walked toward it, she stubbed her toe on a rock outside one of the hogans. 'Dammit.' It hurt like the devil. She peered down and swore at the rock. It reminded her of the rock that killed Flora, but it was smaller. Feldspar or chert? Was that what Jessie said?

She walked over to the place where the weaving shed had stood. The posts that had supported its sunshade were gone. She could see one of them fifty feet or more from where it had once stood.

The clouds were odd shapes, flat on top like anvils, but from their underside, pouches hung as if they had inhaled the red dust of the storm. She remembered that Ryan had told her such clouds were called *Mammatus* clouds – like breasts, of course. Pendulous lobes now bulging with red dust and sand. She looked down at her feet and kicked at a mound of sand. Even the sand had been rearranged into new configurations, some like rippling water, some into soft peaks. She kicked the sand again and heard a click. Must be a rock, she thought. She bent over close to the ground.

'Not a rock!' she said. The words came back to her clear and distinct: 'Wallis and I have the same hair comb . . . except hers are diamonds and mine is mere Bakelite with rhinestones . . . I lost the other one – it must be somewhere, not sure where.'

Georgia's heart was thumping loudly. It was as if the emptiness of the land were filled with the pounding of her heart. Everything had come to a standstill here in this abandoned place that had just been scoured by the dust storm. She reached for the hair comb, then instantly dropped it. Too late! Her fingerprints would be all over it now. Nevertheless, she kicked off her shoe and rolled down her left stocking. Putting it on her hand, she delicately picked up the Bakelite comb.

'Gotcha!' she whispered. And couldn't help but smile as if she had been a lepidopterist who had just come upon the most exotic of butterflies. Hadn't she read – perhaps in the *New Yorker* – about the new young Russian novelist Vladimir Nabokov. He was a lepidopterist.

The sky suddenly darkened, and there was in the distance a shrill whistling wind. *Not again*, she thought as the rain started pelting her. She dashed into the hogan. She would wait it out. She crouched near the doorway. Immediately, she felt the sudden drop in temperature and wished she had a warmer jacket. She blew on her hands, then clenched her knees. Her teeth by this time were chattering.

What would Stieglitz say? He was always telling her she wasn't dressed warmly enough. Ever since the time she had first come to New York and had pneumonia, he was vigilant about her health, her lungs especially. At the slightest cough, he would be pressing his ear to her chest. 'Doesn't sound good in there, Georgia.' He treated her lungs as some separate country from the rest of her, an alien or perhaps rogue nation that might turn on the rest of her body. In a flash, he would run out to the deli around the corner to bring back chicken or matzo ball soup.

The wind began to die down. She rocked herself to keep warm and yawned, then dozed off for a minute – no more. A small, startling sound woke her abruptly. A baby? A baby was outside crying? *Impossible*. The baby cried louder. 'A baby!' she whispered to herself. She got up and, opening the door of the hogan, peeked out. She screamed as a mangy coyote turned his head toward her, bared its teeth and growled. Georgia grabbed her snake stick and roared out the door of the hogan. There was a flash of lightning, and the coyote was gone, gone into the sudden darkness of the day. She ran toward her car. *Zigzag*. The words of the little boy Peter exploded in her head. Would zigzag work for coyotes as it had for alligators? She got back to her car and put her head against the steering wheel.

'A baby, a baby,' she whispered hoarsely. But she knew it was no baby. Skinwalkers, Jessie had said. There were Skinwalkers here, and of course this Skinwalker was custom-made for her, with the whimpering and then the squall of an infant. She felt a cramping in her belly as she had after the abortion. It all came back after so many years.

Twenty-five minutes later, when she drove into the courtyard of Los Gallos, Spud was walking across and waved, then began to make his way toward her. She opened the window.

'Glad to see you, Georgia. You must have got caught in the dust storm out to the north. It delayed Sheriff McCaffrey's departure.'

'He's departed?' She instantly regretted looking so surprised. Spud knew they were together. She should know where her – she paused – 'lover' had gone.

'Some kind of emergency,' Spud offered.

'Oh dear. Could I use your telephone?'

'Certainly.'

She went directly into Spud's office. But just as she picked up the phone, she remembered that Ryan had said the telephone line in Los Gallos was tapped. Tapped why and by whom? He had never fully explained. But did he even know? She thought about it. He first mentioned it to her when he was in San Francisco. There had been the session on wiretapping, and Ryan, being a quick student, had picked up the indications fast enough to realize that the actual line they were speaking on had been tapped. But he hadn't come out here to simply see her or to try to figure out the reasons for the wiretap. There must have been more. She did know that Thomas Dewey, the prosecutor from New York, had given that lecture, and there had been several other sessions with him that had focused on organized crime.

Nevertheless, she dialed the police station in Santa Fe.

'Police station,' Florence Gilbert answered cheerfully.

'Florence, it's Georgia.'

'Oh, Miss O'Keeffe. How you doing, dear?'

'Fine. I was just wondering, has the sheriff come back yet?'

'Ryan back? Not to my knowledge. I must admit our phones here in the office have been in and out of service recently. But ya know Ryan was in San Francisco, something connected with that organized crime conference. Then went to your neck of the woods. Matter of fact, Mr Dewey from New York City called, trying to reach him. Something connected with that conference in California.'

Fib, thought Georgia. What an innocent word to use with something that had suddenly risen to a nearly alarming state.

'Dewey, you said? Thomas Dewey?'

'I believe that was his name.'

'OK, Florence, thanks so much.'

'All right, dear.'

Spud now stuck his head in. 'Everything all right?'

'Oh, yes, yes, Spud. Thank you so much.' She glimpsed a newspaper on a small table, the *San Francisco Chronicle*. A headline caught her eye.

Thomas Dewey Declares War on Organized Crime at San Francisco Cops meeting: Lucky Luciano and Bugsy Siegel top of his list.

'Can I borrow your newspaper, Spud?'

'It's at least a week old.'

'That's OK. Just want to catch up a bit.' She looked down at the tile floor. 'Oh dear, did I track that in?'

'You and Bunny Hatch. She just came back with shoes full of sand.'

'Did she now?'

'Yes, just like Hansel and Gretel and the bread crumbs, I suppose. Now you can make your way back to wherever you were.' Spud chuckled.

Georgia found the remark slightly disturbing. Had Bunny been there to search for her comb? She patted the deep pocket where she had put the comb she had just found.

As she closed the door to Spud's office, she heard a shout.

'Bunny!' It was Eldon Burke. 'Thank God! I was so worried about you when I heard about that dust storm.'

'Oh, it was nothing, sweetie. Just a shoe full of sand.' She took off her shoe and poured a small stream of red sand into the potted cactus. 'Oh, hello, Georgia.'

'Your hair's a mess, darling,' Eldon said.

'Yes, I know.' She raked her fingers through it.

Every nerve cell in Georgia's body tingled as if she had been launched into a frantic electrical jig.

'Hello,' Georgia squeaked. She stuck her hand into her pocket and touched the Bakelite comb.

Once back at the Pink House, she scanned the bedroom for a place to hide the comb. Not under the bed, nor the mattress. The bathroom? Her eyes finally settled on the log rack by the fireplace. Fresh logs had just been delivered, as a chill was expected tonight. She walked over and examined them. She slipped the comb toward the bottom of the stacked logs as far back as possible. Then she went and sat cross-legged on the bed and picked up the *San Francisco Chronicle* she had borrowed from Spud.

THIRTY-THREE

Policemen from all over America gathered in San Francisco for a three-day discussion of organized crime in America. The major speaker was New York City's special prosecutor, Thomas Dewey, who in his relatively short tenure as prosecutor has arrested more than thirty gangland hoodlums.

He vows more arrests are coming. His relentless efforts in prosecuting the Mafia and other criminals are paying off with the recent arrest of Lucky Luciano. This arrest was based on Dewey's wide-ranging evidence of Luciano's call girl empire and related crimes of extortion and bootlegging. Speaking recently at the annual chief of police conference in San Francisco, Dewey said, 'We got Lucky, soon to be incarcerated in Dannemora state prison for a thirty-to-eighty-year term. Next up will be Benjamin Siegel, better known as Bugsy, who is also a kingpin in the prostitution industry.'

Georgia flipped the paper over to read beneath the fold. A somewhat familiar face peered back at her. *Dapper* – that was her first thought when she had seen the man in the hardware store buying the Gilly Teen. Could it be him? There were plenty of handsome men out west but not like this one, with his smooth skin, perfectly barbered black hair and tantalizing eyes. He resembled somewhat the new British movie star, Cary Grant, whom she'd seen in a movie two or three years back. *I'm No Angel* – that was the movie, with Mae West. Stieglitz had walked out, but she hadn't. She had enjoyed the entire show.

Sometimes Stieglitz was too refined for his own good. But the photo on the front page of the newspaper was not Cary Grant but one Bugsy Siegel, and he was a mobster, a mobster out here buying a Gilly Teen. It was as if a lot of disparate pieces of not one but several puzzles had been tossed on the floor. What in the name of God was this Bugsy doing out here? Certainly not a guest at the ranch. This was, after all, Benjamin Siegel, aka Bugsy, that Mr

Dewey supposedly had in his crosshairs when he spoke at the police conference Ryan had attended.

'Ah-ha!' Georgia exclaimed in a muffled voice. 'Gotcha, Ryan.'

It wasn't until she looked up that she spied the note on the bed.

Hi G. Had to scoot out. Business, you know. See you back in Santa Fe.
Ayóó'ánííníshní, R.

Ayóó'ánííníshní meant 'I love you' in Navajo. Ryan's mother had been Navajo and his father half Navajo.

'Oh dear.' Georgia sighed. What would Ryan think if he knew she had crossed paths with this handsome killer and prostitution kingpin?

She walked over to her easel. She was anxious to finish the painting. She wasn't sure if Jessie was at the station today, and she certainly didn't want to drop the hair clip off for those geniuses Harold and Homer.

Taking the tube of paint she had just bought, she began to squeeze some out on to her palette.

She was about to mix in some paint thinner. She wanted the deep blue of the sky to become lighter and lighter as it met the ground behind the shadow of the cross. Then she would darken the blue above it. She needed the black cross to hover like a shadow of . . . of what? Death, she supposed. She reflected on the crucifixion paintings by the old masters that she had seen. It was odd. In most of them, Christ did not appear to be in pain but had a peculiar tranquility, as if he were submitting almost joyfully to death. At worst, Christ looked strangely somnolent. There was only one painting that she could recall that betrayed actual suffering. It was by Rembrandt, and he had painted it when he was barely twenty-five. How strange that no other painters, at least that she knew of, dared reveal actual suffering. Was the agony of Christ unimaginable? Mythic in some strangely contorted way? Had they painted lies to obscure a truth? She stared at the ominous dark cross she had painted that loomed over the landscape like a thin, dark veil. In her own mind, the absence of a Christ figure made the cross even more brutal, and then there was the backdrop of the starry night.

Within two days, the pilgrimage would begin. She looked at

Ryan's note again. 'Business, you know.' What business? She glanced from the note to the newspaper. There was something that was all too convenient, too coincidental, about Ryan's coming here in the first place. Had he dropped into Los Gallos merely to see her? Or was there some other reason for them both to be here at the same time? She looked at the two stars she had painted the day before in the thick midnight blue sky that hung over the cross. *Oh dear*, she thought. *I am heading toward pathetic fallacy here. Ryan and I on a collision course? Two star-crossed lovers? How trite can I get?*

Nevertheless, the feeling haunted her. They both were – or had been – out here away from Santa Fe for different reasons supposedly: the memorial service for Lawrence and the police conference in San Francisco. And then beneath those ostensible reasons, other reasons had evolved, reasons that outwardly seemed unrelated.

Ryan had dismissed her idea about the wig after Emily Bryce had found the suspect's 'hair', and Georgia realized it was very possible that this 'clue' was in fact nothing at all and would lead nowhere. One could not simply turn a clue into something of merit or worth. Apparently, wigs were often worn in Pueblo festivals, particularly by men in the corn and harvest dances. There was even a store over in Alcalde for *chongo*-style wigs worn at the Pueblo and Navajo festivals.

It was probably a silly idea that Georgia had felt that the wig would be some sort of revelatory clue. But the fact remained that a wig was the only point at which her investigation and possibly Ryan's interests had crossed. There was that telephone booth he had told her about, the old codger's gas station where he had stopped to make a phone call. And now there was the hair comb – a wig and a comb. She glanced at the stack of logs where she had hidden the comb. Would one wear a decorative comb with a wig?

The phone booth seemed to be sitting right in the middle of this puzzle. She knew that Ryan had gone there to make his call because he didn't trust the phone at Mabel's. Apparently, Los Burros was the closest safe phone. She went back over to the bed where she had left the newspaper. *Dapper man! Bugsy Siegel. That's who Ryan was looking for, and guess who saw him? ME!* What should she do? Yet again, it all seemed so impossible, so random. How could Bugsy and the path of Flora Namingha cross? Did they cross at all?

Not really. What was the conjunction, the confluence, of her and Ryan's interests? Was she just dreaming all this up?

The dust storm wreaked havoc with Georgia's sleep that night. A stampede of images rampaged through her mind. The swirling red sand of the dust storm, the tines of the Bakelite hair clasp – and spreading over it all, the bruised and smashed face of Flora.

The place where she stubbed her toe began to throb in her sleep. She woke up. A purplish bruise was spreading across her toe and up her foot. It hurt like the devil. She removed the flowers floating in a bowl and filled it with some very cold water and stuck her foot in it, or as much of it as possible.

She then reached for a sketchpad beside her bed and closed her eyes tight. She began to draw the picture in her mind of the tines of the comb. Then, opening her eyes, she drew the shape of the rock that had killed Flora as she remembered it. As she drew, she recalled the contours of the deep bruising that had spread across Flora's face. What did it all mean?

She inhaled sharply. She knew that there was a deadly convergence here. Of this she was certain. Two crimes, one of interest to Ryan and one to herself, with separate origins, were on a collision course of sorts. They were not related in a conventional way, not related at all except that each crime had drawn herself and Ryan to Taos, and she sensed that the worst was yet to come. Her experience during the sandstorm with the coyote seemed to foreshadow this like a macabre, nightmarish dance. The twisted hoodoos like angry dwarves in the swirling winds, the sky splintered by lightning, then crouching in the hogan and hearing the cries of the baby, only to step out and see the coyote. Was blood dripping from its fangs? No! She must have been making up the blood. But there was a coyote there. Of this she was certain. And the coyote was the scheming, self-seeking trickster in Navajo myths.

She sat on the bed and tried to sort out the images that were creating a haboob of their own as they stormed through her head. A pencil was too exact, too bold. A pencil could only reveal a delineated surface image. She sensed that beneath the swirl of images in her mind's eye, there was meaning of some sort – an inscrutable design. A trace of an earlier drawing, a pentimento of sorts, a shadow waiting for light.

Waiting for light . . . Was that not the entire narrative arc of her life? Her life as a painter. Her life as a human being. Her life as a woman.

She got up and fetched a chunk of charcoal to use instead of the pencil. Still with her eyes closed, she began to move it across the pad in small, then larger sweeping circular motions. She tore off a page and, keeping her eyes shut, continued to move the charcoal across the paper. Images stirred beneath her eyelids. Was a design emerging? She opened her eyes slowly and peered down at the papers. Whirlpools of charcoal strokes bled into other forms, all circular but some more clearly defined than others. Funnel-shaped tornadoes, flattened swirling discs and some like an oval disc with a slight indentation. She recognized it, of course. The aborted embryo that had haunted her dreams all this year had come back, now abstracted, but still there.

She knew she wouldn't sleep for the rest of the night. Her mind kept gravitating to the stack of wood and the comb that belonged to Bunny Hatch. She didn't want it in the same space as herself. Too many things were colliding in her mind. As soon as it was light, she would go over to the police station and submit the comb to Jessie. She prayed he would be there early.

At six thirty the next morning, she walked out of the Pink House and glimpsed a truck in the drive. The passenger door opened and Jessie climbed out.

'Take care, brother!' a voice called out and drove off.

'Jessie! Just the man I'm looking for.'

'Hi, Miss O'Keeffe, you're up pretty early.'

'Couldn't sleep.'

'Any particular reason?'

Georgia dug into the canvas bag she had slung over her shoulder. Carefully, she drew out an item wrapped in a scrap of drawing paper and unfolded it.

'Don't touch it. My fingers might have messed up any prints.'

'What is it?' Jessie asked.

'A hair comb.'

Jessie blinked a couple of times. 'Where did you find it?'

'Remember the dust storm yesterday?'

'Yeah, it was a doozy.'

'I was out at those hogans where we were the other day, out on the Old Santa Ana Road. That's where I found it.'

'Yeah?'

'Yeah, Jessie. It's not just any hair comb.'

'Uh, not quite following you.'

'It's Bunny's hair comb.'

'What the hell was she doing out there?' He stopped abruptly. He suddenly recalled the odd, arched fingerprints on the fragment of black pottery. He stared down at the comb. 'What's this material?'

'Bakelite, a kind of plastic. More and more things are being made from it now. It's almost unbreakable.'

'Unbreakable,' Jessie murmured. 'But very smooth.' Smooth like the black pottery from which he lifted the odd fingerprints. 'I gotta take this into the station and look at it with my loupe. Right away.'

'I'll drive you in.'

An hour later, Georgia sat bent over with a loupe and peered down at the steep arches of the fingerprints. They reminded her of the country in the Panhandle when she was teaching at a Texas normal college. There was a short range of hills that were of a completely different contour from the others. They rose abruptly, breaking against the skyline like the serrated edge of a gigantic knife.

'And what percentage of fingerprints are arches, did you say?'

'Only four percent. Whorl patterns are thirty-four percent and loops are about sixty percent. And remember, no two are ever identical.' He inhaled deeply. 'Just think about it. In New Mexico, one of the least populous states in the country, how many arches do you think we might find?'

'No idea.'

'I figured it out. Less than point-one percent. So now we have three objects here, one from the black clay vase, one or rather several from the latents from the car at Jonno's and now this one from the hair comb that belongs to . . .'

'Bunny Hatch.'

'Exactly!' Jessie said.

'Does this mean Bunny murdered Flora?'

'I'm not a judge. But I am a numbers guy, and this is evidence.'

'You'd better call Santa Fe,' Georgia said.

THIRTY-FOUR

'Well, speaking of the devil!' Florence Gilbert exclaimed as Ryan walked into the Santa Fe police station. 'Here he is right now, Agent Stone.' She turned to the sheriff. 'He's called twice already, but the phones aren't working very well.'

Ryan jerked his head up. 'Linc Stone on the line?'

'Indeed, Sheriff. Another call too from Taos, but the connection was lost before they could say who was calling. The phones have been spotty this week.'

He nodded and went into his office. Closing the door, he picked up his phone.

'Happy Maundy Thursday to you, Linc.'

'You want me to wash your feet?'

'Very funny. So, what do you have for me?'

'Probably not the first thing on your list after foot washing.'

'OK, tell me what the second thing is, then?'

'About that agent, Doctor Bernard Ellington – double agent.'

'Yes, so I heard from Fritzy Freihoff over at SIS.'

'Yeah, well, he was picked up crossing the Mexican border by Wolf Boy. It seems like Mrs Simpson had been sleeping with Doctor Ellington as well as with a bona fide Nazi, one Joachim von Ribbentrop. Ellington told us this. He's hoping that this information will get him on the good side.'

'Good side? Good side of what? Honestly, Lincoln, I'm not looking for Nazis now. I'm looking for Bugsy Siegel. What does this have to do with Bugsy? Bugsy trying to recruit Mrs Simpson for the prostitution businesses he's supposedly opening in Las Vegas. Is that it? If so, I doubt it. I cha-cha'd with her.'

'You what with her? Is that dirty?'

'No, it's a dance they were teaching at – never mind. It's not related at all.'

'I don't know about Bugsy, but this Nazi thing with Mrs Simpson and Ribbentrop, SIS is very upset. This isn't simply gangsters, it's national security. But Ryan, you don't get it.'

'I don't get what?'

Linc took a deep breath. 'Look, I know that you found out about Ellington being a double agent from Fritzy over at SIS when you were supposed to get Bugsy in your crosshairs. So do I have to draw you a diagram? Ellington was at Los Gallos, the Mabel Dodge Luhan place. Wallis Simpson was there as well – and she'd been sleeping with Ribbentrop before that. And you're out west trying to track down Bugsy for Mr Dewey. It's becoming a hot spot out there.' He paused. 'And, Ryan, who else do you think is out there?'

'Let me guess. Eliot Ness?'

'Close but no cigar. Alexander Jamie,' Linc replied

'Who?'

'Alexander Jamie, Ness's brother-in-law. He's in the Chicago field office and of course is part of Ness's bunch, the Untouchables. They're not just focused on whisky anymore, what with Prohibition being over. So you got the mob and the House of Windsor in their crosshairs. What a combination!'

'OK, Linc. Let me think about all this. I'll get back to you.'

'You bet, buddy.'

The conversation ended, Ryan's mind wandered off. He scratched his chin. All that was needed to throw into this mess of pottage was the murder of Flora Namingha. Then it struck him – was there any chance that while Georgia was so focused on Flora, his own investigation could have somehow become entangled? One had to think out of the box. And for Ryan, that box had become deductive reasoning. But the box was simply too small for all these crimes or would-be crimes that were pouring into it.

He thought about Georgia. She was trying to figure out who killed Flora. Then he thought about himself. Where did Bugsy Siegel, one of the most ruthless murderers in the organized crime world, fit in here? His mind skipped ahead to Georgia at the Pink House, their legs entangled, while he was trying coyly to steer the conversation to his own reasons to be in Taos. He picked up the phone and pressed the button.

'Florence!' he roared.

'I'm right outside. You don't have to scream.'

'Florence, come in here.'

She flew in the door of his office. She had never heard him in such an agitated state.

'That fellow we have in jail for the murder of the girl up in Taos.'

'Yes, sir, Mateo Chee. They don't have room for him yet in Albuquerque.'

'Has the public defender shown up yet?'

'Not yet.'

'Who's it supposed to be? Roscoe Biddle?'

'Yes.'

'That dumb cluck.'

'Yes. He's never seemed that bright to me.'

'I want to talk to the prisoner myself. Which cell is he in?'

'Five-W.'

'Tell Jason to let me in. I'm coming down to speak to him.'

THIRTY-FIVE

A gnes Brown, better known as Rosamond at the Desert Lily, loved fucking Benjamin. He was the handsomest dude that had ever tumbled into the Lily. She looked at his buttocks – they were so perfect – and lord, that dick! He called it a *schlong*. In all the fellows she had ever fucked, she'd never heard anyone who called his dick a *schlong*. When she told him that, he merely smiled and said, 'So you never fucked a Jew before?'

'I must have, but I've never heard that word *schlong*. It's a Jewish word?'

'Yep.'

'I thought maybe so. 'Cause, you know, you're circumcised.'

'Yes, I know that, Rosamond.'

'I guess you do.' She giggled. She shouldn't smile, as she was missing a few teeth. If she wanted to work in Vegas, she should invest in some dentistry. 'Did it hurt when they did that to you?' she asked.

'Heck, I don't remember. I was only eight days old.'

'Oh, poor baby.'

'There are certain advantages to being an infant, I guess.' He smiled. He was in a shack just a half-mile out of Los Burros. He couldn't wait to get out. Pissing in the sagebrush, sleeping with a two-bit whore, that was not his style. And if there was anything Bugsy cared about, it was style. She definitely was not going to make the cut for Vegas, although she kept pestering him about it.

'You know, a guy came into the Lily the other day and he was wearing those things on his shoes like you first wore when you came into the Lily. And I say to him, "I only ever saw one fellow with those gadgets on his shoes."'

'What gadgets?'

'Those things you wore the first time you came to the Desert Lily – very classy, you know.'

'Spats?'

'Yeah, that's what they're called. I forgot. Classy, as I said.'

Yes, too classy, he thought. The only guy anywhere close to here that he could think of was Alexander Jamie, Eliot Ness's brother-in-law, who had been at that San Francisco police conference, and both he and his brother-in-law were out of Chicago. Jamie was known as a snazzy dresser. And he was in the Bureau, the new Federal Bureau of Investigation.

'Did you sleep with him?'

'Not really.'

Not really. What the fuck did that mean?

'Naw, he just wanted to talk to Lily about something.'

Bugsy cursed himself now for dressing up. Why had he done that? Well, he knew why. While he was on this mission for Chance Burke, he thought he might as well check out the possible candidates for the Vegas prostitution work. Efficient. Killing two birds with one stone.

'Did you tell him who else you knew who wore spats?'

A look of fear flashed across her face. 'Well, not exactly.'

Bugsy's eyes narrowed. He slipped his hand into his pants pocket and walked around behind her. Crouching over her, he nuzzled her behind the ear, licked her earlobe. She tipped her head up to the perfect angle. In a second, he had the knotted wire across her throat and wrenched it. There was a small crack, an infinitesimally tiny sound, as the hyoid bone fractured. She didn't look horrified. Not even frightened. Just slightly confused. Then she slumped against him.

He dragged her body out of the shack. He left her in a nearby arroyo where he had seen some wolves the previous night. They'd find her soon enough. They would go for her neck and the tantalizing necklace of blood. He could imagine their teeth tearing at her throat, destroying all evidence of his handiwork. But now he would have to find a new place to hide out for the next few days until his business out here was done.

Ryan stood in the shadow of the west-wing prison corridor that gave him a perfect view of Mateo Chee in his cell. He wanted to observe him quietly for a minute or so. Mateo sat very still and appeared to be looking at an object in his lap. With his left hand, he began moving something across what he was holding. Was he sketching? But pens and pencils weren't permitted. He soon realized it was in fact a drawing instrument of sorts that he had in his fist. It appeared to be a chunk of charcoal.

He felt a little pang as he recalled watching Georgia work with charcoal. There was something infinitely mesmerizing watching her hand hold the charcoal and traverse the paper in sweeping strokes. The marks she made were all very abstract. She said it was the music in her head that guided her hand. The pressure with which she applied the charcoal varied greatly, so with simply one color, pressure and line, she created images that lurked in the most hidden parts of her brain. At least, that was how Ryan felt when he looked at the charcoal drawings.

'Interested?' Mateo's voice came out of the shadows. Ryan startled.

'So, you can see me?'

'I can feel you, and I have very good hearing.'

Ryan walked over to the cell and put his hand on the bars. 'I understand that you have not yet met your public defender.'

'Nope.' There was a pause. 'Will it make any difference?'

'Depends on who you get.'

There was no reply.

'You want to say anything to me – off the record?'

'I loved Flora.'

'All right.' Silence followed. 'Anything else?'

'Nope.'

'You were there at the time of the murder.'

'Nope again. We made love in the chapel. She was tired and stayed on. Said she wanted to take a short nap. I left. That about sums it up.'

'Not really,' the sheriff replied. He waited. But Mateo said nothing.

'Can you prove she was still alive when you left?'

He shook his head. 'Not really.'

'The report says a heavy object was smashed on her head – repeatedly. Although, according to the coroner's report, the first blows would have done it.'

Mateo crunched over as if he'd just received a gut punch. His shoulders heaved, and then came a strangled sob. He lifted his face which now appeared ravaged. There was no trace of the previous placidity.

'OK, I'm going to get a public defender over here right away.'

'And I'm supposed to thank you for that?'

Ryan sighed. 'Actually, if I were in your shoes, I wouldn't. Nobody's done you any favors around here. According to New Mexico law, a public defender should have been in here within the first twenty-four hours of your arrest.'

'Since when has New Mexico law abided by the rules with Indian people?'

Ryan sighed, scratching his head. 'OK,' He was about to say 'son', but he didn't want to be taken for a fool.

He turned and roared back into Florence's office. 'Where the hell is Collins?'

'His grandmother died, so he's off today. Good Friday coming up tomorrow and all, I thought it would be OK.'

'Oh, yeah.' The sheriff rubbed his chin. 'Well, how about Montarlo?'

'Montarlo is around.'

'Tell me this, Florence. Why the hell did no one think of calling in a public defender?' Florence's eyes opened wide. She'd never seen Ryan in such a state.

'I–I'm not sure, sir.'

'Get me Albuquerque on the phone immediately. They'd better send one down here on the double. Yes! On the double and not on a pack mule.' He was tempted to say, *We've got an innocent man rotting in there.* But he didn't, even though he was sure that Mateo Chee was innocent. He'd never been more sure of anything in his life.

'Also, call Coroner Bryce. Tell her I'm coming over.'

'Hope I can. These phones are miserable now on calls. I was surprised Mr Stone could get through.'

Ryan went back into his office and sat down. His mind was like a maelstrom. A goddamn haboob. He felt he was on a collision course with unknown and uncontrollable forces. Four days ago, when he had arrived in Taos, he could not have imagined how his business – tracking down a mobster – could have crossed paths with Flora's murder. It was uncanny, but maybe not. Hadn't Sherlock Holmes said that crime was common, but logic was rare? Therefore, it was on logic that one must focus. However, the sheriff thought, isn't it human, deeply human in our unconscious, to seek and need a logical universe? And hadn't Albert Einstein said, 'Logic will get you from A to B, but imagination will take you everywhere'?

The sheriff groaned. Sherlock Holmes meet Albert Einstein. Then he thought to himself how they had stumbled accidentally, quite accidentally, into this situation of two seemingly unrelated crimes meeting up. That truly was beyond, by a step or two, the boundaries of logic.

THIRTY-SIX

'Yes, just like Hansel and Gretel and the bread crumbs, I suppose,' Spud had said when he told Georgia that Bunny had also tracked in sand when she returned somewhat earlier. Georgia was sitting on the bed as she recalled Spud's words when she had apologized for tracking the red sand into his office. But there was also the hair comb and red dust, another odd collision of facts. Georgia thought about this as she saw some remnant red sand on the floor that she must have tracked into the Pink House. Was it a collision per se or was it more like a logical set of overlapping facts? *A Venn diagram*, she thought, as she recalled her high school math. Two intersecting circles that would show the logical relation between two sets. She peered down at the comb and the red sand. She knew from her years as an artist that everything in life does have a pattern. She had spent a lifetime looking for patterns to put on paper or canvas. And she knew that often, in the brief moment when a pattern becomes visible, it was in fact a simple coincidence, or at least indecipherable in terms of its significance or reason. Now they had proof, but because the phones were out at the Santa Fe police station, she had been unable to call Ryan. She had thought of driving there. She'd wait and try again.

'All right,' she muttered to herself. She'd go to the damn cocktail hour this evening. She would wear something beautiful – beautiful and interesting. Props you could call them – something to talk about that was relatively meaningless or at least serve as a subterfuge for getting at something more meaningful.

As Georgia approached, she saw that cocktails were being served on the patio.

'Oh, my darling Georgia,' Mabel cooed. 'Aren't you a lovely sight. That dress, those silver bracelets. Now, don't tell me you made that dress.'

'I did, indeed.'

'Oh, Bunny, come over here, and yes, you too, Sybil.' Bunny walked over with Eldon and her mother.

Georgia felt a tremor rise within her. She had to play this right. Maybe she shouldn't have come. She was such a poor actress.

'Is Georgia not a picture?' Mabel asked. 'How would this work as a wedding dress for you, Bunny, but longer, with a train?'

'Oh, it's lovely,' Bunny cooed. 'And I love the silver and turquoise hair clip. I so miss mine. Although mine was just Bakelite. This looks like it came out of a Navajo silversmith shop.'

'Yes, it did.' Georgia paused. 'You lost yours?' she uttered in barely a whisper. *Come on, Georgia, get hold of yourself!*

'Yes, and I have no idea where? May I take a closer look?'

'Certainly.' Georgia began to lift her arms to remove the clip. Her hands were trembling. *Stop it, goddamnit!*

'Oh, don't bother. I can see it without you removing it. Just turn around.'

She felt Bunny's breath on her neck. A chill ran through her. Those fingers with the strange arched fingerprints, so close to her own skin. She imagined them grasping her neck and strangling her. Was this the closest she'd ever been to a killer? Bunny was the killer. She knew that now. The fragment from Flora's vase was the conclusive evidence.

'Oh, the stones are Bisbee turquoise,' Bunny said.

'I believe so,' Georgia whispered hoarsely. She could feel Bunny's breath on the back of her neck as she spoke. Was there a scent with it? A wild scent but not of the high desert, rather woodsy, moss – did moss have a scent?

'Yes, there is no turquoise on earth that is comparable. It has very unusual characteristics.' Bunny paused. 'Lovely.'

Another exhalation of warm breath on her neck and with it that scent. *Stay calm*, Georgia told herself.

'Often called smoky turquoise because of those markings. To me, they look like clouds.'

'An apt description,' Georgia replied softly as Bunny came around to stand in front of her.

'There's a dealer in Arizona that I have sometimes contacted when I go to the NAC.'

'NAC?' Eldon asked.

'Native American Crafts show, darling.'

'Oh, of course, now I remember, and you introduced me to that – if I may say – that very handsome young man.'

Bunny's face went white. 'I–I don't know who you mean, darling.'

Was it Georgia's imagination, but did people say 'darling' in this tone when they were about to kill them? Bunny twisted the engagement ring on her finger furiously.

'The glassmaker. You said he did stained glass.'

'Oh, that must have been Mateo Chee,' Georgia offered.

'Oh, him,' Bunny replied in a whisper.

'It was his girlfriend, Flora Namingha, who was murdered,' Georgia said. Her voice was low and steady now as she slid her eyes toward Bunny, who remained as tranquil as a breezeless lake.

'Murdered?' Eldon gasped.

Bunny slipped her arm through Eldon's and sighed. 'Very shocking.' She paused. 'But, Eldon, just look at that sunset!'

'Yes!' Mabel said. 'Sunsets are always quite interesting after a "weather event". I heard there was a dust storm today out north. A real haboob, as they say out here.' She turned to Eldon. 'Did you know the origin of the word "haboob" is actually Arabic?'

'No, ma'am, I did not. How interesting.' He paused. 'Now, can I ask you where Mrs Simpson disappeared to? I was having a very interesting discussion with her the other evening.'

'Lord knows where she went, and I don't care,' Mabel answered tersely and turned her head to watch the sunset.

'Did I anger her?' Eldon whispered to Sybil.

'Oh no, dear boy,' Sybil replied. 'None of us cared much for Mrs Simpson, including Mabel. She was so awful to that nice girl Maudie, whom she brought as her lady's maid.'

'Oh yes, Maudie!' Bunny exclaimed. 'What happened to her?'

'She was taken ill and is in the hospital.'

'Mrs Simpson left her behind?'

'Apparently so,' Sybil replied and pursed her lips as if to indicate that the subject was closed.

'Talking about Wallis Simpson?' Frieda Lawrence said, coming up to the group.

'Yes,' Sybil sniffed.

'That whore!' Frieda hissed. 'I heard she learned her tricks in a brothel in Shanghai.'

'Really, Frieda!' Mabel exclaimed.

'Yes, really.'

'Let's change the subject, please,' Mabel said.

'Yes,' Georgia said. 'So, you never found your Bakelite comb, Bunny?'

'No,' she said somewhat defiantly.

She took Eldon's arm and led him to the edge of the patio to look at the sunset. Sybil followed.

'Wonder if it will last?' Frieda murmured.

'What?' Georgia asked.

'Their marriage.'

'Well, aren't you being cynical!' Georgia gave a soft chuckle.

'Not at all. Sybil and Bunny need the money that Eldon Burke comes with.'

'And what does he need?'

'A wife and an heir.'

Georgia looked at Frieda blankly.

'Georgia, you're such an innocent. He needs a wife to prove he's not a fairy. Light in his loafers and all that.'

'Really?' Georgia replied, trying to feign surprise. 'You think he's queer?'

'He is. Believe me.'

Twenty minutes later, Mabel Dodge Luhan stood before the fireplace and clinked a wine glass with a spoon. 'Quiet please, quiet! As many of you know, tomorrow is Good Friday, and many of our staff are already absent this evening as they begin the last part of the pilgrimage route attending the elder members of their families. We here at Los Gallos try to help out as we can by sending over water and food along the route. So tonight, Holy Thursday, and tomorrow, Good Friday, we are short-staffed. Jessie is accompanying his elderly aunt, Mariel, her grandmother, and Cowboy is walking with his grandmother and others. But we're all pitching in as best we can. Georgia is working in the kitchen tonight with Luis. Tony is taking over the bar, and tomorrow morning you'll have to make your own beds!' She paused and gave a sly smile. 'We'll have inspection.' There was a ripple of laughter through the main salon.

'If any of you are interested in walking the last two miles, Spud will be leading a group. Most important, bring water. We have a lot of canteens here. Spud will be departing at five o'clock tomorrow morning.'

'Any tea sandwiches?' Bunny's voice rang out, and there was a burst of laughter.

'No, dear, it's not high tea in the desert,' Mabel snapped. She seemed slightly annoyed. 'Remember, this is a serious event, a reverent event. The people who take this journey are called Penitentes. You will see people carrying heavy crosses, flagellating themselves with ropes. The Penitentes first appeared in New Mexico almost two hundred years ago. They are dedicated to service and Jesus Christ through acts of penance.'

Mabel is really something, Georgia thought. She was glad that she had reminded the guests that this was a reverent occasion.

Ansel Adams leaned over and whispered in Georgia's ear, 'She is quite a wonder. Good for her.'

Georgia nodded. 'Indeed, I was just thinking that myself.'

As they were going in for dinner, Georgia turned to Ansel. 'When are you getting up to catch the light?'

'Before there is light.'

'Good idea.'

'How about you?'

'Well, I really want to get a close view and a long view. Cowboy has invited me to walk with him and his grandmother and aunt. So I might for a little while, but someone told me that the best view is from Punto Rojo.'

'You bringing a sketch book or anything?'

'Don't think so. I just want to absorb the whole scene.' She paused. 'Lens-less, I guess one might say.'

'Lens-less? That's an interesting word.'

'Hard to describe. It's just that I think going into a situation without the tools of my trade is exciting. Freeing, in a sense. It's just a way of amplifying the possible randomness of a situation. And I firmly believe that at the heart of randomness there can be treasures.' She thought at this moment of the wild winds of the haboob that uncovered the comb, not to mention her stubbed toe that encountered the rock so similar to the one that had smashed Flora's head. Random acts of wind and sand that possibly under-scored the crime of murder. 'I'll just go and see what I can see, not particularly what I want to see.'

'Interesting, Georgia. And I am restricted to the confines of this lens with a diameter of two inches.'

'You do all right, Ansel.'

'So do you, my friend.'

When she returned to her room that night, she stopped short as she entered. An uncanny feeling swept over her. Had someone been in here? It was not a scent, just a feeling. She flicked on a lamp.

Everything appeared normal. Her paintbrushes were arranged as she had left them. The extra wood where she had hidden the comb appeared untouched. Yet the ghost of a presence lingered.

As she undressed and got into bed, one streak of moonlight against the walls animated the shadows of a bristlecone pine outside an east-facing window. Crouched and hunched, it looked like a figure from a fairy tale, one of the seven dwarves or perhaps the greedy Rumpelstiltskin. The squeal of a building wind lashed around the corners of the Pink House and set the impish shadow of the bristlecone into a grotesque jig. *Tonight, tonight, my plans I make, tomorrow, tomorrow, the baby I take. The queen will never win the game, for Rumpelstiltskin is my name.* Now how in the hell did she remember that ghoulish song?

A flickering light now seemed to skitter across the room.

She wanted to get up or to turn over and shut her eyes, but she couldn't move. It was as if she were paralyzed – sleep paralysis? She had heard of this but never experienced it. There was a presence, a presence invading the Pink House. Her eyes were locked on the stack of wood by the fireplace. Then the floorboards creaked as someone approached slowly but not furtively. She felt a breath on the back of her neck, a familiar breath. Words came back to her, the feeling on the back of her neck as those words were whispered: 'Oh, don't bother. I can see. Just turn around.' A chill ran through her. 'Oh, the stones are Bisbee turquoise.'

The scent came back to her in full force.

'Move!' she commanded herself. 'Move!'

She jerked up in bed. It was almost as if she had broken through a glass cage. But she could breathe, and with a stunning clarity, the realization broke upon her. Had Bunny been in this room? Was she in this room now? The scent wafted over her. Her eyes opened wide now, as if some compartment in her mind had opened up and spilled out odd bits of information she had sequestered away, perhaps in denial or simply fear. What was the difference? It was the same inscrutable scent she had detected at the hogan. Yet when she had returned after finding the comb, she had hardly noticed it, but that was during the hoodoo, of course. The rain or the wind might have carried it off. But that scent was in this room. It seemed almost to saturate it. She had to call Ryan immediately.

Five minutes later, she stood in the office of Los Gallos and quickly dialed Ryan's home phone. He answered on the fourth ring.

'Ryan,' she gasped.

'Georgia, what's wrong?'

'I know who the killer is.'

'Wait, wait. Who are you talking about? Bugsy?'

'No, Bunny, not Bugsy.' Was this conversation in some way turning comical?

Two minutes after they hung up, Ryan's phone rang again.

'Hi, boss, Joe Descheeni here. Heading out to Taos. Got a tip that Bugsy's out there.'

'Christ almighty. Meet you there.' That was all he said as he reached for his shoulder holster and gun.

THIRTY-SEVEN

D r Jules Goldstein held Maudie's wrist and looked at his watch as he checked her pulse.

'Doing very well, my dear. Very well.'

'But Doctor Goldstein, I'm not sure I want to get well.'

'Of course you do, my dear.'

'But where will I be safe?'

'For now, just where you are: out here in our house on the Punto Rojo Road,' the doctor replied.

'You let us worry about that, miss,' the large black FBI agent said. 'We've got you protected here for now.'

'For now? Is now forever?'

'Not forever, Maudie,' Dr Goldstein said. 'And you know, Maudie, I think you're filling a place in my wife's heart since our two daughters upped and left to get married all in the space of a year.'

Maudie wondered who would have ever thought that what she knew about Mrs Simpson and this man Ribbentrop would have been so important. 'Vital' was the word that Lincoln Stone used. She had never felt vital or important, never even necessary, except maybe for ironing and keeping a lady's clothing in order.

She had grown stronger in the two days she had been at the Goldstein house. Today, just her second day here, she was permitted to go out on to their patio and the garden surrounding it, but no farther.

Milly, the doctor's wife, could tell that she was getting restless. She especially enjoyed walking in the garden, which was lovely.

'We have none of these flowers or plants back in England,' Maudie said. 'They are so beautiful. I'd like to draw them.'

'Well, I can certainly arrange that. I'll pick up some paper and watercolors or pencils in town.'

'Really, Mrs Goldstein?'

'Just call me Milly. Yes, I'll get them when I go to town today.'

'Now, what's that over there?' Maudie pointed. 'Toward the far left of that church with the big cross. That twisted thing.'

'Oh, that. It's an almost dead bristlecone tree. It's rather amazing.

The top – the canopy, I guess you call it – was blown off in a storm, but the trunk in my mind is simply astonishing, like a sculpture of some sort. It prevails! And that is the only word I can think of. It has this elegant presence. The people around here call it Methuselah. In very old trees, only a narrow strip of living tissue connects the roots to a few live branches, and yet it defies death. There's something noble in that, isn't there? A life force.'

'Life force.' Maudie whispered the words to herself. 'Could we walk over there to see it?'

Milly picked up Maudie's hand and gave it a squeeze. 'Sorry, dear, but that's off limits for now. How about I get you Jules's binoculars and you can see it better from here with them?'

'Yes, that might be good. So kind of you, Mrs Goldstein.'

'Milly, please.' She got up to leave and was back within a minute. Maudie lifted the binoculars to her eyes.

'Oh, my goodness.' She sighed when she drew the tree into focus through the binoculars. 'Just look at that. The trunk so wrinkled – as wrinkled as my gran's cheeks,' she whispered softly. 'And those gnarly limbs. How old do you think it is, Milly?'

'Not sure, but people say over one thousand years old.'

'My goodness.' She put the binoculars down. 'Would you want to live one thousand years, Milly?'

'I don't think so. I . . . I think it must be lonely. I would miss too many people.'

Then, out of the blue, Maudie said, 'Rodney wouldn't miss me.'

Milly caught her breath. So it was Rodney whose child she had been pregnant with. Jules had told Milly that Maudie had suffered a miscarriage. That was what brought her into the hospital. No one mentioned it, of course. It was Jules's idea, and he was most likely right, that if Maudie wanted to say something, she would. She didn't need the stress of having other people pry into her private life. The Bureau and the deputy from Santa Fe were doing enough prying concerning this Ellington man, who was a double agent and connected with high-ranking Nazis.

Maudie was so charmed by the view through the binoculars that Jules got out his telescope for her in the evening when he came back from the hospital. Maudie was mesmerized from the first glimpse.

When darkness fell, they went out on to the patio.

'This is the best place to watch stars right here in New Mexico,' Jules Goldstein said.

'Why's that?'

'No light pollution, and the air is so clean. The skyline spic and span. No city lights or soot.'

'We don't see the stars often in England, especially in London,' said Maudie.

The doctor took a step away from the telescope. 'Take a look – Orion has a surprise for you tonight.'

'Oh, what's that?' Maudie laughed softly. To think that a few days ago she had never even heard the word, the name Orion.

'See the nebula, just south of Orion's belt in the constellation?'

'That sort of misty cloud? That's a nebula?'

'Yes, a cloud of dust and gas. It's where new stars are being forged.'

'You mean like baby stars?'

'Yes,' the doctor said softly. 'Like baby stars, I suppose.' He knew what she was thinking about but did not say a word.

The doctor gave her several astronomy books. She was content, perfectly content. Her life had become so different, as they would not allow her to lift a finger. She had gone from serving to being served. From servant, a being that people looked through and saw nothing, to an individual who had worth beyond her simple skills of serving. However, they were constantly apologizing for not allowing her the freedom to roam beyond their house.

'We can't let you out on your own. Not for a while,' Milly said that first evening when she was at the Goldstein home.

'Not until they nail down what the hell is going on with these Nazis,' Dr Goldstein growled as he clamped down with his teeth on his after-dinner pipe. 'Now they're talking about Race Laws in Germany.'

'What's that?' Maudie said.

'If, say, Milly and I were in Germany, we would not be allowed to be married.'

'Why ever not?'

'Because Milly isn't Jewish.'

'How ridiculous,' Milly said. She was mending a shirt of her husband's and broke the thread with her teeth.

'Looks like Jewish doctors are not going to be able to practice,' Jules Goldstein growled. 'And Jews cannot use public recreational bathing facilities. The Nuremberg Laws, they are calling these restrictions. And they are expected to be passed by September.'

Maudie was uncomfortable. She had heard Wallis Simpson and her lover Ribbentrop discussing such matters when he would visit the apartment in Belgravia.

'I think we should change the subject,' Milly said abruptly.

'Milly,' Maudie said, 'let me finish sewing on those buttons for you. I finished this shirt and have nothing to do with my hands.'

She saw Milly and her husband exchange a nervous glance. They generally tried to steer clear of not only political discussions but any references to Wallis Simpson. They had been told the identity of Wallis's lover and how Maudie had served in the household when he visited Mrs Simpson. Maudie herself had been grilled endlessly by the agents from the FBI as well as another secret American agency called the SIS.

On the second night at the Goldstein house, Jessie Yazzie, who was also part of the surveillance team, rounded the patio through the garden. He stopped by three clumps of sagebrush and looked down. There were footprints. He crouched closer to the ground and studied the imprint of the heel – a Roper heel, flat and stable. Good when a cowboy was roping cattle and had to jump off the horse to drop a steer. Not a very common boot around here.

At the same moment, Maudie wandered out on to the patio.

'How ya' doin', Maudie? And Happy Maundy.'

'Oh my goodness, is it Maundy? I've kind of lost track.'

'So tomorrow's Good Friday, and you'll have a great view from here.'

'Great view of what?'

'The pilgrimage.'

'Pilgrimage? Like in the days of the Crusaders in Europe?'

'Not exactly, but close. People walk to the morada from all over. They call them Penitentes, not Crusaders. But kind of the same idea.'

Jessie smiled and dipped his chin. The patio that Maudie stood on was about three feet higher than where he was standing on the garden path.

'Anybody walking out here today aside from myself?' he asked.

'Not that I know of. Why?'

'I found some footprints.'

'Well, Jose sometimes walks around. He's the gardener.'

'I doubt Jose wears boots like these.'

'Why?'

'Fancy, expensive – dude ranch kind of cowboy.'

'Maybe Cowboy from Los Gallos wears them.'

'Naw, Cowboy couldn't afford these and probably wouldn't wear them if he could. He's not a show cowboy. He's the real deal.'

'He was always very nice to me,' Maudie said. 'He even tried to get me out on the dance floor that night when he had finished dancing with Lady Sybil. But Mrs Simpson wouldn't hear of it.'

'I remember that!' Jessie said. 'Mrs Luhan was shocked. She was about to ask you to dance herself, but you disappeared.'

'I seem to be good at that – disappearing. Now, nobody – except you and Doctor and Mrs Goldstein – knows where I am.'

'And the FBI, and Harold and Homer when they're sober.' He sighed. 'I thought you'd be out here earlier.'

'It was cloudy until about ten minutes ago. So nothing to see. But now the sky is flowing with stars.'

'That's pretty, Maudie.'

'What's pretty?'

'Your words – a night flowing with stars.' He paused. 'Sounds like a river of stars up there.' He tipped his head toward the sky. 'You're kind of a poet, you know.'

'No, I'm not. I just . . . just . . .'

'Just what?'

'I just love the sky, I guess. Never stopped to really look at it until Doctor Jules showed things to me.'

'Doctor Jules.' Jessie laughed softly. 'I like that.'

'You know, nobody has ever treated me like Doctor Jules and his wife, Milly. Nobody ever.' She bit her lip lightly. It seemed to her suddenly that a huge piece of her life had been missing. Not even Rodney had treated her in this way. And what exactly was 'this way'? She wasn't sure, but it had something to do with being valued as a human being and for herself, not simply what she might provide for others. 'In service' was the expression for people like Maudie and her parents. And so it had been for generations. And now that she thought of it, the term might as well be translated as meaning 'into a dead end'. It designated her place in life forever, like it or not. No one could even dream of a life beyond, beyond serving those above. It was a term used for work horses, farm equipment and, of course, human servants. She pressed her face closer to the eyepiece of the telescope and adjusted the focus.

'Oh, Jessie,' she said suddenly. 'I think I see Virgo rising. This is really exciting.' She adjusted the telescope again and tipped up her chin slightly.

Bugsy sighed as he rotated the focusing screw on his binoculars and sharpened the lovely vision of this girl. What luck that he had found the cave beneath a cliff overhang.

As far as he could tell, there had been no reports of the missing Rosamond. What a ridiculous name for a whore that was short a half-dozen teeth. Well, he couldn't stay here forever. He had to climb halfway up this goddamn heap of rock to Punto Rojo for a good vantage point for the pilgrimage tomorrow. He wanted to do it in daylight. Less chance of stepping on a snake. He hoped to God this Gilly Teen worked if he needed it.

THIRTY-EIGHT

E mily Bryce looked up from the report she was reading.
'What brings you here, Sheriff? On Good Friday, no less!'
'What brings me here? The usual,' Ryan answered.
'Well, seeing as I have three statewide murders and one from
Arizona because the coroner there had a family emergency and no
one to stand in, can you fill me in? What murder in the state brings
you here?'

'Flora Namingha.'

'Shipped her off a few days ago for burial or whatever over in
Taos. Sometimes Navajos set them up in trees. Don't like to think
of what the vultures have done to her.'

'Can I see any of the photographs of the body?'

'Sure.' She pressed a button on her telephone. 'Irma, can you
bring me the file on Flora Namingha?'

Two minutes later, Irma Greyeyes came in with the file. 'Hello,
Sheriff,' she said. 'We got the negatives in there, too. It might help
you to look at them on the light table. There's some grit – rock
grit.'

'Thanks, Irma.'

'They say that Cain murdered Abel with a rock,' Irma offered.

'Actually, no,' Emily interjected. 'It was the bone of an ass.'

'Now, how do you know that, Emily?' The sheriff chuckled.

'My superb convent education.' She inhaled. 'It was beaten into
me by Sister Amelia. Fabulous education.'

As he looked at the negatives on the light table, the sheriff saw
that the forensic geologist had made a check mark.

'You sent this over to Gregory at rocks?'

'Yes, sir, but just recently. It took the Taos police forever to get
the rock to us,' Irma replied. 'Gregory said that the rock that killed
her came from at least twenty miles away from the murder site.'

'Anything else?'

'He said it was a kind of chert that was often used in whetstones
for sharpening knives. But that kid over in Taos said the same thing.'

'What kid?'

Now Emily spoke up. 'Jessie Yazzie, smartest kid you ever met. Gregory didn't find out anything that Jessie hadn't. Jessie's report is in that file, too.'

Ryan realized that this must be the same Jessie who worked at Los Gallos. He scratched his chin. 'That's ironic.' He paused. 'Normally, it's the knife that does the killing and not the whetstone.' He skimmed the next page of the report. 'What's this about fibers?'

'Oh, yeah,' Emily said. 'We found under the victim's fingernail some fibers that looked like human hair before we got them under the microscope. Not human at all. More like horsehair.'

'She tangled with a horse?'

'Doubtful. Rather someone wearing a horsehair wig. They use horsehair, sheep, goats, for wigs. You know, for all the corn dance festivals and that.'

'She flipped her wig!' Ryan recalled Walk's comment about the woman rushing out of the phone booth. Then he recalled his conversation with Georgia and how she had told him about Emily's call and the wig fibers. How dumb did he have to be! Not just dumb, but behaving like Georgia said all men behaved – deaf to women! Devaluing whatever women said. He was mortified by his own behavior.

His thoughts were interrupted by Irma.

'Sheriff, there's another note here from the geologist,' she said as she handed him a sheet of paper.

'Grit particles found in abrasions include CBN,' the sheriff murmured. 'What's CBN?'

'Cubic boron nitride,' Irma replied.

The sheriff gave a low whistle. 'Irma Greyeyes, you are something!'

'I've just been taking a geology course at the extension school in Albuquerque.'

'I should retire right now, Irma, and turn it all over to you,' Emily said with a chuckle.

'Before you retire, Emily, do you have the number for Gregory Peterson?' Ryan asked. 'I'd like to give him a call and see where rocks with CBN can be found.'

Five minutes later, he was on the phone.

'Hi, Greg. Ryan McCaffrey here.'

'Yes, Sheriff, what can I do for you?'

'This report on the murder over in Taos – Flora Namingha.'

'Oh yes, very sad and very unusual. Murder weapon a whetstone and not a knife. A reversal of sorts.'

'I'd say.' Ryan paused. 'So, tell me, Greg, where would one go for good whetstone rocks out near Taos?'

'Most likely the Questa basin.'

'Where's that?'

'You'd have to go northeast out the Old Santa Ana Road from Taos about sixteen miles.'

The Old Santa Ana Road. It rang a bell for Ryan. Wasn't that the road Georgia had mentioned going on to find some weaver's house?

The door opened, and Emily stuck her head in. 'Joe Descheeni's on the other line for you. Urgent. Follow me to the second phone on my desk.'

'OK, thanks for talking with me, Greg. Gotta go.' He picked up the other phone as he sat down behind the desk. It was incredibly neat. No photos, mementos of any sort. Just barren, scrubbed like an operating table.

'Yeah, Joe, I'm here. What's up?'

'You know that kid in the Taos office?'

'You mean the only one with a functioning brain?'

'Yeah, that's the one – Jesus Yazzie. Well, he's picked up some interesting fingerprints.'

'Whose?'

'Possibly the murderer of Flora Namingha.'

'Possibly?'

'They're arches.'

'Arches? I don't believe we've ever had a set of arches here in New Mexico, at least not in my time.'

'You're right. But we got some now.'

'Who discovered them?'

'Close friend of yours.'

'Who are you talking about?'

'Georgia O'Keeffe.'

Jesus Christ, he thought. Then he laughed. *She beat me at my own game!*

THIRTY-NINE

That morning, the sun was just rising, and there was a definite chill in the air when Georgia arrived at the junction between the roads leading into Taos from Espanola, Oja Caliente and Santa Fe. Gradually, as the darkness seeped away, she could see the lines of people advancing. Some wore backpacks and some carried large crosses across their backs. Some used walking sticks and others ski poles. They walked in an odd silence. But nearby, Georgia heard a child arguing in Tewa with an old lady. She realized suddenly as the sky lightened that the little girl was Elena, Flora's sister. Her grandmother looked up at Georgia and smiled.

'The cross is too big for her,' the old woman said.

'No, it's not, *Sani*.'

'But I helped you, and so did Marcus.'

Marcus . . . Cowboy! Georgia realized.

And soon enough, Cowboy arrived. 'Hello, Miss O'Keeffe.'

'Hello, Marcus.' She hesitated. 'Have you seen Sheriff McCaffrey around?'

'No, but some of his deputies are here.' He turned toward the grandmother.

'So, you found the cross all right, Auntie Ava?'

'Yes, but now she wants to carry it by herself.'

'Well, let's let her have a try. I can strap it on to her back.'

Elena smiled broadly as Cowboy began getting out some rope and tied it on to her back at an angle. The little girl hunched under the weight and staggered a bit.

'I can help you,' Cowboy said.

'No, I don't want any help. I want to do it all by myself, for Flora.'

'All right.' He winked at Georgia and the grandmother as Elena began walking. Surreptitiously, Cowboy put a couple of his fingers under the junction of the horizontal and vertical pieces of the cross.

'See, I can do it!' Elena said triumphantly. She still staggered a bit.

The image of her little body bent under the weight dug deep into Georgia's mind.

Georgia glanced around for Bunny. There were an awful lot of people. Who knew if she and Eldon would get up this early? If she headed up the hill as she had planned to for the view, she might have a better chance of spotting Ryan at least. He was a large man and would stand head and shoulders above the throng. She started up a narrow path, using her snake stick as a walking stick now. She felt a crick in her hip and remembered what her mother had said: 'Getting old is not for sissies.' But her mother was hardly that old when she died, not old enough to witness her daughter's success.

What is success anyhow? she wondered. All she wanted right now was to see a killer arrested. She paused and looked out from a clearing where she could see the crowds below. No sign of Ryan. But she might have glimpsed Bunny.

'Goddammit,' she muttered. 'If I have to, I'll run down and arrest her myself.'

FORTY

Bugsy laid out what he thought of as the vitals of the rifle from a canvas bag he carried – the stock, breech, barrel, the telescopic sight and the silencer. He slid bullets into the chamber, then fit on the silencer; last, he clipped on the telescopic sight.

Fuck! he muttered as he saw the little girl struggling with a cross on her back. Imagine having kids staggering around with crucifixes. *Goyische little kids.* Would Jews ever do a thing like that? 'Not on your life,' he muttered. This little kid was screwing up his meticulous preparations. Damn, why was his target, this cowboy fairy, sticking so close to the little girl? Probably a child molester to boot.

Concentrate, he told himself. *Don't get distracted.* Twenty thousand dollars in his pocket! He could buy Esty that house in LA that she craved. And if the Vegas deal worked out, he'd build what Esty called his Sand Castle in Nevada. She wouldn't come. She hated sand, the desert. She'd stay in LA. Fine with him. But he didn't tell her that, of course. She knew about the gambling part of the Vegas venture but not the prostitution. He told her he'd only have to be there a couple of weekends a month. Fine with her. All things considered, they had a very good marriage, he mused.

Damn that kid. Why didn't she move with that fucking cross and give him a clear shot at Cowboy? The little girl began to walk away from Cowboy just a bit. She was pointing to a tall blond lady. Now some old codger had come up to them and was blocking his view of the fairy. Damn. A man with a badge now began to make his way toward the blond woman. Why were all these people suddenly in his crosshairs? He was just after one stupid guy. A slight commotion was going on down there. Someone was yelling, but at the same time he heard something closer moving through the brush.

Goddamn if it was a snake! His hands began to shake. He put the rifle down and reached for the snake killer.

As Georgia came up the path, she thought she heard a rather human-like grunt. Someone else must be up here trying to watch the pilgrimage – it was bound to be a good perch for the overall view. She could have sworn she heard a car engine in the distance coming up a rather rough road. She rounded a bend and gasped as she tried to make order out of the scene that confronted her. The man from the hardware store was shaking like a leaf with a rifle in one hand and the snake killer in the other.

'Oh, Jesus!' He gasped as she stepped toward him. 'What the fuck are you doing here?'

She waited for several seconds to reply. 'I might ask the same of you.'

'Don't,' he replied.

The coldness in his voice was frightening. It was as if with that single word he was disconnecting himself from the human race. His handsome face darkened. There was a deadly glint in his eyes. She felt the warmth of the sun rising behind her in the east. In another few seconds, it would be right behind her, and if she kept facing this way, it would be blinding for the man. He set down the Gilly Teen, pushed it aside and raised the rifle. She saw the fierce glare of the sun off the barrel and immediately crouched and rolled aside. The gunfire was deafening despite the silencer. She raced up to him, kicked the rifle out of his hands and reached for the Gilly Teen.

'What are you doing?' he asked as she stood over him. In one hand, she had her own snake killer stick and in the other the Gilly Teen. She stood directly over him now. He tried to reach for the Gilly Teen. There was a click as she unlocked the trigger, followed by a snap as she jabbed the Gilly Teen. An agonizing scream tore through the air, then a geyser of blood spurted into the air as the double blade snapped off Bugsy's index finger.

There was more rustling in the brush. A shadow stretched across, blotting out Georgia's shadow and that of Bugsy Siegel.

'Miss O'Keeffe!' Joe Descheeni stepped forward.

'Well . . .' She exhaled and leaned on her own snake stick. 'It seems I have come across an errant pilgrim. One who was about to shoot somebody. Me!'

'You came across Bugsy Siegel.' He bent over and picked up the rifle. At that moment, Eddie Collins stepped out of the brush.

'Jesus Christ!' he said, looking at the man on the ground. His hand was spurting blood. 'You did that, Miss O'Keeffe?' he asked, looking at Georgia.

'Yep, his finger should be down there someplace. His trigger finger at that!' she exclaimed.

'Fuck you, Georgia O'Keeffe!' Bugsy roared.

'No way to speak to a lady, or we'll snap off that finger, too!' Walk Howson cackled as he stepped out of the scrub and raised his middle finger. 'Always enjoyed a pun, ma'am,' he said, winking at Georgia. 'Yep, that's the fellow, officer. He came in to use my phone. Told you that was the guy,' he said, looking at Descheeni.

'Where is Ryan? Sheriff McCaffrey, I mean,' Georgia asked.

'Oh, he's down at the pilgrimage making another arrest.'

'Another arrest?' she asked.

'A lady. Miss Barbara – or Bunny, as she is better known – Hatch.' Descheeni paused. 'For the murder of Flora Namingha.'

'I led him right to her,' Walk said. 'About ten minutes before I caught sight of this guy. Got a ride up with these cops.'

The bread crumbs – like Hansel and Gretel, like the crosspieces of the crucifix, like all things divergent – had come together.

There was a moment, and she must have swayed, for Collins reached to grab her elbow.

'No, no, Eddie, I'm fine.' But how could she explain this? Even hope to explain how the bread crumbs had crossed paths. That all the divergent elements had come together, woven together in a deadly but beautiful design.

As they arrived at the junction where the roads leading into Taos met, Georgia saw two police cars and an ambulance.

'There must be a mistake,' Eldon Burke was saying. 'My fiancée has done nothing wrong. What are you talking about murder charges? What murder?'

'The murder of Flora Namingha,' the sheriff said. It was as if Bunny had turned to stone. She had manacles on both her hands and feet. She said nothing as Ryan pushed her head down and firmly propelled her into the car.

'But she's my fiancée. This is impossible.'

Not at all, Georgia thought. A little hand slipped into hers. She looked down. It was Elena, and she was pointing at Bunny Hatch.

'That's the lady who gave me the doll. The truth doll, she called it.' She sighed – a sigh too deep and too old for such a young child.

'But I told her the truth,' she whispered. 'I said that Mateo loved Flora. That was the truth. And now I hope that lady dies.'

'Hush, Elena. Don't say such things,' her grandmother chastised gently.

'But it is the truth, *sani – áá aaníinii!*'

'Yes, I agree, Elena,' Georgia said as she bent down to hug the child.

FORTY-ONE

British aristocrat's daughter arrested for murder.

'Oh my,' Eleanor Burke whispered to herself as her maid set down the teapot and biscuits. She looked up. 'No butter, please, I'm on a diet.'

'Oh, sorry, ma'am, I forgot.'

'It's just your second day here. Don't worry about it.' She smiled a tight little smile. She was less than a week out of plastic surgery with the same plastic surgeon that had operated on Wallis Simpson. She and Wallis had become quite chummy after they had met at the party where Eleanor was wearing the lobster dress. Indeed, she had invited Wallis to come and stay with her and Chance the next time she visited Palm Beach. Not only that, but Wallis knew Bunny's mother. They would definitely put her on the guest list for the wedding. She got out her reading glasses now to look at the article.

A blood-curdling scream tore through Arenas Doradas.

The new maid and Chance Burke burst into the breakfast room.

'What the devil, Eleanor?' Chance said.

'Our son! Our son!'

'What about our son?'

'He's marrying a, a murderer.'

'No, my dear. You've got it all wrong. Eldon is fine.'

The butler now came into the breakfast room followed by two Palm Beach police officers.

'Mr Burke?'

'Yes,' he replied as he put a shaking hand on the back of his wife's chair.

'We are here to arrest you in connection with the attempted murder of Marcus Willis. Come with us, please.'

Eleanor heard the click of the handcuffs. With a policeman on either side of him, Chance Burke was marched out of Arenas Doradas.

A small contingent of photographers descended on him in the

portico. Like a mid-morning electrical storm, the flashbulbs from their cameras greeted him.

Georgia walked up the path to Mateo's house and jingled the small bells of the front door.

'Come in,' he called.

She walked through the house toward the studio. He came out, wiping his hands on a towel.

'Come with me, Georgia. I'll show you something.'

She followed him to the drafting table. The drawing was of Flora, but next to it on a board were the cut pieces of the stained glass.

'Lovely, Mateo.'

'Yeah, next step is the copper foiling. It will be easy on this one, but the next one will be very hard.'

'You're making two of these?'

'Yes, one for Elena. A little pendant to wear around her neck.'

'Oh, like you made for me of the east-facing window.'

'Exactly. Much harder to work small than large.'

He was quiet for a long time as he gathered a few materials for the foiling process.

He sighed. 'So, you want to know about Barbara? Bunny.'

'You don't have to tell me anything, Mateo.'

'I don't, but I will. I met her at that New York craft fair. It was maybe three or four years ago. It was long before Flora. We slept together a few times – when she would come to New York, the craft shows, and a few times when she came out here on her buying trips. I was never in love with her.' He shrugged. 'She was good in bed. What can I tell you? But then maybe two years ago, I noticed that Flora had grown up. It seemed like overnight. She was such a talented artist, and we fell in love. Bunny was furious. She didn't come back for a couple of years. By that time, she was buying a lot of rugs from Malinda Chee for her gallery. I think they had become quite close. Then Malinda died. There were rumors that Malinda's *chindi* – her ghost – haunted those hogans out on the Old Santa Ana Road where she had lived. But that proved a convenience for Bunny. So, when she came back last year, she saw that Flora and I were still together. Not only that, but we planned to get married. I thought she had reconciled herself to the idea. But apparently not. I felt from the start that it could have been Bunny who killed Flora.'

'And you didn't say anything?'

'Those fools, Homer and Harold, they don't know anything. The law is not on our side out here.' He paused. 'But Sheriff McCaffrey. He's a smart guy. He must have sensed something wasn't right.' He closed his eyes and took a deep breath. 'He got it right. And so did you.' He paused. 'You were the one who figured it all out with the fingerprints.'

'Don't give me too much credit. It was really Jessie Yazzie who figured it out. I just somehow stumbled into the crosshairs where the paths of two very different species of murderer connected.' She inhaled deeply. 'But what will you do now, my friend?'

'I'll go on. Go on making my glass. Mrs Luhan is working on getting me some commissions.' He didn't say anything for a minute or more.

'But, Mateo, aren't you angry?'

'Of course, but you know what the old Navajos say?'

'What's that?'

'If a man is as wise as a serpent, he can afford to be as harmless as a dove.' He sighed and picked up a sketch from a pile. It was a dove in flight. 'I'm making this for the morada.'

'It's lovely, Mateo.'

'The wings are difficult because they are white, and white stained glass is hard to do. You can't make it too white. I have to fool the eye by making the surrounding glass pieces more vibrant.'

'Of course, we all have our tricks, you know.' She gave him a sly wink.

EPILOGUE

The Ghost Ranch, Abiquiu, New Mexico, October 1935

They were on the rooftop of Georgia's casita at the Ghost Ranch, leaning against the chimney. She was reflecting on this view – how she loved it! She turned her head toward the Pedernal, the mesa that she had become absorbed with from the first time she came out to this high, wild country. How many times now had she painted it, sketched it? Changing Woman was what the people called the mesa. She was the daughter of Earth and Sun. Georgia now looked down at her own hands, deeply tanned, wrinkled, the veins bumping up. The leathery hand of an old lady – an old lady artist and as corrugated as this landscape.

'What are you thinking about, Georgia?' Ryan asked.

'Her.' She nodded toward the Pedernal.

'Yes,' he said softly and gave her cheek a kiss.

Her . . . her . . . her. The word threaded the air like a silent echo. This was the profound pleasure of love. One didn't need to explain too much. Ryan understood. Words become superfluous. He just knew what she was thinking. He knew about the Pedernal and the Changing Woman, and that she was in fact that woman. That *her.*

AUTHOR'S NOTE

While many of the characters in this book are fictional, some are based on real people:

D.H. Lawrence died in France in 1930 and was buried there. His wife Frieda Lawrence, five years later, in 1935 decided to exhume the body, cremate the remains and bring them to New Mexico where Mabel Dodge Luhan had given them a house some years before. Frieda decided to build a chapel in his honor and inter the ashes there. Many of her friends objected and felt the ashes should be scattered in the Kiowa Hills behind their house. Frieda became fed up with all the suggestions, and in fact did dump his ashes in a cement mixer which settled the issue. The cement was used in the construction of the chapel.

J. Edgar Hoover was an American law enforcement administrator who served as the first Director of the Federal Bureau of Investigation of the United States beginning in 1924 when it was then called The Bureau of Investigation. In 1935 it was re-named the Federal Bureau of Investigation and Hoover served as its director until his death in 1972.

Mable Dodge Luhan was a wealthy American patron of the arts, who was particularly associated with the Taos art colony. She was a friend of Georgia O'Keeffe.

Georgia Totto O'Keeffe (November 15, 1887 – March 6, 1986) was an American artist. She was known for her paintings of enlarged flowers, New York sky scrapers and New Mexican landscapes. O'Keeffe has been recognized as the "Mother of American modernism". When she was called the best woman painter her response was: "The men like to put me down as the best woman painter. I think I'm one of the best painters." She was married to Alfred Stieglitz from 1924 to 1946.

Alfred Stieglitz was an American photographer and modern art promoter who was instrumental over his fifty-year career in making photography an accepted art form. He supported such photographers as Paul Strand and Charles Sheeler. In 1916 Georgia O'Keeffe and Stieglitz met for the first time. He was entranced with her work. In 1917 Stieglitz gave her first show at his gallery 291. They fell in love. Stieglitz left his wife Emmeline Obermeyer Stieglitz and he and Georgia subsequently began living together. They married in 1924.

Benjamin "Bugsy" Siegel was an American mobster. He was enormously influential in the development of the Las Vegas strip. He was also a bootlegger during prohibition in the United States.

Wallis Simpson was an American socialite, twice divorced before she married the former King Edward VIII. Her status as a divorced woman caused a constitutional crisis leading to his abdication. When they did marry she became the Duchess of Windsor and the former king, the Duke of Windsor. They were both rumored to have Nazi sympathies.

Further historical notes:

The Duquesne Spy Ring is the largest espionage case in United States history. A total of thirty-three members of a German espionage network were convicted by the FBI. Of those indicted, nineteen pleaded guilty. The remaining fourteen were brought to jury trial in Federal District Court, Brooklyn, New York, on September 3, 1941; all were found guilty on December 13, 1941. On January 2, 1942, the group members were sentenced to serve a total of over 300 years in prison. The Duquesne Spy Ring became the basis for the Lutzen Ring in *Light On Bone* and *Mortal Radiance*. I advanced its espionage to a few years earlier.

The Special Intelligence Service was a covert counterintelligence branch of the United States Federal Bureau of Investigation during World War II. It was established to monitor the activities of Nazi and pro-Nazi groups in Central and South America. It was a predecessor to the Central Intelligence Agency.

The British also at this time had an SIS agency which evolved into MI6, the present-day foreign intelligence service of the United Kingdom.

Special Operations Executive was a secret British World War II operation. Its purpose was to conduct espionage, sabotage and reconnaissance in occupied Europe (and later, also in occupied Southeast Asia) against the Axis powers, and to aid local resistance movements.

The Ghost Ranch was originally won in a poker game in 1928 by Roy Pfaffle. His wife Carol Stanley named it the Ghost Ranch. They planned to develop it as an exclusive dude ranch. One of the guests in those early years was Arthur Newton Pack, an environmentalist and editor of Nature Magazine. He bought it from Carol Stanley when she began to have financial problems. Georgia O'Keeffe first visited the Ghost Ranch in 1934. In 1940 she convinced Arthur Pack to sell her a small house and seven acres of property on the ranch. Many famous people came to the ranch during those early years including Charles Lindbergh and his wife, Ansel Adams and John Wayne. In later years distinguished scientists who worked at Los Alamos and others found their way there.

In 1955 Arthur Pack and his wife Phoebe gave the ranch to the Presbyterian Church with the express mandate that it would be a place for "spiritual development, peace and justice, honoring the environment and exploring family through the celebration of art, culture and nature".